For family … the most precious of gifts

Power tends to corrupt, and absolute power corrupts absolutely. Great men are almost always bad men, even when they exercise influence and not authority: still more when you superadd the tendency or the certainty of corruption by authority. There is no worse heresy than that the office sanctifies the holder of it. That is the point at which — the end learns to justify the means.

John Emerich Edward Dalberg, Lord Acton

PROLOGUE

It was cold.

Angry fingers of wind poked and pulled at his thin t-shirt, making another shiver irresistible. Eric adjusted position on his perch and looked down with weary eyes.

Far below, lurid patterns formed and disappeared in the briefest of moments as strobing blues and reds collided with the grey oxide metalwork of the bridge. Everything else had stopped, and only the headlights of stationary vehicles stretching into the distance like daisy-chains hinted at the disruption he was causing.

He shivered again.

"At least let me get you a blanket, Eric?" a grey-haired man in a brown suit called over, buttoning his jacket and turning up the collar. "It's getting chilly up here now. Just while you think. That can't hurt, can it?"

Eric had to admit the offer was tempting. The guy, Dean, said he was a negotiator, said he was there to help. But the young wetware specialist couldn't even remember how he'd gotten to this place, let alone what needed negotiating.

For the last hour he'd rambled, more to himself than Dean, and the older man had listened with quiet sympathy to the confused mixture of statements and questions. Every so often affirming Eric's safety. Gently repeating that friends were worried and wanted him to come home. Softly asserting, while the young man looked towards the city in bewilderment, that no *good* answers would be found at the top of a bridge in the middle of the night.

"Eric," the negotiator called again. "The blanket?"

On a conscious level, the twenty-six-year-old understood the sensible option was to go with Dean. But something was stopping him; something was off. A certainty he couldn't quite grasp gnawed at the edges of his mind, and the wetware creator felt trapped.

That had to be an odd feeling when people were only trying to help — didn't it?

He stared over at the greying guy in the brown suit again, a growing sense of unease about the man belying what his senses were telling him.

"This isn't real," he heard himself murmur, turning away and beginning to rock. "This isn't real."

"Eric," Dean shouted over, noticing the change and trying to re-focus the younger man. "That isn't the answer. It's never an answer. Stay with me and let's figure this out. There has to be something I can do?"

Stopping his swaying, the exhausted engineer looked back again. "You could let me go."

A sincere smile spread across the negotiator's rugged face and he held out a reassuring hand. "Hey, you're not under arrest. You've done nothing wrong. Of course you can go. Let's just get you down. Warm. Safe. Figure the rest out from there?"

But the older man's smile didn't extend to his eyes, and Eric's cold lips slowly stretched into a manic grin of their own; fragments of memory beginning to surface like flotsam.

"Did you think I wouldn't remember we've been here before, *Dean*?" he spat back through the wind, only processing what he was saying as the words fell out of him.

The grey-haired man gave a visible sigh and shook his head. "Then why do it again? Let me help you." He looked down at the tarmac one hundred and fifty feet below. "We both know you won't find what you're looking for like this."

Now focused solely on the negotiator, a parade of fear and resolve battled across Eric's features in involuntary response to a body preparing to defy all of its natural programming. Adrenalin exploded through his system and energy surged into the cold, aching muscles of both arms, which then bunched for one final act.

He pushed forward on that moment's instinct, and as gravity took his body beyond the possibility of any change of mind, a resolute Eric, who in those last seconds seemed to remember himself, called back, "Neither will you."

Face now expressionless, Dean watched the wetware designer fall. He'd been so close this time.

With an irritated sigh, the man in the brown suit looked up at the starless sky above him and said, "Reset."

PARTITION ONE

Eric jumped.

"Jeeze," he said, pulling off his haptic cap and looking at the feedback screens.

"Sade, what the hell was that?"

The petite mech opened a vidstream on the wall between them which showed the young engineer working moments earlier; eyes closed, arms outstretched, fingers twisting and seeming to pull at nothing, while the holo over his shoulder showed a pair of microscopic tweezers delicately lifting a nanometre thick filament of the chipset embedded in his brain and separating it from the nerve ending it was buried in.

"Yes there, look." She froze the recording following an almost imperceptible jerk and re-played it. "What happened?"

Eric shook his head. "I don't know. It felt like I'd lost my balance; like I was falling."

"And now?"

He balled his left hand into a fist and released it. "Edgy."

A gentle blue light fanned out from a nearby emitter and swept over the wetware specialist's body. "Wow. Yes," she said. "You're awash with adrenalin, and there was a slight electrical surge nanoseconds before your neurotransmitters fired up."

"What do you think it means?" Eric asked, turning to study the screen she was updating.

Shaking her head, Sade pulled the PDrive connectors from the port behind his left ear and sat down next to him, cupping her chin between thumb and forefinger as she examined the data again. "There's going to be a correlation, some sort of stimulus that triggered your body's fight-or-flight response, but I'll need to run more checks to be certain. For now at least, I think we take the warning and stop trying to remove that chip."

"Agreed," Eric said, rubbing the heels of both palms into gritty eyes and stretching.

Turning the brain into a literal computer had sounded amazing in concept, a real gift to the world, so of course he'd been interested when Fenton approached him to revisit the work. And frankly, it had only taken a subtle adaptation of the tech billionaire's chipset infrastructure and a minor re-write of his own Total Immersion wetware to get basic binary communication running between it and his test construct.

But that was the easy bit.

The hard bit, the bit few did well, was the subsequent modelling and development of epigenetic coding at a molecular level that would allow the chip to read and translate machine language to a form the human brain could understand, and then facilitate that brain's responses in a likewise manner.

So while his PDrive was limited to perceptual immersion in bespoke programmes and needed a hardwired connection to a computer or techdeck with corresponding software, MindMerge had a suite of pseudo dendrite extensions that harvested and utilised electricity generated by its host for power; creating, in theory, a self-sustaining wireless computer connection within a person's head. It was a true stroke of genius. Then again, so was the amphiconductive neurochemical he'd created to make it work.

But when two data sets began emerging as he nuanced the new *ampware's* syntax and semantics protocols, Eric discovered the clever little implant wasn't just reading and translating commands as they passed through its membrane, it was also *writing* new data — his memories of the testing process were being captured and encoded as well.

At first, that had seemed like a holy grail moment for neurolinguistic engineering, opening all kinds of doors for medical and technological progress. They'd even completed a survey of Eric's brain before a joke about body-snatchers stopped the wetware engineer in his tracks, and he realised with a terrible certainty what the polycorps would do with the revolutionary chipset.

The corpos wouldn't use the technology to create equality of education or resolve the poverty gap — they would monetise it. Worse still, weaponise it; take all that wonderful potential and distil it, in only the way self-destructive humans can do, into the most frightening form of control.

Expecting agreement, he'd led with that epiphany in his last vid call with Fenton. But the tech billionaire hadn't liked it, hadn't liked it at all; moving rapidly and with uncharacteristic hostility from telling Eric it wasn't his place to play God because of short-sighted philosophical anxieties, to accusing him of trying to steal the chip for himself.

Shocked by the vehement attack from the man he'd thought of as a friend, in the heated exchange that followed, Eric told Fenton to poke his chip — he was done, and good luck finding someone else.

Problem was, although Fenton didn't know it, the prototype was now firmly lodged in Eric's brain, and getting the damn thing back out after its filaments had threaded across his cortex was proving a whole lot more complicated than getting it in.

With a sigh, the tired engineer took off his holo-gloves and unjacked from the construct interface. "I'm gonna go freshen up," he said, shutting down his deck. "You okay to work through those glitches by yourself?"

"Yeah, sure. You go."

Sade had started *life* as one of the tech entrepreneur's ideas for traditional AI replacement; a digital entity that could also inhabit a mechanical body, be a companion. But as the months passed, her evolutionary algorithms developed a personality even Pascal, his lead roboticist, hesitated to call mimicry. It was far too complex, too human — and right now, she'd gone oddly quiet.

"You okay?" he asked.

The mech's imipolymer skin flushed and her beautiful, handcrafted eyes remained fixed on the screen as her fingers tapped over the results of Eric's scan.

"I'm still trying to understand how," she began. "But the checks I'm running indicate similar incidents have occurred six times in the last ten hours. Each time a subroutine has logged the event as nothing more than a spike train and blocked escalation to my conscious awareness." She sniffed;

an action Eric had come to equate with upset. "Had you not specifically asked just now, I'd have done it again."

The poor mech looked mortified.

"Your serotonin and melatonin levels are suppressed, and your cortisol count has been climbing for hours. None of that should be possible without me knowing. I'm sorry."

A forlorn Sade finally made eye contact.

"Once I've got to the bottom of the surges, I'll run a self-diagnostic to establish how, or why, parts of my programme have become corrupted." She sniffed again and Eric raised an eyebrow, glad he'd not created tear ducts in her bodies.

"Come on now," he said, pulling her into a hug. "We've talked about this before, haven't we? It's great your personality continues to grow, but there are some emotions I don't want you overindulging in. They won't be helpful to either of us."

Sade nodded, leaning into the embrace; enjoying the warmth of the engineer's body pressed against hers, and the steady, calming thump of his heart.

"We've had a long night. Let's both just slow down and take a breath. I mean, how bad can it be?" Eric looked down into her near perfect violet eyes and winked as he ran a hand through her short silver hair.

"That's better," he grinned as the mech offered a demure smile, unable to resist a dab at tears that weren't there.

"Go get your shower," she said. "I'll be able to tell you more when you come back down."

Half an hour later and still the wrong side of 6am, the twenty-six-year-old rising star of the tech development world had showered and thrown on a comfy pair of joggers and

5

sloppy blue t-shirt. If he fancied a nap after eating something, it was just a matter of kicking off his slippers and falling back into bed.

He headed down to the ground floor, where a nod at the wall in the lounge put on the morning newsfeeds, and in the kitchen a thought both opened the patio doors to the beach and turned on the coffeemaker to begin its first brew of the day. Within moments the room filled with the rhythmic soundtrack of the ocean and unmistakable aroma of ground arabica beans. Sade had even made a start on breakfast.

But as Eric's toast popped, the door entry system chimed, and a glance at the clock told him it was only 05:57. Who the hell expects someone to answer their door at that kind of time?

Anticipating his question, Sade opened a vidstream on the kitchen wall of a heavyset, middle-aged woman with short, dark hair. "I don't recognise her," she said through one of the kitchen's com nodes.

"No, neither do I," Eric agreed, leaning closer to look at the untanned face and sharp features. "Clearly not from round here though."

"Do you want me to send her away?"

The tech entrepreneur looked at his toast and toyed with the idea of ignoring the big stranger. Then the entry chime rang out for a second time, and he put down his butter knife with an annoyed sigh.

"Hello?" he said. Sade relaying his image to the front door.

"Dr Thorne?"

"Yes," Eric replied. "And you are?"

"My name is Miah Hargreaves, Doctor. Sorry about the time. I'm here because Mr Whittaker of the Eden polycorp believes you might be in trouble."

"Daran Whittaker? Fenton's CEO? Wait, what do you mean, trouble?"

She looked over her shoulder up 34th Street. "Yes, that's him. It's a little complicated, but he's concerned your security may have been compromised. So sent me to, um … assist."

"My security? How so?" Eric stirred from his stool and began walking towards the hallway. "Is this about Fenton? And what do you mean *assist*?"

"Lots of questions, Doctor," Hargreaves answered. "It's not so much your home we're worried about. At least not here." She looked up the road again. "It's you, or more specifically, your mind. And Mr Whittaker is handling this, as yes, it seems Dr White is part of the problem."

Eric's stride faltered; he and Fenton hadn't spoken since their argument, and though the wetware designer was expecting repercussions, lawyers or something, surely the man wouldn't do anything crazy?

"Okay, that doesn't sound good," he said. "What are you saying I need to do?"

"Opening the door would be a useful start, Doctor, and please, call me Miah."

Frowning, Eric resumed his walk down the hallway. "Sade, open the door and then begin a deep scan, full system, including my lab. This may be connected to those surges."

"Will do, Eric," the mech replied as the door swung inward.

Standing in the dim light of the porch, Miah Hargreaves created an intimidating first impression. She was a

7

tall, wide-shouldered woman, whose muscular body wreaked of military enhancements and was punctuated by a buzz-cut, black fatigues and jackboots.

"So what the hell's going on?" the entrepreneur said, ignoring her offered hand as he reached the doorway.

A muscle in the big woman's jaw tightened, but she ignored the slight. "That's a good question, Doctor. We're still working out those details ourselves. What I can tell you is yesterday your house — your real house that is, went into lockdown and you disappeared."

"*Disappeared*?" Eric snorted, raising an eyebrow and making a show of examining both hands.

"I understand that sounds ridiculous."

"You think?" he laughed, irritation turning to sarcasm. "So you're saying … what? That I've been abducted? That this is some type of immersion programme?"

"Yes, Doctor Thorne. That's exactly what I'm saying."

Beginning to suspect this was another example of Hiro's wayward sense of humour, Eric pulled the door wide, fully expecting to see his crazy, offbeat coder friend hiding somewhere nearby.

"If I wasn't already up *Miah Hargreaves*, this wouldn't be funny," he said. "You do look the part though, I'll give you that. How'd he talk you into it? You lose a bet?"

Before Hargreaves could reply, the high-pitched whine of a maxed-out motor cut through the pre-dawn gloom, and they both looked out to see a dark-coloured sedan hurtling down 34th Street.

"Argh shit, that can't be good," the big woman grumbled, reflexively shoving the engineer inside and pushing the door closed.

"Hey —" Eric began, then spotted his visitor now had a gun in her hands.

"You recognise those guys?"

"I'm not cool with that!" he pointed, more interested in addressing the unwelcome presence of a gun in his house. But as the young engineer's eyes flicked to the vidstream on the wall beside the door, he noticed the wiry man in a brown suit and two large, uniformed cops getting out of the car.

"That's odd," he said, a mixture of déjà vu and fear washing through his system. "I … This sounds insane, but maybe the one in the suit?"

A bark of laughter escaped from Hargreaves. "Well, you must have really pissed off Fenton White, Doc, because that man's an assassin; a corpo hitman, and if he's tearing up outside your house — whether this place is real or not, you are in the shit my friend!"

Eric's gaze shifted from the vidstream to the woman and back, stomach tightening as he started to realise this might not be a fucked-up joke.

"You're not serious, right?" he asked, hoping the woman's face would crease into a wide grin; that she'd say *'got ya'* or something.

She didn't.

Instead, powerful fingers ejected a bullet from the Glock G40 in her hand and waved it in front of the rapidly paling man's face.

"I have no idea what damage these things will do to a human body *in this place*, Doctor. But unless you have another way out of here, I figure we have about a minute before we find out?"

Eric stared on in dumbstruck silence, unable to take in what seemed to be happening as deft fingers re-chambered

9

the10mm round. He and Fenton were friends. They'd known each other for years — they weren't the kind of guys that hired gunmen to solve minor disagreements for Christ's sake.

"This is madness," he said, an edge of panic entering his voice. "I need to speak to Fenton. Straighten this out."

Hargreaves gave another bark of laughter. "Oh okay. You wanna go tell him that?" she asked, tapping the bit of wall showing the corporate killer walking up the path outside.

They had about fifty seconds.

"Doctor Thorne?" she stepped up to the immobile tech entrepreneur. "I really would prefer not to try going through those guys. Is there another way out?"

Forty-five.

"DOCTOR THORNE!"

That seemed to penetrate, and the engineer's eyes refocused on the strong, angular face now just inches from his own.

"We could go through the garage?" Eric suggested, swallowing hard and running a dry tongue over his teeth, trying to get some moisture back into his mouth. "It's below the house. Comes out on Ocean Drive."

The muscular woman dipped her head in agreement as a chime announced the three men had reached Eric's front door. He tapped at glyphs on his cuff and a section of wall ten feet away began sinking back before sliding to one side. Then he tapped again, instructing Sade to deactivate her bodies and secure the house servers.

Thirty.

Miah shepherded the frightened engineer along the hallway and through the newly formed gap as rows of automatic lighting activated to reveal a staircase leading down to an enormous basement and its collection of expensive cars.

Whistling in appreciation, the big woman pointed at a grey Range Rover opposite the up ramp. "That one," she said, pulling Eric behind her. "I'll drive."

Ten.

A single shot ricocheted off the garage door as the sleek SUV swung out onto Ocean Drive and the creeping shadows of dawn. Several quick turns then helped the near silent vehicle disappear among Manhattan Beach's maze of streets, and a terrified Eric, who was on his knees watching out of the rear window, finally let go of the breath he hadn't realised he was holding.

PARTITION ONE   Cluster 1   **Sector i**

July 31, 2042.
10:56H [Tiananmen Square, Beijing]

Li sat outside his father's office in the Great Hall of the People watching the ponderous third hand of an enormous clock set above the doorway to the old man's lair as it lumbered through another rotation; the twenty-sixth since his arrival. Time, he knew, was the most valuable of commodities, and Cheng Jianzhu enjoyed demonstrating his power over others by making them watch it tick by as they waited on his pleasure.

The young colonel sighed and switched his gaze back to the scene made from thousands of coloured ceramic pieces on the opposite wall. It depicted the PRC's two greatest leaders, Ye Janpeng and Mao Zedong, waving above soldiers of the People's Liberation Army. The mural had garnered an

11

approving comment from Chairman Ye when his father unveiled it, and while that was a useful sycophantic bonus, Li knew the true purpose of the piece was to remind everyone about to see Councillor Cheng Jianzhu of his status and enduring connection to *both* Paramount Leaders.

China's uprising against the bourgeois three generations earlier had offered Li's grandfather an unprecedented opportunity to rip many men he hated or envied from power, and over the following ten bloody years, the onetime murderer and guttergang leader was repeatedly rewarded for the relish with which he *purged* China in the name of Chairman Mao. So when the country's next all-powerful despot emerged, it came as no great surprise to Beijing's bureaucrats that Li's father, a nefarious chip off the old block, rose to become Ye's most trusted enforcer and confidant. The Chairman even gave him a wife from one of the old dynastic families.

But whether through fear or contempt, despite proving himself utterly shameless in attempts to climb both political and social ladders, no one in polite society truly accepted the ill-mannered thug; and it was Li, the third generation of Cheng since their ascension from the streets, who broke through that class barrier to be welcomed by Beijing's social elite. People liked the sharp-witted neurobiologist who'd inherited his mother's good looks — and he knew that was why the aging henchman despised him.

At 11am, the huge oak doors swung inward and the once intimidating form of Cheng Jianzhu, one of China's five State Councillors, stepped out to greet his son with a perfunctory nod. Like Li, the old man was taller than average, and though his frame no longer supported chords of thick muscle, his eyes remained cold and hard.

There was no greeting, just a command.

"Come."

Li stood and bowed in required subservience. "Thank you, father."

Adopting a timid, deferential posture had become his camouflage of choice years ago. It didn't get insulted, rebuked or attacked.

Jianzhu grunted and gestured towards a lavish, leather upholstered chesterfield set on its own in the middle of the large office. "Sit down," he said, closing the doors and walking around the desk to arrange his wiry body in the throne-like chair opposite.

"The Chairman asked after your work yesterday," he continued without preamble. "Y*our* minister drivelled on about progress, though said little if anything concrete and was typically evasive over finer details." Leaning forward, the aging hardman turned politician gave a vulturous smile. "I'm certain the Great One grows weary of his excuses."

Li felt compelled to meet his father's gaze, and saw the flame of avarice still burned savage and bright in that bony, grey skull. The man hated Yung Zhu and, given the chance, would delight in taking his life, his job, and his seat on the Standing Committee.

"So what can I tell the Paramount Leader about the work of our family that is more encouraging than the pellucid stalling of that nauseating minister?" he demanded. "It's time to show me the years and money spent on your soft, privileged education were worth it."

Li shifted, looking uncomfortable as he found a place to the side of Jianzhu's head to focus on.

"Father," he affected a weak tone. "You know my work is classified. The Minister—"

"I don't give a rat's dropping what that man says or thinks," Jianzhu stormed, standing to bang the desk between them with a fist. "He means nothing. Is nothing. Tianzi presents an opportunity I will not miss. My reward for a life's service, and I will not let you or that pathetic example of a spineless spook ruin it. I have worked too hard for too long. Given *everything* to elevate our family —"

Struggling to breathe, the angry old man paused, spittle glistening on his chin as shallow breaths rattled in and out of tobacco damaged lungs. Then he stabbed a gnarled, claw-like finger at Li: his uniform, his rank.

"— Moved heaven and earth to get you where you are," he finished with a sneer, leaving the accusing digit hanging as hard, hateful eyes bored into those of the child who'd proved such an intense disappointment. "So... *boy*, you will not refuse me!"

Li's gaze fell to his lap. "No, of course not, father," he said in a quiet voice.

Satisfied the younger Cheng now remembered his place, Ye's confidant took a calming breath and lowered himself back onto his aspirant's throne.

"Then speak," he ordered more softly.

Until two months ago, Li had been happy to simply wait for the old man to run out of time. Yung Zhu was the only member of the Standing Committee below the age of seventy, and when Chairman Ye, the oldest of them all by quite some margin, shuffled off, no one would be around to protect his unpopular bruiser anymore.

But it seemed *yuanfen* was not about to make the young social climber's life that easy; and when, because of his brainless father's ambitions, Li was promoted to colonel and placed in charge of Project Tianzi, the capable scientist with a bright future knew he'd just been royally fucked.

Tianzi was the Chinese attempt to get a neural implant conceptualised by the Eden polycorp, working. But the position was no honour; it was a curse. The Americans had abandoned their research almost immediately, claiming language interface tech was nowhere near evolved enough to make the device operable. And despite that unambiguous intelligence, at the Paramount Leader's insistence, a Bureau 3 operative had infiltrated the polycorp and stolen the chipset's schematics.

Since then, four project leads had tried, and failed, to get the damn thing working. Three now lived in disgrace, their lives ruined — and most of China's scientific community believed the fourth to be buried in a shallow grave somewhere outside Beijing.

Li had no intention of following in any of their footsteps. Especially not for the hateful bag of bones sat across from him.

He cleared his throat.

"To be honest, father, the Minister's assessment of progress is rather optimistic. I've read all the research notes from the last seven months, and aside from continuing Tze's process of trial and error, which had zero success but caused permanent functional impairment in ninety-two percent of test subjects, I have nothing from a neuro-engineering viewpoint to add to the work of my predecessors."

That wasn't what Jianzhu had been expecting to hear, and dangerous looking folds appeared in the paper-thin skin of the old councillor's face as he banged his fist on the desk again. "I can't tell the Paramount Leader that," he stormed. "I promised him results."

Li re-adopted his submissive posture. "I understand that father, and I am grateful for the opportunity you have given me. So when I saw the data and realised we could not solve Tianzi's issues ourselves, I tried to think past the problem — as you would."

He made the slightest eye contact.

"I even approached the Minister with a plan. But he dismissed the whole thing out of hand."

From the edges of his vision, Li noticed the feral grin grow on the bony skull opposite.

"Fuck him," Jianzhu growled. "The man's an idiot. What was your plan?"

"But he's already said no —" Li persisted.

"And I already said *fuck him*." The old man's lip curled into a snarl, his fist rising in anger again. "You are a Cheng. You work for me! What..is..it?"

Suppressing the desire to smile, Li took a slow breath, not wishing to sound too eager. "Fenton White will be attending the Taipei Technology Expo next month."

"Who?"

"The tech giant whose plans we built the Tianzi chip from."

That focused the aging brute's attention; greedy, scheming eyes coming alive. He waved a hand, wanting more.

"Our greatest problem with Tianzi is getting the chipset to interface. The plans we have are detailed, but incomplete."

Li paused, deliberately waiting for his father to make the leap.

Moments later, Jianzhu sat forward, perching elbows on the desk and his head in liver-spotted hands, re-appraising his son. "And you intend to get the rest from him?"

16

"Something like that, father," Li allowed himself the slightest of smiles. "But we'd need to move quickly."

"From the horse's mouth." Jianzhu inclined his head in approval. "Where better? What was the idiot's problem with that?"

"The Minister thought the plan risked an international incident," Li said in a meek voice. "While offering no guarantee we would get the data required. He was quite rude."

"Pah!" Jianzhu exclaimed. "He's a coward and will soon be dead. The Chairman has no time left for half measures." With a satisfied nod, the old man pressed a button on his desk.

"Councillor?" a female voice enquired.

"Miss Wong, would you bring tea for my son and I please," the onetime enforcer said, cutting the line without waiting for a response. Then he re-opened it. "And see when the Paramount Leader is available. Tell his staff it's urgent. I wish to speak with him about the Tianzi project."

As he cut the line again, Cheng Jianzhu realised with surprise he didn't feel utter disappointment in his son for a change.

"A chance to screw over that sanctimonious prick Yung, and a plan to achieve our Great Leader's ambitions, all in one?" He gave a wolfish grin. "I'm finally starting to like the way you think, boy. Maybe you have Cheng balls after all."

The old man re-arranged himself in his cavernous chair and waved a hand at Li again.

"Go on, impress me."

Aug 13, 2042
18:25H [South Blade Military Base, Guangzhou]

Li came too and threw up. There was a sucking, gurgling sound his mind absently connected with a visit to the dentist, then the world went dark again.

The Executive had flown him to the Special Forces base in Guangzhou straight after the procedure was sanctioned, and just an hour later, two multi-limbed MedBots hung over the unconscious man in the Ministry's clandestine body shop.

Three days of surgery followed. Spindly appendages, bristling with myriad surgical tools, working with efficient mechanical detachment to open and close skin, shave bone and add prostheses; completely remaking the body suspended in the diamagnetic field of their tableless, windowless, soundproofed room.

They created big round eyes and altered Li's iris colour. They shaped a long bulbous nose and square jaw. They removed his thick, black mane and replaced it with a scalp of fine blond hair. Then finally, while the poor wretch underwent a bleaching that made every one of the two billion nerve endings in his skin scream, they laser-cut new fingerprints, changed the tone, pitch and range of his voice, and modified both DNA and retinal profiles.

By the time the giant spider-like machines had finished, the only bits of Li that remained truly Cheng were his thoughts — and even those fell silent during the week his ravaged body spent floating unconscious in a re-gen tank.

18

After two more heavily sedated days wrapped in DermaGel, a medtec was finally in the anonymous operative's room removing the last of his face coverings. What lay beneath those bandages would decide his future. If the surgery had gone well the young scientist might just become the most famous of Chinese heroes; the Paramount Leader's own personal saviour. But if it had gone wrong, and he'd heard a lot of horror stories, Li figured he'd be dead before the day was over.

Taking a deep breath, he opened his eyes.

Though set low, the light in the room felt intense at first, and the Chinaman in the gweilo body furiously blinked away tears, praying blurs were not how he'd see the world from now on. But over the next couple of minutes, just as the medtec had said they would, his eyes adjusted, and the anxious colonel took the mirror held out by the mech — nerves replaced with a simple need to know his fate.

Silence filled the room for several long seconds, then the low rumble of a very western laugh started; staring back at the now nameless agent in that eight-inch looking glass was a scarless, tanned white man with fine, sandy blond hair and big blue eyes.

"Amazing isn't it," a rugged-looking guy with an unshaved face and greying hair said from the doorway, cutting through the younger man's elation.

Li hadn't seen a *real* person since arriving at the body shop, and assumed the man was a doctor. "Yes," he replied with a wide smile. "Yes, it is."

"You should only speak in English from now on," the man continued, switching to a gravelly American accent as he approached Li's bed and took his hand. "Make your handshake firm and maintain eye contact, irrespective of a

19

person's rank or position. You're an American now my friend, and we don't go in for exaggerated acts of humility."

Piercing grey eyes held Li's as the older man spoke.

"Good," he added with a crooked smile. "Welcome to the debauched land of the iniquitously free, and home of the largely disenfranchised."

Grunting a half-laugh at his own joke, the scruffy man wearing a dated brown suit popped a Marlboro into his mouth and sat down in the chair beside Li's bed. Ignoring the disapproval on the face of the retreating mech, he then produced an old silver coloured zippo from his jacket pocket, lit the cigarette with one fluid flip and strike, took a long drag, and blew the smoke towards an air-recirculator set above the simulated window and its view of Baiyun Mountain.

"You can call me Dean. They sure did a decent job on you, kid. Still hurt?"

"A bit," Li answered, beginning to realise this was no doctor. "I'm sorry *Dean*, I've no idea who you are or why you're here?"

The scruffy man smiled again. "Yeah, I get that a lot. I'm a last-minute addition to your mission, compliments of the Minister for State Security."

He took some folded documents from an inside pocket and handed them to Li. The papers included a set of orders from the Executive for Dean, which as he'd said, spelt out specific directions for his involvement in Li's mission, and then went on to instruct Li himself concerning their respective responsibilities.

After reading the documents through twice, the younger man nodded and passed them back.

"So in short," he frowned. "You're my babysitter."

"Pretty much," the older man agreed, taking another drag on his cigarette. "But I'm not here to steal your glory, kid. I've had my fill of that, and to be honest it's not all it's cracked up to be. From what I've been told, your specialism is wetware — yes?"

Li nodded.

"Well, mine is wetwork. Consider me an insurance policy; an extra bit of cover to make sure you can do your job without … interruptions."

Dean leaned forward in the chair, waving the two fingers holding his Marlboro. "Until two days ago, I was looking forward to retirement." His face betrayed the depth of his disappointment. "So I don't want to gatecrash your little trip any more than you want me tagging along. But if you encounter people-problems or someone needs removing from the country — that's my area of speciality, not yours."

Li couldn't argue with that. Colonel in the MSS or not, he was no trained killer or spy. He was a scientist whose reckless ambition had blinded him to the realities of the Premier's plan until he was on a plane, and even then, it was only while lying on a MedBed with every part of his body on fire that he began to realise just looking like Fenton White was never going to be enough.

"I know you know nothing about me, lad," Dean continued. "And to be honest, you don't need to. A heavily redacted summary of my career would go something like 'has been working in intelligence for a very long time and keeps a bunch of medals no one will ever see in a box gathering dust under the bed of a home he's never at.'" The veteran spy chuckled at his own humour again, then added. "The only bit of my story that really matters to you is, after all those years — I'm still here to tell the tale.

21

"This," he circled his face, "is all people need to see. And when you're good, it's all they *can* see."

The greying agent smiled at Li's obvious confusion.

"Okay, listen. Despite getting off a military transport from Beijing, it's taken four hours of checks and a vidcall direct to the Minister for State Security for me to walk into this room today. Why? Because I look nothing like a Major in the MSS; like a person who anyone needs to salute or call 'Sir.' And even now, with my ID confirmed, I remain a source of side glances and whispered conversations."

Dean ran a hand through his chalky, uncombed hair. "But that's as it should be. That's the trade-off we make to do our job. The price paid for staying alive. Pack Cheng Li away in your mind-vault, my friend. You're not that person anymore."

After taking a last long tug on his Marlboro, the mysterious American got up and walked through to the wetroom where he threw the butt of his cigarette into the toilet.

"You're a chameleon now," he said as he re-emerged. "Albeit one with no previous experience. So over the next couple of days the both of us will study your alpha's habits and mannerisms, and I will teach you some essential field craft. You can't just wear his skin lad; you have to become him.

"Trust me when I say it will be the smallest of mistakes that gets someone suspicious — and neither you or I can afford that."

The grey-haired spy eyed the other man as he walked towards the door, and although senior in rank, Li gave a short, deferential bow of the head.

22

"Like that," Dean pointed. "Remember what I just told you. You're not Chinese anymore. Get some rest. I'll come find you again in the morning."

Dean's accommodation was in the same annexe as Li's specialised medical unit, and his bags, which he noticed had been searched, were sitting on the bed when he entered.

Like the younger man's room, the solid concrete square had a simulated view of the mountain with an air-recirculator above it. A standard modular wet room cut clean straight lines into and across half the small box, separating the bed from a polymer desk, and frameless mirrors set in the wall above each, broke up the greyness of the walls while creating an illusion of space.

The veteran operative had stayed in many such rooms during his career and liked the lack of fuss. He went to the control panel by the door, turned the air-con down to eighteen, and after a rummage in his jacket pocket, ran a scanner over every surface.

No telltale signal spikes were a good thing and the old spy took off his jacket, pulled the tie around his neck loose, undid his collar button, and retrieved a bottle of Johnnie Walker from the centre of his duffel. In practiced routine he then walked into the small ensuite, got a glass from the shelf above the sink and took it, along with the whisky, his Marlboros and zippo, over to the desk; where he sat down, poured a drink, lit a cigarette, and let out the frustrated sigh he'd been holding in for two days.

Unlike the badly out-of-place scientist whose father bought him a position in the MSS following his graduation from Beijing's prestigious Tsinghua University, Dean's early life wasn't one of effortless privilege. The ironic thing being

23

his grandfather was among those vilified as bourgeois capitalists during Mao's cultural revolution some seventy years earlier, while Cheng's was a murderous low-life who became one of the so-called *revolutionaries* that hunted them like dogs.

In short order, the fate and fortune of each family had been reversed, and the Chengs went on to do very well thank you, with their sticky fingers in many pies and sycophantic empowerment of a senile old dictator — while all but a few admitted to remembering the now destitute Wu's.

But Dean, or Shen as he'd been back then, refused to let the hand fate dealt his family hold him back, and like his father before him, had simply gritted his teeth; always prepared to work harder, faster, longer than those around him.

That single-minded determination saw the young Wu win a scholarship to the university of Fujian, where he graduated with a first in dynamic psychology before outscoring twelve thousand other applicants to gain a place on the coveted MSS Special Operative training programme.

He laughed to himself. That now felt a long, lonely time ago, and despite the augmentations and jacked reflexes, the veteran field officer now felt far older than his fifty-two years.

At some point, it seemed overnight, his black hair streaked with grey had become grey hair streaked with black, and the price of one too many surgeries began to emerge, leaching elasticity from his skin and giving his face a parchment like texture he kidded himself translated into a mature, rugged look.

Anyway, it was in those first two years of training that he'd met Yung Zhu; a similarly disaffected, dispossessed overachiever who, though twelve years Shen's senior, shared

24

not only the younger man's determination to set certain records straight, but also his sexual orientation.

They'd climbed through the ranks together, one assignment after another, and now Zhu was the Minister for State Security, while Shen, who'd undergone the same procedure as Li four years earlier to assume the identity of a dead US agent, was now, at least outwardly, Dean Reynolds, a double agent only the Minister and a handful of the Chairman's inner circle knew existed.

The boy, on the other hand, was a colonel after just three years of pen pushing in a lab, and that was just ridiculous. Then again, so was the Executive signing off on the deployment of an untrained scientist.

Dean shook his head and offered an angry toast to the young officer, adding an ironic salute before swallowing his whisky in a single gulp.

The halfwit was certain to get them both killed.

But as the grey eyes in the mirror scolded him for being petty, the emotionally exhausted operative conceded it wasn't really Li he was pissed at — Zhu had promised him retirement … knew all the names and faces were catching up, and the man who'd given him *everything* was dangerously close to falling apart.

The aging spy suppressed an unwelcome tear with a snarl. He'd been going to return to the smallholding his father had bought in Yunnan and a mother who wouldn't recognise his face. He'd hoped to reconcile those long years of service to restore his family name, with the things that really mattered when weighing the soul of a man. But then Cheng Jianzhu took his son's ridiculous proposal to the Paramount Leader … and fate once again chose to take a giant shit on the meagre *hopes* of a Wu.

25

Consciously pulling his game-face back into place, Dean forced the unhelpful emotions down — they were more likely to get him killed than that idiot boy.

With a grim smile, he refilled the glass and lit another Marlboro. At least the three worms would rejoice — grateful for another chance to feast upon his guilt ravaged corpse.

This time he toasted the Minister.

PARTITION ONE   Cluster 1   **Sector iii**

Aug 18, 2042
11:15H [Chek Lap Kok, Hong Kong]

Four days later, Dean and Li were in a car headed towards Hong Kong airport. They could have taken a bullet train, but Dean was keen to limit the inexperienced scientist's exposure; who's name, at least for this part of the journey, was now Christopher Jacobs — a corpo exec from San Francisco travelling with his business partner to the Innovex Expo in Taipei. Both men had the requisite invitations, tickets and itineraries, along with records on their pads of booked accommodation and planned excursions while staying for one of Asia's pre-eminent technology conferences.

As Dean had promised, they'd practised for hours each day before leaving the safety of the base. Questions about home, about the business, about each other. Bit by bit, Li's rough edges broke away; the stiffness and wide eyes of a liar relaxing into casual confidence.

Now, sitting in the back of an executive Mercedes wearing a tailored linen suit and Ray Bans, the young blond-haired American cradling a panama hat in his lap looked every bit the successful executive on an all-expenses paid trip abroad.

"You feeling alright kiddo?" Dean asked.

"Yeah sure," Li said. "Just a little sticky."

The older man reached for the blower controls. "It's like they mess with your internal plumbing along with everything else during that op, isn't it?" he grinned. "Bet you didn't sweat like this before, gweilo." They both laughed as he turned up the stream of cool air circulating in the rear of the car.

"We'll be on a plane in three hours, and in the hotel by six. You're doing great, kid. Just keep breathing and remember what I told you."

Li nodded. "Perfect chance for me to settle into my new skin."

"You got it," the veteran spy said.

The sun was high in a cloudless sky as the long, black limousine glided over the Tsing Ma Bridge. Container ships navigated the Ma Wan Channel below at a leisurely pace, and men with long rods were visible on the craggy rocks either side, fishing in the bright blue waters. Li was getting nervous now. He'd soon be standing in one of the busiest airports in the world, exposed for the first time to the scrutiny of others. He felt naked without his uniform, his *own* skin, and fully expected someone to point at him as he left the safety of the car; accusing eyes questioning who that man over there was — the one pretending to be someone else?

Hong Kong International was enormous. Built on the artificial island of Chek Lap Kok, it was the third largest airport in the world, and as the Mercedes pulled up outside Terminal One, people and cars were everywhere.

Their driver got out and opened Li's door with a bow. Fighting the urge to bow back, the fake American said thank you in what he hoped was a bad enough Cantonese accent and pressed two hundred Hong Kong dollars into the hand of the small, weathered looking chauffeur. As Dean got out and also thanked the driver, a porter emerged from the terminal entrance steering a maglev cart and offering warm greetings.

"Mister Jacobs? Mister Matthews?"

Li nodded, and as he and Dean then moved to the pavement beside the car, a fast-paced conversation ensued between driver and porter as the boot opened with a gentle whine; the driver waving a hand in Li's direction as he told his countryman to look after them — they were big tippers. A smile spread across Dean's face and he winked an 'I told you so' at Li. Despite his anxiety, the younger man couldn't help but grin back. Maybe this wouldn't be so bad after all.

Inside, it was like someone had kicked an ant's nest. Thousands of people dragging luggage and screaming children in their wake milled backwards and forwards with no obvious sign of organisation. The terminal was a battleground, and while conditioning units blasting tepid air from large overhead pipes fought valiantly to keep both the building and tempers cool, not a single one of its economically disadvantaged belligerents seemed to be having any fun.

On the back of the maglev, none of that bothered Li or Dean as their porter manoeuvred his way through the masses towards Cathay Pacific's executive lounge; the vehicle's amber light, and leathery man's near constant use of horn and vigorous arm-waving, easily parting the human tide before them. With each passing moment, Li's nerves calmed.

Yes, people were staring. But they were staring with looks he could tell were annoyance or envy, not suspicion.

Ten minutes later, a very attractive attendant had checked their boarding passes, taken their lunch orders and escorted them through to the Pier Lounge, where an equally human waiter was just delivering two large, cold beers. Dean held up his glass, clinking the top of Li's. "Notice the lack of mechs in your life today?" he said. "You're going to like the *executive* lifestyle, my friend."

Li hadn't noticed. But now the older operative had snapped him out of his fugue, it seemed almost obscene *real* people were waiting on them and so few passengers got to enjoy the decadent space; its one-way floor to ceiling visi-steel walls providing the privileged few with a zoo-like viewing experience between their quiet, airy oasis, and the marauding hordes beyond. A lone corpo sat on a stool at the marble-topped bar, sipping coffee and tapping away on his pad, while perhaps a dozen other execs and wealthy couples occupied no more than a handful of the lounge's sumptuous sofas, either engaged in quiet conversation or simply enjoying the comedic chaos *relative poverty* was inflicting on those beyond the boundary of their sanctuary.

Aside from the occasional nod or wave of a hand, no one was interested in Li, and the young man who now enjoyed the casual good looks of a western billionaire decided he already liked the *executive* lifestyle. He liked it a lot.

Passage through Songshan Airport was equally trouble-free, and within half an hour of landing, another old man in a chauffeur's uniform was loading their bags into another limousine, and they were on their way to the hotel.

Taipei was beautiful, and the people there thrived despite everything the PRC had done to thwart them. Dean respected that. He saw in Taiwan the realisation of a dream his people once sought; a co-existence with the wider world that wasn't built on fear or suspicion, but rather on mutual co-operation and success.

Socialism didn't demand totalitarianism. In fact, the opposite was true. Though somehow the PRC, like the Russians, North Koreans and a raft of other countries who'd since been swallowed up by the polycorps, had warped that beautiful dream into thinly veiled dictatorships.

In contrast, Taiwan was a true democracy, where everyone had a say in their government, not just a hand-picked group of elites who served a *leader* no common citizen had voted for in decades.

The veteran intelligence operative looked over at his travelling companion. History was littered with the stories of *visionary* leaders like the one Li's family served; men inflated to a godlike status by reshaping society to propagate views and beliefs designed solely to reinforce their control. Those stories were always, without fail, accompanied by ethnic or political *cleansing*, and the general loss of an entire population's freedom to think anything other than what they were told to think.

That's what made time, or at least its passage, so important. It always levelled the field. Those men eventually died, and in doing so, created change — allowed different outlooks to flourish. Even during war, time provided a rock for people to cling to; sowing the seeds of futures where hope could take root and thrive.

So when, if, man became the master of death and time's passage of little consequence — what then?

Dean couldn't begin to fathom all the ramifications. He just knew in his heart, as did the Minister, that no man should be allowed that kind of dominion over nature.

He glanced again at the young scientist who hoped to usher in that new age, wondering if the lad had stopped to think about the consequences; about the people that had, and would, die for his ambitions; about a world where old men like Ye never died and guarded their power jealously.

He doubted it.

But none of that really mattered anymore — both of them were trapped: Li by naive desire and Dean by loyalty. Neither could escape his fate, and as the car continued its shaded journey among the glass and steel giants, the aging spy sighed in rueful anticipation of what lay ahead.

Access to their suite on the top floor of the Mandarin Oriental had been arranged via a staff entrance, and eight hours after leaving the spartan utility of Guangzhou, the two men were standing in the second-best suite of Taipei's finest hotel looking out at the magnificence of the 101 Tower. They were now, at least according to the mission briefing, in enemy territory.

The corridor and guest lift outside their door serviced only one other set of rooms, the Presidential Suite, and Dean had ensured the butler servicing both was on the MSS payroll.

In fact, the veteran operative had been very busy indeed since the Minister drafted him into the mission, and several cases of equipment were waiting for them on arrival. He didn't discuss their contents with Li, and the rookie agent already knew better than to ask.

From the ones he did open, the chiselled older man removed a ceramic Glock 17 and several types of ammunition;

31

checking the weapon and magazines before slipping off his jacket to put the covert holster on. He then took out a document pouch and slid the contents, a wallet and another passport, into his inner jacket pocket before putting the one he'd used to travel to Taipei into the pouch and waving at China's newest and least prepared operative to hand his over too.

A second case contained three digipads displaying camfeeds from the corridor outside and suite of rooms next door. And from a third, Dean removed a digestible BeiDou tracker, which he told Li to swallow. "Just in case we get separated."

But when the aging spook reached the last two cases, he stopped, and it became obvious to the younger man he wouldn't get to see what they contained. So he took himself off for a shower.

Contesting fingers of shade and painful brightness groped along the suite's white ceilings as Taipei's long afternoon wore into evening. But when the sky finally darkened enough to give the gentle breeze a chance, both men took their equipment out onto the terrace with a bottle of Johnnie Walker, and watched as lights across the city began blinking into existence like will-o'-the-wisps.

At ten o'clock Dean received a call, and moments later an alarm on one of the digipads indicated movement on their floor. As they both sat watching, a man and woman entered the corridor and approached the Presidential Suite. Within the apartment, the pair then sat in the lounge overlooking Taipei and discussed the day while Yu-En, the butler, arrived and served coffee. Both were well dressed, and Li watched their behaviour with nervous, professional interest; breathing a sigh of relief when things didn't get intimate.

The conference it seemed, had gone well, and they agreed she'd collect him in the morning at 10:15 for an excursion to the Taroko National Park before their flight home. Dean looked at Li and he nodded. He knew the plan. The woman then left with a stroke of the man's arm and a request he not stay up too late working.

They watched her enter the lift. Then all was quiet again.

PARTITION ONE   Cluster 1   **Sector iv**

Aug 18, 2042
23:30H [Mandarin Oriental, Taipei]

In the dim light of the office area, Fenton hunched over a portable techdeck, eyes closed to the outside world as he rotated the molecular model his mind's eye could see, and removed the errant carbon atom.

"Your work is truly inspiring, Doctor," an American voice said, breaking through his concentration.

"Thank you," he answered.

But as the time and place registered, the tech entrepreneur pulled off his synaptic cap to see a shadow spilling out from the doorway. "I'm sorry, I don't think I know you?"

As he moved into the room, the lights revealed a chalky-haired white man in perhaps his mid-fifties wearing a dated brown suit who was carrying a gun. "Yeah, I get that a lot."

The billionaire inventor felt the dull thud of something hitting his chest, and in less than a heartbeat he was lying paralysed on the plush beige carpet.

"Don't worry, Doctor." The American's voice sounded a little distant. "You're not dying. In fact, you'll be feeling rather good in about a minute."

Then another, more familiar face appeared in Fenton's view.

He was feeling woozy now.

"Hello me," he mumbled as his breathing deepened.

The other person laughed and stroked his hair before taking his cuff. "Hello me," they responded in the entrepreneur's own voice.

Fenton giggled at that. Then everything went dark.

PARTITION ONE   Cluster 1   **Sector v**

Aug 19, 2042
10:15H [Mandarin Oriental, Taipei]

Lucy Grey, Fenton's PA, arrived on the floor at precisely 10:15, and Yu-En opened the door to the Presidential Suite.

"Good morning, Miss. Have you breakfasted?"

"Thank you Yu-En, yes I have. Although I'll take a coffee if there's any going?"

"Of course, Miss." Yu-En showed Lucy into the suite and she sat down on a sofa, flicking through the day's itinerary on her cuff.

Fenton appeared moments later, buttoning his shirt. "Be with you in a sec. Might have stayed up a little late last night messing with molecules."

Lucy rolled her eyes, and Dean, watching on his digipad, nodded in approval.

Twenty minutes later, as Fenton White and Lucy Grey left the Mandarin Oriental for their helicopter flight to Taroko, the aging spook went into the master bedroom of the suite next-door and sat on the huge emperor-size bed occupied by the man who'd inherited Christopher Jacobs passport and identity.

Before interrogating the privileged executive with the contents of the bags Li hadn't seen opened, Dean had been worried he'd have to kill the billionaire to stop him from co-operating. But the plucky lad had proved to be both brave and resourceful; defiantly informing the greying spy during a lucid moment, that he'd activated a kill switch which would prevent even his own access if neural countermeasures detected any further physical or chemical compromise. Satisfied his next move would invoke those protocols and lockdown any files in White's brain, Dean rendered the tech genius catatonic again and packed away his head-breaking equipment.

Once Li had left with Fenton's PA, Yu-En informed the veteran operative that four associates had arrived and were travelling up in the service elevator to assist with Mr Jacobs. Dean nodded and looked over at the unfortunate, immobile soul staring at him with mute, accusing eyes. Perhaps killing him would have been the kinder thing to do.

"Have you heard of Qincheng?" the aging operative asked. "My Grandfather was sent there —." His voice trailed off, and he cleared his throat.

"As a lad, *The Man in the Iron Mask* captivated me. Do you know the book, Doctor? I felt a sense of great pity for the man who'd not only been unfairly imprisoned, but also had everything he was stolen from him."

He sighed and nudged Fenton's leg.

"That said, I also thought such a man, a man with no identity, could become anything he wanted — could perhaps escape his fate."

His digipad showed four men getting out of the elevator.

"You're now Christopher Jacobs, my friend. A no one from Frisco whose record will soon show was convicted of drug smuggling."

Dean gave Fenton an apologetic look as the MSS agents entered the bedroom with a wheelchair and face covering. He gave them strict instructions not to talk with the prisoner or show his face to anyone. "Keep him isolated and medicated until the Minister decides what to do with him." Then to Fenton he added, "Goodbye, Mr Jacobs."

There was an edge of sadness to Reynolds' voice as they picked the tech billionaire up from the bed and put him in the wheelchair.

"Pray for Musketeers."

Unable to move or speak, a single tear travelled down Fenton's right cheek as one of the men covered his face.

Aug 18, 2042
20:00H [Eden campus, California]

The deskcom chimed and Maggie's wiry face blinked up amid the trail of green and red numbers scrolling over the plexiglass of Daran Whittaker's desk. "Sorry, I know it's late, but you're going to want to see this."

Eden's Chief Executive nodded, acknowledging his sister considered whatever it was urgent, and made a hand gesture for the office AI to activate the link she'd sent to his deck. The windows transitioned, shutting out the molten bronze sky of a long Californian evening, and as the excited voice of an Asian reporter invaded that sudden darkness, he turned his attention towards the section of wall now displaying what seemed to be a live newsfeed.

"That's Fenton's chopper, isn't it?" Maggie stated rather than asked.

Whittaker ignored her, transfixed by the vid as news drones hovered over a scythe-like furrow cutting through the treeline of a heavily forested area before following its path to an abrupt end, where a burnt-out helicopter fuselage lay on one side among shattered sections of tail and rotor. After several seconds, he turned his fleshy face back to his sister. "Are they alive?"

"The newsfeeds aren't saying," Maggie said. "But I've got the entire back office working every comlink to find out more."

He stared at the scene a moment longer, considering his response. Western news channels would be all over it soon; the Board of Directors and other polycorps not long after.

"Get me out there," he growled, snatching his pad from its dock and sliding the accompanying cuff back onto his wrist.

"Already on it," the near skeletal woman said. "Frank in administration is filing a flight plan as we speak. I'll grab a few aids from those still in the office, and draft something for the media that says Eden is aware of a crash and is making further enquiries?"

Whittaker made a conscious effort to remove the scowl from his face and looked down at her image.

"Always a step ahead, little sister. What would I do without you?"

He gave her a subdued smile.

"Arrange some feet on the ground as well. If we've got no assets out that way, hire them. But by the time we land, I want to know what happened. I want to know how it happened. And I want to know if we need to fuck someone up for attacking Eden."

Maggie nodded, and he cut the link.

Aside from the seclusion and natural beauty of the two hundred and forty square kilometres Daran and Fenton had created the Eden campus on, the deal with Riverside County included a former military air base and agreement with the FAA that the polycorp could use it if they funded necessary air traffic control staff. So, little more than fifteen minutes after leaving his suite, Eden's CEO, together with his sister and seven aids, was aboard the corporation's Stratoflyer as the sleek low-orbit shuttle taxied onto the old World War Two runway.

The cost of the jet was phenomenal, and the carbon footprint obscene. But Whittaker was happy to atone by funding a forest or two in the orbital agri-domes if it meant his transit time between appointments stayed to a minimum.

He smiled to himself in anticipation as the engine noise and vibrations converged to a single thrum of readiness while Maggie settled her excited gaggle of aids in seat restraints. "I'll allocate tasks once we're in the air," she told them. "Just sit down. Mr Whittaker doesn't like waiting."

In fact, the Chief Executive's impatience had turned into a competition between flight crews to earn his recognition and a regular spot on the company flagship. They knew, after getting aboard, the boss counted each second in his head until the pilot released the snarling Pratt & Whitney engines and sent the aircraft hurtling down its four thousand metre concrete strip.

This evening though, he reached fifty-two before the soft leather seat swallowed his ample body as the Stratoflyer surged forward. Not the best by a long stretch.

Moments later a slight lurch of the stomach reported they were off the ground and climbing sharply towards the edge of darkness, where they'd skim Earth's atmosphere at five times the speed of sound.

Some people, including Fenton, had called the increasingly autocratic CEO's acquisition of the aircraft needlessly decadent. But as none of them had built one of Earth's largest polycorps in just ten years, Whittaker felt perfectly justified in telling them all to go fuck themselves; time was money, and the heavy-set magnate would be in Taipei in under two hours.

He'd once tried to explain to Fenton how precious time, well *their time* at least, was: the better they used it, the

39

closer they came to achieving goals. While the lad had stated he agreed, he then wanted to debate what constituted a *good* use of precious time, and Whittaker had thrown his hands up at the futility of arguing with the intractable genius — choosing instead to show him by simply walking away.

That had made Fenton laugh, and clap as he acknowledged the point being made.

They'd both enjoyed those early years.

Whittaker gambled both his future and fortune to finance the talented engineer's crazy dreams, and in turn, those crazy dreams had revolutionised the use of smart tech for people with enough credit to access it.

But as their various companies grew and diversified, the wily CEO came to realise that while his protégé was truly gifted, and there was no doubt about that, the younger man was also supremely naïve and opinionated in the way only truly gifted people could be. So the weathered businessman adapted, as he always had, and sought to keep Fenton away from the grittier realities of a polycorp's growth.

PARTITION ONE   Cluster 2   **Sector ii**

Aug 18, 2042
22:45H [Near Earth Orbit, California time]

Twenty-five minutes after take-off, Maggie threw the image of a thin-faced, rugged looking man onto the section of wall between her and her brother.

"This is Dean Reynolds." She scanned to see whether any of Daran's aids were in earshot. "The, err ... investigator we engaged in Taiwan."

The man on the other end of the link was older than Whittaker was expecting, but had a military bearing and searching grey eyes.

"Mr Reynolds," he greeted, looking at the notes Maggie was flagging on his pad. "Thanks for the quick response. Though I thought we were reaching out to MacKenzie Security?"

Reynolds gave a disarming smile and nodded. "Mr Whittaker," he responded in a gravelly mid-west baritone. "It's a pleasure to make your acquaintance. I'm a senior associate with MacKenzie, so rest assured, you have. The Colonel would usually greet such a prominent client as yourself, but he's in the field at the moment so the office matched your needs with my skills. I hope that's acceptable?"

The corpulent executive nodded, keen to know what the man had established. "Yes. Yes, of course. What have you managed to find out so far?"

"Well, it's early days, and the Taiwanese are always tight-lipped when something bad happens to a foreigner. Particularly a polycorp exec," Reynolds said. "But I guess the most important and immediate news we've been able to gather so far, is that by some miracle your man is alive — thrown clear as the helicopter went down. Though I can't tell you much more than that because, despite the authorisations your office sent, the staff at the Taiwan University Hospital and local security services have refused me access to Dr White himself. So the best I've been able to do for security at this time is post a team of ... investigators," he adopted Maggie's word, "around the facility he's in."

Annoyed, Daran looked over to his sister, but could see in the corner of their comlink she was already typing a simple instruction to his pool of aids — *make the position of Taipei's leadership clear; resisting the wishes of one of the world's most powerful CEO's will have dire individual, political and economic consequences.*

"I think you'll find them more compliant now," he said, turning back to the military contractor. "Have you got any information on Fenton's actual condition? The drone footage from the accident site didn't look encouraging."

Reynolds nodded in affirmation. "Though he refused to go into any detail, I did get the hospital administrator to confirm Dr White's injuries weren't life threatening. Regarding the *accident* though," the man's thin brows twitched upward. "I'd prefer to give you some solid facts once we've made a few more enquiries. But you're right, it does seem Dr White has been unimaginably lucky."

Whittaker's eyes narrowed as he considered the other man's words.

"And Lucy, his PA?" Maggie interrupted.

Reynolds' voice altered slightly, inflecting a tone of sympathy. "I'm sorry ma'am, both the pilot and Dr White's companion died in a fire that started when the aircraft's fuel cells ruptured."

The wiry woman caught her breath and sat back out of image capture, adjusting the tint of her glasses to hide the moisture gathering behind them. Daran reached out to take her hand, but she pulled it away, refusing to make eye contact. Sighing heavily, the thickset businessman placed his elbows on the table and returned his gaze to the mercenary. "I'm guessing you don't think this is an accident then?"

Reynolds hesitated, then shrugged, as if deciding to say something. "I don't, Mr Whittaker." He leaned out of camshot to pick something up. "These are the tech specs for the aircraft Dr White and his companion were in."

"And?" Daran enquired.

"And one of the manufacturer's main boasts is that a fire, any kind of fire, just isn't possible in that model of chopper." The security contractor held up a hand. "But like I said, we need a proper look at the wreckage with specialists to fully understand what happened. The manufacturer and operator both know who was on that bird, so I guarantee they will be climbing all over it too. It won't be hard to isolate the cause."

Maggie was watching her brother from behind darkened glasses now. He left responding for the briefest moment, then acknowledged the gravity of Reynolds' words. "What are the Taiwanese authorities saying?"

"Nothing at the moment. They won't even talk off the record yet." The dangerous-looking man suppressed another shrug. "But that's normal, they'll be worrying about repercussions too. Give me a day and I'll get you answers … if that's what you want?"

"Yes," Daran replied without hesitation, locking eyes with the other man. "Yes, of course that's what I want. What Fenton and Lucy's parents will want."

Maggie's hand was back on the table now and he reached over, successfully gathering it up and squeezing gently.

"I know you've not worked for Eden before, Mr Reynolds, but nothing is too much in your pursuit of this matter. Nothing. I don't care what you have to do, or what it costs." Whittaker dabbed his cuff twice and swiped towards the display. "I'm sending you my private comlink and want you to contact me directly with any updates or requirements. Just get me answers and get them soon. Do that, and you can expect many more lucrative contracts. Understand?"

The other man acknowledged receipt of the Chief Exec's secure comlink with a corresponding swipe on his own cuff. "I think I do, Mr Whittaker."

"Good. We'll be at the hospital in a couple of hours. Hopefully, my sister has now resolved your access issues, so I'd be grateful if you could see to Fenton's security and get us an update on his condition."

Reynolds nodded, and Maggie cut the connection.

The exhausted, desperately thin woman could see anger sitting behind her brother's eyes and hoped it was the righteous kind, the kind that would pursue justice for Fenton and that poor dead girl. He got up, issued several further orders to his clutch of aids and poured himself a brandy from the bar before returning.

"You okay?" he asked, standing over the backrest of his seat.

"I will be," she answered in a flat, quiet voice.

The powerful businessman gave a wan smile, absorbing her mood. "Well, get some rest for what's left of the flight. It's going to be a long couple of days." Then he left for one of the private cabins in the rear.

After her brother had gone, Maggie sat staring out of the window, watching the blue-white halo they were hurtling along and trying to convince herself the icy feeling in her gut was wrong. Through her AR connection she saw Daran open and close several encrypted comlinks, and tried not to think of who he might be talking to.

Please don't have anything to do with this, she thought.

There were a lot of skeletons in the Whittaker family closet. Most of them bastards who deserved it. But some didn't, and she fervently hoped the death of that beautiful young girl had nothing to do with her brother or his scheming.

Her hands were shaking like they used to in the old days, and she hooked a couple of moggies out of her purse to take the edge off...then she blurred the rest with a bottle of red.

Aug 19, 2042
15:20H [Chang Gung Memorial Hospital, Taipei]

Fenton looked banged up. A jagged gash traversed his forehead under the unruly mop of blond hair, and bruising had begun blooming along the line of his jaw to merge with a puffy purple-black mass laying siege to his bloodshot left eye.

Whittaker stared at the forlorn figure half lying, half sitting on the bed in a pale blue dressing gown and shook his head. The young billionaire had spent the night in a sedation tank which had completed most of the recuperative work, but a DermaGel chest cast continued to protect and set broken ribs, while a thick, nanite-filled donut encasing his right knee would remain in place for another two days to rebuild the shattered joint.

"How are you doing, kiddo?" he asked. "You scared the living shit out of me there."

Ravaged eyes left the spot on the floor they'd been staring at to travel up Daran's thick, fine-suited frame. "Have they told you about Lucy?"

The big man swallowed and nodded. He felt bad about the girl. "Yes, I spoke to her father on the way here. We'll get to the bottom of what happened, Fenton. I promise."

The tormented young man's face twisted in obvious self-loathing. "It's my fault Daran. She wouldn't have been in that damn helicopter if I hadn't wanted to see the temple at Taroko."

The older man reached out to touch Fenton, then stopped short, unsure of what might hurt. "Hey, come on, don't do that to yourself," he said in a soft voice. "No one could have known this was going to happen." His rounded face affected a look of reproachful sympathy. "In fact, I'm told the manufacturer had boasted fire is impossible in that model of aircraft. So, while I'm certain someone is to blame for this, Fenton, either through negligence or malice — I can tell you now son, it isn't you."

A knock at the door brought a habitual "Come" from Eden's Chief Exec, and Reynolds entered, flanked by two men with carbines strapped across armoured chests. "It's good to meet you in person, Mr Whittaker," he said, offering his hand.

"Likewise," Daran responded, exchanging a brisk shake while glancing left and right at the mercs. "I was just telling Fenton here of your concerns about his *accident*. But I'm guessing the additional muscle points to something more concrete?"

The security consultant nodded to the battered-looking man on the bed before returning his gaze to the big CEO. "Yes, I'm afraid it does. I'm now confident we can draw a line under any question of an accident," he said. "I've had an

46

expert working with the manufacturer of that aircraft, and their claims are sound. We've also inspected the operator's maintenance and safety records, which are exemplary."

"Meaning?"

"Meaning," Reynolds continued. "That even if we somehow establish pilot error as a significant factor in the crash, Dr White's chopper should not have been able to catch fire. Leaving just one viable conclusion — sabotage."

"What?" Fenton stiffened, shock evident on his bruised face. "What are you saying?"

Reynolds fixed his winter grey eyes on Whittaker, interested in the big man's reaction. "I'm saying, Dr White, that I think someone tried to kill you."

PARTITION TWO

Sector [U/K]

[QUARANTINED: Bad Sector: timestamp error: location error]

As the Range Rover picked its way through the back streets of Manhattan Beach, Eric looked at the driver, still unable to fathom how the powerhouse of a woman could be there in the manner she'd described or what the hell she could do for him if, as she'd suggested, they were stuck inside a program neither of them controlled.

In standard Total Immersion, he'd be hooked up to a deck, and while the game might be multi-player, each person within the environment would be able to come and go as they pleased. Here though, if he was genuinely immersed, it seemed someone or something prevented participant commands, well his at least, and he had no idea how to get out. That said, whoever or whatever it was, couldn't have complete control. As surely, if they did, they'd just reset the programme now or … *shit*, he realised perhaps things were going exactly the way they wanted them to.

This was serious Descartes territory; a TI programmer's dream; a place where you couldn't tell real from artificial; a place where you couldn't trust your senses one bit — and the only thing you knew with any certainty was that you, the thing doing the thinking, existed.

He couldn't even rely on Sade if he was in TI. She'd just be another NPC, a projection.

"I know, right," Miah said, eyes flicking in his direction before returning to the road.

"What?" Eric asked, realising his thoughts must be plastered all over his face.

"This is a hot mess," she replied. "I have no idea what that guy will try. No idea what I can and can't do in this environment. No idea how to protect you. And no idea how to get you out. I don't even know where here is?"

She eyed him again.

Eric appreciated the apparent sincerity, even if a little anxious Whittaker had sent her into this with no plan of what to do next. And while something in his gut or the depths of his cognition told him the guy in the suit was bad news, it was important he kept some perspective around the *bodyguard* sent to *protect* him; he didn't know a damn thing about her either — especially whether he could trust her. Hell, he didn't even know if she was real or just part of the programme. But, if she was to be believed, more than one person or group were playing around inside his head, and Eric needed to know more about who and why if he was going to get out.

"To be honest, Miah, I'm desperate to get my head around all this too. You need to start at the beginning for me. Maybe we can figure some of this stuff out together?"

Miah's head bobbed in agreement with the common sense of Eric's request. "Okay, that's fair. I'm a security consultant contracted by Mr Whittaker to keep you safe," she said, looking over at him again. "He, Mr Whittaker that is, was contacted by government officials a couple of weeks back

49

over concerns regarding both the project you have been working on, and the intentions of Doctor White."

"Wait, what?" Eric cut in. "The government? How are they involved? How do they even know? Why —"

"Lots of questions again, Doctor," Miah observed.

"Yes, right. Sorry. Go on."

"I can only go from the briefing I was given, okay?" He nodded again.

"According to Mr Whittaker, the US government became aware that Dr White had resumed work on something called the MindMerge chip. Whether that intelligence was provided to them or intercepted, I don't know," she said. "And while he didn't go into the specifics with me, Mr Whittaker had developed his own concerns regarding Dr White's recent behaviour. Particularly his obsession with that same project — which I understand he'd been quite emphatic about shutting down several months earlier."

"Yes, yes he was," the wetware engineer agreed.

Miah turned the Range Rover onto the 405, heading north.

"As I understand it, Mr Whittaker agreed to work with a government computer scientist, and gave him a position in one of the labs at Eden so he could have a poke around. Anyway, someone tried to kill that fed in the early hours this morning, and then your house went into lockdown."

Eric swallowed. "Wow," was initially all he could find to say. "So, you being here? Can you shed any light on that? This?" He waved an arm at the reality they seemed to be driving through, and the big woman nodded.

"When your place went into lockdown, so did Eden. Dr White even tried to freeze Mr Whittaker out of the corporation's systems. But it seems he's unaware of several

50

backdoors into the mainframe, which have allowed those now working for Mr Whittaker in San Francisco to isolate and recode aspects of your neural pattern as it travels through the Eden servers. That, I'm told, should mean the bad guys can't reset the immersion processes anymore." She gave him another quick glance. "I hope that makes some kind of sense to you, Doc. Because, to be honest, most of what they said before I put on the cap of wires went way over my head. I'm good at keeping people alive — but I'm no techie.

"I was just told to keep *the you* running around in here out of White's hands, while the people out there try to regain control of Eden. Which, if I had to guess, is where they must think your body is."

Miah blew out a breath, puffing both cheeks, and gave the wetware entrepreneur an enigmatic smile. "So here I am. Doing something I would never have imagined possible or necessary — playing someone's bodyguard in what I understand is essentially a high stakes computer game."

The whole point of total immersion was to create a seamless interaction with other people in a digital environment that seemed real. Hell, alongside the PDrive that created the necessary perceptual connections, developing the concept and subsequent gaming platforms are what made Eric rich. But, and it was a big *but*, if what the big woman had just said was true, he couldn't think of a way anyone would be able to hack a live TI stream; it was end to end encrypted with algorithms even he couldn't break. No invite — no entry. The only way he figured this could be happening was if he was jacked in somewhere, and all the other *players* had been granted access.

If the programme was running through Eden servers, he supposed some sort of backdoor entry might be possible; like two gamers running off one deck. But what were the odds

51

of Fenton White not being able to freeze someone out of a computer if he wanted to? A lot of Miah's story, Eric decided, just didn't add up.

"Do you know why all this is happening?" he asked.

"Mr Whittaker was hoping *you'd* be able to shed some light on that?" Miah responded. "I mean, it's clear Fenton White had a bad reaction to something connected to the MindMerge project, and as you're now missing — it seems reasonable to assume that *something* is related to you?"

They drove in silence for a few seconds, then the hired gun added, "One thing is for sure though, whatever triggered this, there's no going back for Fenton White. He may be a corpo big shot, but even if the US isn't what it used to be, trying to disappear a federal agent isn't something their government will take lying down."

She was concentrating on the road now. Deliberately not looking at him.

"So, any idea what you might have said or done to piss him off in such a spectacular way?"

Eric hesitated, reluctant to answer. "That wasn't part of your briefing?"

"No." The security consultant gave a single shake of her head. "As I said, Mr Whittaker knows Dr White approached you, and you were working with him. He knows someone took a shot at the scientist, that you are missing, and both your house and Eden are now in lockdown. He also knows that since then, the only statement released by White has been to the effect that he's taken pre-emptive measures to prevent his *former* CEO and as yet unspecified others from stealing Eden property — and, as Mr Whittaker hasn't tried to *steal* anything from his *own* polycorp, he was kinda hoping you might be able to fill in some of the blanks?" She paused for a reply, and Eric sighed, feeling compelled to answer.

"Fenton approached me last month and asked me to look over a chipset he'd developed but shelved as he couldn't get it to talk with the brain. Wetware is my thing."

"Yes, I know that bit." Miah waved a dismissive hand. "Moving on from there though, it seems pretty clear something happened over the last few days to change your relationship. Did you get his chip to work and then try to renege? Is that what this is all about?"

The big woman's directness shocked Eric, and he eyed her with caution. "Why would you ask that?"

"Look," she went on, holding up an apologetic hand, "I'm not trying to offend you, Doctor. And I don't give a shit if you tried to pull a fast one or not. Not my business. My point was, knowing what his beef is may help me protect you."

The agitated wetware specialist rubbed at gritty eyes, shaking his head. "Of course I didn't try to *pull a fast one*. I was trying to help a friend. Now I wish I'd never got involved!" He took a shaky breath, "Sorry Miah, I'm just —"

"Hey, no problem, Doc," the mercenary interjected. "Forget I asked."

But now Eric had started, the words continued to fall from him. "We had an argument about it. The chipset I mean. I thought, still think, the thing is dangerous. I suggested perhaps it would be for the best if it never worked, and he went crazy at me. Totally flipped. So I said I wanted out. Told him to stick his chip and find someone else."

Miah gave a sympathetic nod. "So why not just send it back to him?"

"Believe me," Eric said, shifting position in the SUV's well-padded seat. "I wish it was that simple."

Sensing that was all she was going to get from the man, the muscular merc gave him a roguish smile. "Well, looking on the bright side, I'd say if he wanted you dead — you'd be dead already."

The confused twenty-six-year-old couldn't see any bright side to that news and turned his head to stare out of the window, desperate to piece together a credible series of events.

As they passed LAX, a jet climbed ponderously into the air, and he marvelled at the intuitive impossibility of the metal giant defying gravity; brute force it thrusting heavenward.

Their conversation hadn't taken the tired tech engineer any closer to understanding who he was stuck in a car with, and as none of his comms worked, he couldn't call his dad for help. Brute force wasn't going to break him free of this nightmare. He had to think his way out, and that meant, for the time being at least, just sitting tight, playing dumb, and fishing for information.

"So, where are we going?" he asked.

"Unless you tell me there's a point to heading somewhere specific, I'm just going to drive until Whittaker gets in touch." Miah tapped a bud in her left ear. "I can't call out, but he can call in."

Aug 25, 2042
14:35H [Eden Campus, California]

A comfortable breeze from the mountain rippled
across the surface of Mystic Lake, creating miniature waves
which lapped against the causeway he'd crossed to reach
Fenton's island retreat.

"I thought you shelved this last year?" Eric said,
pointing to the schematics spread across the table with his
fork, before skewering an onion ring and resuming work on
the marbled slab of ribeye dominating his plate.

The tech billionaire nodded, his nose lost within the
bowl of a large glass of red. "I did," he agreed. "Well, kind of.
But the idea never really left me. And then the crash …"
Fenton's eyes lost focus and strayed across the water as his
smile faded and mood darkened. "The crash taught me it was
best not to leave things that needed doing, undone."

Eric had read about the helicopter accident that
claimed the life of Fenton's aid a week earlier. He'd not
known her, but Maggie, who was covering the poor young
woman's duties until a more appropriate time to replace her,
had told him his old college friend and partner had not been
the same since. Unsure of what he should or shouldn't say,
Eric opted for candour. "I was truly sorry to hear about Lucy
—"

"Yes," Fenton cut across him in a tone that said the
topic was off limits. "She was like a sister to me."

Eric nodded in understanding. "Well, I'm here if you
ever want to chat," he said, letting the subject go.

Fenton raised his glass in thanks, saying nothing more.

The two of them then sat in silence while Eric finished his meal. Fenton watched the geese come and go from a nesting spot in the nearby reeds, and Eric watched him. It was undoubtedly the same blond haired, blue eyed, easy-smiling tech giant who'd funded his Total Immersion business until Eric could buy him out. But there was something off about the other man; something missing.

Daran Whittaker had intercepted the wetware specialist on arrival, telling him to expect some erratic behaviour and memory blank spots from his friend.

"Just go with it," the hefty CEO said in a fatherlike way. "Try not to make him feel too self-conscious. He's his own worst enemy at the moment."

And even with that warning, Eric had found it hard to hide his surprise. The poor bastard was a mess, and his mind — that beautiful billion-dollar mind, seemed to struggle with much of the technical banter they'd always traded in. It soon became embarrassing, and Eric had stopped.

He put down the knife and fork and wiped his mouth with the napkin. "So what would you like from me?" he asked. "We both know there's nothing I can do that isn't within your reach."

"Well, that's a little self-deprecating, Eric," Fenton replied with a disarming smile. "You were always better with neurolinguistics than me, and you've built a worldwide reputation for innovative wetware design. That's where I'm falling down. If I'd continued with the project first time around, you know I would still have called you." He raised his glass again, this time in salute, and though Eric gave a gracious incline of the head, he was certain that would not have been the case.

Fenton tapped the schematics. "MindMerge works in concept, and it works solely as a microscopic computing device. What it doesn't do is respond to organic commands. That's where your very special skill set comes in."

The tech genius he'd first met at MIT gave Eric a tight look and moved his head a little closer, even though they were the only two there.

"Please Eric," he added in a near whisper. "Everyone's tiptoeing around it, but I know I'm not myself." The billionaire bit his bottom lip, fighting to hold back tears. "I think this will help. Working with you again, I mean."

Eric smiled and reached across the table to take his old friend's hand. "I'll help in any way I can, buddy," he said.

Whittaker watched from the comfort of a large cream sofa in the conservatory as Fenton bid the wetware engineer a fond farewell, and the man walked over the causeway to climb into a maglev cart that would take him back to his own vehicle. As the one-hundred-and-fifty-foot path slipped below the water's surface, once again isolating the island from the rest of Eden, he poured himself another glass of bourbon and went to join the young pretender as he sat back down in the afternoon sunshine.

"That was very well done," he congratulated. "You're a natural."

Li smiled up at Eden's Chief Exec with the lopsided grin Fenton's hordes of fans and media trolls so adored. "Why thank you, Daran," he drawled. "My chopper crash and PTSD are making it all rather easy."

Salesman's genes providing an air of conspiratorial sincerity, Whittaker smiled back. His relationship with Fenton, the real Fenton, had grown more and more strained over the last year. The tech genius's once insatiable appetite for success having been ironically castrated by egalitarian nonsense as soon as Whittaker made him rich enough to become that self-righteous.

The older entrepreneur, who'd ploughed every cent he had and a lot more he didn't to back the young dreamer's visions, had gently tried to remind his protégé of who did what in their businesses. But mistakes he'd made early in their relationship, coddling the man and his ego, had created a sanctimonious prick with a redeemer complex, rather than the winner obsessed with fame and fortune he'd intended.

Fenton's lack of gratitude had needled him at first. But that sense of mild irritation blossomed into total animosity when the arrogant young fool began asserting in board meetings that, as Eden's founder and controlling shareholder, *he* called the shots. And when *he* then went on to openly defy Whittaker, withdrawing from a project that would have cemented the polycorp's relationship with the only two nation-states still strong enough to resist de facto corporate control, the veteran CEO, the man who *created* Fenton White, had been forced to accept his golden goose had laid its last egg.

Of course, he'd still sought to broker a deal with the Americans and Chinese, and while neither government's best or brightest had managed to get the damn chip working, the time spent in discussion with various officials from both had made some interesting connections; one of which led to China's Premier offering to deal with his *Fenton problem.*

So, a couple of months after signing what had grown into a very attractive agreement with the politician, Whittaker

58

was more than a little annoyed when he departed Eden to retrieve a fake tech genius lying on a hospital bed licking self-inflicted wounds — the deal had been for a dead Fenton in return for his support.

But when Wei Han explained why he'd made the last-minute amendment, while the hard-nosed businessman made it clear he didn't like being leveraged, he had to concede the ruse was a clever way of rooting out the Premier's main rivals without risking a costly civil war… and because their contract granted Eden sole rights to what was effectively the economic behemoth's corporate integration, Whittaker decided he could roll with it — for now.

What neither one of them had ever truly envisaged though, was Cheng Li *actually* delivering a working chipset. The ambitious young scientist was nothing more than bait; a worm dangled to draw out Yung Zhu and his allies. But because the damn near perfect replica of the tech billionaire believed he was on a genuine mission, the poor bastard was trying to succeed… and that, it turned out, was yielding unexpected fruit for Whittaker. Eric Thorne would never, ever, have worked for him — But, the little prick couldn't resist the forlorn pleas of a sad and emotionally damaged friend.

The thick waisted executive chuckled inwardly; fortune favoured the bold, and with a little fancy footwork he might yet land a working chip. '*How do you like them apples Fenton, you smug bastard?*' he thought as he sat down in the seat vacated by the wetware guru.

"We're going to want to keep an eye on Thorne though," he added, shifting his weight to get comfortable.

"We are?"

Whittaker offered a paternal smile and took a sip from the heavy crystal tumbler he was holding. "Even if the guy plays it straight with you. Which is a fairly big if. This won't go unnoticed. As soon as they hear what you're doing, the other polycorps will be plotting to steal that chip."

Li nodded his understanding. "That's why Dean's here."

"You trust that guy?"

Fenton's double raised an eyebrow. "Of course, he was handpicked to support me. My people are nothing like your deceitful execs, Daran."

The ruthless perpetrator of numerous hostile takeovers gave the naïve young lookalike an oblique smile. "Good to know. But I'll go ahead and hire some additional eyes, ears and muscle anyway — just in case."

PARTITION TWO   Cluster 2   **Sector i**

Aug 27, 2042
17:08H [Federal Building, Los Angeles, California]

From the visi-steel windows of the seventeenth floor, the small symmetrical gravestones set in a sea of lush green grass opposite the Federal Building made the cemetery look like a giant circuit board; it's perfect straight avenues like traces running between thousands and thousands of printed components. It had just gone five, and Fisher, who'd been waiting outside the office commandeered by the counter-intelligence Deputy Director for almost two hours, was running out of things to stare at.

Since his arrival, three older agents had turned up and been told to go straight through. None bothered acknowledging Fisher, and two had since left again, still without a glance in his direction. It was kind of rude, but then the onetime undercover operative had cultivated a nerdish outer layer years earlier that was hard to shake off, and tended to encouraged others to avoid eye contact.

Finally, the oversize opaque glass door swung inward, and the swarthy CIA legend Fisher had worked for when he was Unit Chief in New York made an apologetic face, before turning his attention to the woman who'd kept the younger man company for much of the afternoon.

"Grace, I know you've got places to be. I'll handle it from here." He gave a warm smile, and the secretary nodded her thanks as she began closing down the workstation.

"Simon," he went on, giving the younger agent's hand a brisk shake. "Long time no see. I'm sorry for the delay, but you've presented an interesting problem. Come on in and meet Jerry from the FBI." Fisher waved farewell to the secretary and followed his old boss into the large corner office.

Jerry Weinberg was the gigantic bear of a man who had been the last guy to walk past him half an hour before. He nodded his wide box of a head at the DARPA deck jockey and pointed towards a vacant chair at the conference table.

"Hello Dr Fisher, I'm Jim's opposite number at the FBI. He invited me over so we could figure out who this little problem belongs to."

The computer specialist unbuttoned a jacket he wasn't used to wearing and sat down. "I take it this is about my report then, Sir?"

Johnson nodded an affirmative as Weinberg threw a mugshot of a well-dressed, middle-aged white man up to the polymer wall of the office. "Is this the man your sifting programme captured entering the Taipei Mandarin Oriental?"

Fisher shifted his gaze to the wall. "Younger there. But yes, that's the file photo my programme locked onto," he said. "When I tried to access his record though, I got frozen out and informed the attempt had been passed to your office. Am I in trouble?"

"Depends on how you look at trouble, Doctor," the big FBI agent rumbled. "I've not had a chance to read the report in detail, so I'd be grateful if you'd summarise the key points of your analysis for me."

The DARPA field office manager looked to Johnson, who nodded assent. "Sure," he said. "No problem. I don't know how tech savvy you are though, so tell me to dial it up or down as we go?"

Weinberg presented a row of slab-like teeth in a meaty smile. "I'll try to keep up."

Leaning forward, Fisher rested both elbows on the conference table and pushed his glasses further up the bridge of his nose. "The Taipei Technology Expo took place two weeks ago, and as it's one of the biggest events in the industry for emerging tech, who does and doesn't attend always attracts our attention. Of interest, in terms of my report, was that Fenton White, the semi reclusive founder of Eden and undoubtedly the world's most talented tech developer, not only attended, but also walked away from a helicopter crash while out there."

Weinberg nodded for him to continue.

"Now, although coincidences can happen, I couldn't see one of the world's richest men getting into a poorly maintained, ropey old gas guzzler. But by the same token, if it wasn't an accident, any attempt on his life raises serious questions concerning who went after him, why, and what the repercussions will be.

"So, because the main Eden campus is on my patch I did some digging and, to cut a long story short, my search through the databases of the manufacturer and operator of that helicopter led me to discover Eden had hired a security company called MacKenzie to complete an investigation. As I'm sure you know, that's not unusual, the polycorps often use merc companies to establish facts and then enact whatever they deem appropriate retribution.

"Anyway, each of those companies provided evidence to MacKenzie showing that neither the aircraft or pilot could have been responsible for the type of accident that occurred. Now, I clearly haven't had access to the final report; Eden's ICE is too good —"

"ICE?" Weinberg interrupted.

"Intrusion countermeasures," Fisher explained. "— and I didn't want them detecting a breach. So I can't say what MacKenzie learned concerning who might have done what, or what retribution is planned. But the fact foul play was confirmed legitimised a more invasive search of foreign databases."

Again, the FBI deputy director just nodded that Fisher continue.

"I created a bespoke sifter programme to retrace White's footsteps through the hotel and expo, to establish if I could identify any data correlations. There was, of course, an enormous amount of information, and every connection the program established over the week White was there could be explained — until yesterday, when it identified a statistically non-coincidental link to every one of the hotel camfeeds getting corrupted during the last night of his stay."

63

That caused Weinberg's bushy eyebrows to raise.

"Yeah, exactly," Fisher said, waving a slender finger at the big man. "I've yet to give it a thorough examination. But we're not talking accidental deletion. We're talking about a logic bomb that activated an adaptive worm, which then propagated throughout the vid servers, literally scrambling their code. I'm confident my programme didn't trigger it, so someone else, maybe MacKenzie, had pawed through their security vid before me.

"Anyway, that rather unsubtle act prompted me to check the hotel's manifest for the night in question, and the only other suite on that floor was rented out for one night. Though unsurprisingly, information on its occupants was also scrambled.

"Satisfied someone had taken deliberate steps to conceal what had occurred over those twenty-four hours, I felt justified in re-programming the sifter to its widest settings for collateral intrusion, and broke into restricted data from all the surrounding buildings.

"That search flagged a vidstream from the entrycam of an apartment across from the hotel's loading dock which recorded a limo arriving at six thirty on the evening before White's crash, and two well-dressed western men entering the hotel via a staff entrance. It's a fleeting side view, but our pattern recognition software indicated an eighty-seven percent probability that your guy on the wall there was one of them."

Weinberg spoke up again. "And the other one?"

"Can't tell I'm afraid. This guy obscures his head going in."

"And you couldn't find either of them leaving?"

Simon shook his head. "I can't say. The data on the hotel image server is corrupted until after midday. However, the entrycam across the road does capture someone being wheeled out to an ambulance on the morning of the crash. That may have been one of them. Again, no face was visible, and I need more time to work through the data to see whether the movement ties into any hospital admissions."

Weinberg looked thoughtfully at Johnson, who was staring at the image on the wall with his chin cradled in his right hand. Then turned his attention back to Simon. "So what dots have you joined from this, Dr Fisher?"

The tech specialist, who hadn't worn a suit for so long in years, pulled the tie around his neck loose and unbuttoned the collar of his shirt. "That's better," he said unapologetically. "Well, the involvement of that man on the wall has clearly grabbed you attention. But rather than him being above my paygrade to read about or the evidence of foul play, it's the behaviour of Doctor White *since* the crash that rings alarm bells for me."

"Okay, go on."

Fisher adjusted his glasses again. "About a year ago, Fenton White unveiled an ambitious project to build a neural implant he claimed would revolutionise personal computing. He said it was his dream to ensure every human could enjoy free, unrestricted access to education and the metaverse, irrespective of wealth and station in life."

The DARPA agent didn't try to hide his respect for the man.

"That's the kind of guy he is. But of course, just like any other truly ground-breaking technological development in mankind's history, it didn't take long for the *defence* gnomes in Virginia, and no doubt every other weapons developer, to see the military potential in his concept.

"So my boss was ordered to approach Eden and offer to partner with them; said we'd even pay all the research and development costs. Now, the Chief Executive, who is a total dirtbag by the way, was *very* keen. But White overruled him, and one week later announced via his personal account, not Eden official channels, that the project had been permanently abandoned.

"He said the technology was beyond our reach and would stay that way for some time. But pretty much everyone in the industry could see there was friction between him and Daran Whittaker, his CEO, and most of us figured he'd chosen to bury the chip rather than let the military at it.

"Moral compasses, eh? Anyway, didn't matter — or so the gnomes thought. Because with a little help from Whittaker, we *borrowed* the initial research before White could delete it."

Fisher gave a brief chuckle.

"… And that's when you begin to appreciate the gulf that exists between brilliant minds and genius. Because eight months later, none of our guys, and I'm talking about some of the best and brightest outside of the polycorps, were any closer to making a vaguely viable prototype. So, we accepted that if White didn't make one, no one else was going to.

"But, and this is the thing, when he returned to California a couple of weeks back with your guy there in tow." He pointed at the image on the wall. "Fenton White resurrected that research and, with no announcement or reason why, started work on the chip again."

"So what are you saying, Doctor?" Weinberg asked.

Fisher frowned and pulled at his collar again. "I'm saying Sir, that while I still can't point to a clear 'who or why,' I'm convinced Fenton White has been gotten to, and is

66

being controlled or manipulated somehow. Because that's just not how the guy operates, he wouldn't do that."

The big FBI agent gave a grave nod as he digested those last words.

"Well done, Simon. This is a fantastic catch," Johnson said. "But we have no authority over Eden, so how do we go about unpicking what's happened?"

"Well, you won't manage it remotely, that's for sure." Fisher took his glasses off and rubbed the bridge of his nose. "Their comms are the tightest in the industry. Other corps have tried, and several top jocks have disappeared: accounts, profiles, history — everything. Just gone like they never existed."

Johnson's bony head bobbed. "So that means trusting someone, or getting our own eyes and ears in there. Tell me, how well do you know Fenton White, Simon?"

"I've never met the guy, if that's what you're getting at," the government deck jockey answered. "Dr Clements, our lead in the Defence Sciences Office, dealt with that."

"—and Daran Whittaker," Weinberg asked. "What about him?"

Fisher let out a bark of laughter. "Oh yes," he said. "Mr Whittaker was very keen to build a relationship with DARPA. We spoke *a lot*."

Weinberg's look grew calculating. "Can we trust him?"

The continued laughter provided the burly agent's answer.

"As a patriot, absolutely not," Fisher said. "The man believes corporate giants like him are above the law. Well, our law anyway. But," his eyes narrowed, "as an avaricious megalomaniac?" He smiled and began nodding. "Yeah, I think you could find a way to align his interests with ours."

"Manipulate him, you mean?"

"Play him, Sir," the thin-boned programmer corrected. "And anyone who goes in needs to understand that's exactly what he'll be doing to us."

The two Deputy Directors looked at each other and shared a nod. Then Johnson asked, "How long is it since you transferred from Cyber Ops, Simon?"

"Two years, Sir."

"Any problems during that time?"

"None. The new name, re-location and job stuck behind a computer in a restricted lab on the opposite side of the country have kept me mostly out of trouble," the younger man said with more than a hint of sarcasm.

"Fancy coming back?"

Fisher raised an eyebrow, and a slight grin tugged at the corners of his mouth. "Seriously?"

Johnson bared his teeth and pointed at the image on the wall. "That man is, or perhaps now *was*, one of ours. He went dark six months ago, and while you don't need to know the finer details of *his* assignment, it's fair to say that if he's turned up on American soil babysitting one of our corporate billionaires, something is very wrong."

The CIA Deputy Director paused for a moment, then continued. "You've put your neck in a noose for me before Simon, and it almost got you dead. So I hate asking. But your skill set and pre-existing relationship with Whittaker might well allow us to insert you into Eden without too much fuss or notice — if he's willing to play ball, that is. What do you think?"

The skinny tech nerd pushed a strand of lank, mousy hair out of his eyeline and couldn't help smiling as he reached to shake his old boss's hand.

"I think you should tell me what you need doing, Sir."

Sept 17, 2042
15.18H [Manhattan Beach, California]

Charlie was sitting at a small, shaded table on the corner of the terrace. The afternoon sun was beating down and he was grateful for the gentle breeze coming off the Pacific. It had been a long hot summer, and September showed no signs of giving way to California's more balmy autumn.

An unremarkable, unrememberable older man, Charlie watched as wave after wave of beautiful bodies strolled by on the promenade — invisible to those around him. It was a gift he'd had since childhood, a form of crypsis that allowed him to disappear into the white noise of other people's perception. He was a ghost; a man with a wealth of experience in covert ops who, for one reason or another, was paid to watch others. Usually without them knowing.

Reynolds had said this particular assignment was to monitor and maintain the subject's safety, and that he knew about the surveillance wrapped around him. But Charlie very much doubted it was, or that he did. Not that the details mattered. His team worked on a no questions basis: plausible deniability always meant a bigger payday.

69

He'd worked with the ex-CIA spook years ago, when they were both on the right side of the line and rewarded with meagre government wages. Now, neither cared much for lines, and given what Reynolds had paid Charlie for their last several jobs, the man was doing very well.

The greying spook called himself a security consultant, though in corpo terms that title covered a multitude of sins, and none of the jobs Charlie had worked on for him were close to legit. In fact, they'd all needed a little lateral thinking and a lot of money to moralise. No, he knew Reynolds was a killer. His team got contracted, they watched, built profiles, identified security or competition … then one day the subject would disappear or have an accident — and they got paid.

The briefing they received this time described Thorne as a successful wetware entrepreneur who was involved in the development of some ground-breaking bit of tech. A piece of kit so revolutionary, Reynolds had said, that he considered it likely competitors would go to *extreme lengths* to steal it. That, of course, was a trade euphemism suggesting several unpleasant futures awaiting the hapless engineer. Which again, wasn't Charlie's problem. His team's job was simple: stay invisible, identify any other eyes on or approaches to Thorne, and report them back to Reynolds. The *approaches to* bit suggested concerns over Thorne's intentions, and it wasn't clear to Charlie if he was considered *a* risk, as well as *at* risk; Reynolds didn't elaborate; Charlie didn't ask.

One thing was clear though, if Thorne *had* been warned of his company's concerns, the guy was one lazy sonofabitch and seemed oblivious of the several ghosts now following him around each day.

70

Ray had followed the woman and man currently shadowing Thorne back to separate properties in the area last week, and the team had since established the man worked for one of the European polycorps, while the woman was in the pay of Uncle Sam. A bit of careful cambot placement then led them to six other regular faces connected to the European house, and four to the American.

Reynolds had reviewed the images they'd gathered and didn't seem concerned. "Carry on," was all he'd said.

With a blink, Charlie sent the optic captures of this afternoon's watchers to the others, left ten bucks under the ashtray for his bagel and coffee, waved a goodbye to the waitress, and ambled onto the promenade. As he then stood there like a navigational hazard, parting the moving tide of people while putting on his fedora, Ray strolled past and on to the patio, scansheet underarm, to sit at the table he'd just vacated.

The best, like them, made surveillance look easy, and once Thorne had gone back to his uber expensive slice of privilege that evening, they watched several walls slide open in different rooms before he appeared on a first-floor balcony with a cold drink and his pretty little mech. The man had proved to be a straightforward assignment who didn't tend to go out much of an evening, and the team had settled into a comfortable night-time rhythm that allowed for one of them to rotate out for some personal R&R. Tonight was Charlie's turn; Ray would watch the feeds while Dale bunked down in the ready room for a few hours, and then they'd swap.

Watch, eat, sleep, repeat.

That was the thing about surveillance. It was, for the most part, mind-numbingly boring. But it almost always carried high stakes. If you showed out to the subject, you blew your job. If you showed out to other watchers on the wrong kind of job, you ended up dead.

Charlie, Ray and Dale knew the risks and, even if now advanced in years, prided themselves on still being up there with the best. Getting old in this game was its own badge of honour, and the trick to staying alive was never becoming complacent, no matter how time may have passed without incident.

They'd been watching Thorne for two weeks now, and aside from the small swarm of ghosts he'd attracted, the team hadn't identified any other overt activity around the man until yesterday, when Charlie captured images of two people snooping around Ocean Drive in the middle of the night. And now, as Ray watched the camfeeds, that same young couple was back, paying particular attention to security patrols and visible cams.

No interference with Thorne's property was apparent, but a single flash of light suggested they'd painted his garage before returning to a vehicle parked two streets over.

They might, of course, just be better-than-average burglars interested in one of Thorne's millionaire neighbours. But Ray's experienced gut said two nights in a row felt very much like someone dangling bait in a deliberate attempt to draw out watchers, and while he wouldn't be falling for it, he did give the couple a grateful salute as he joined them in looking for those who might.

No one showed out.

In the morning, Thorne left home at 11am, following a common routine which would see him wander along the seafront to Uncle Bill's Pancake House for a waffle and coffee. Dale chose a cap and sunglasses from the wardrobe and went mobile, looping past the scansheet stand for his free daily read before falling into a steady stroll some forty metres behind the wetware engineer on the busy promenade. But just as Charlie was about to leave the screens to rouse Ray, he noticed a grey Toyota pull up alongside the absent engineer's garage.

It was an odd thing to do.

No one got out; it just sat there for a minute and then pulled away again.

People didn't stop to make a call anymore. In fact, most people didn't even bother driving; they left it to their AI. So Charlie was sure they'd been up to no good. Ray had said something was brewing, and he was right — this was unmistakably hostile reconnaissance, and he tapped his cuff to call Reynolds.

The wetwork specialist looked tired, and the old ghost figured the lean, greying killer had been doing his own snooping last night.

It was funny really, Charlie and his boys looked like your average, everyday wheezer, growing leathery and senile in the Californian sunshine — the kind of folks younger generations tried to avoid eye contact with, just in case they started talking about weak bladders or what funeral they were going to next. But Reynolds — getting on or not, Reynolds was the kind of guy you could dress up in a faery costume, and he'd still look like one dangerous sonofabitch a group of teenage thugs would hesitate to argue with.

"Damn," he said, as the watcher relayed his news. "You're sure? I was hoping it wouldn't come to this."

"I'm certain." Charlie replied. "While I can't say who or why, someone is clearly prepping for entry. If not tonight, tomorrow."

"Any read on who they might be?"

"Nothing on the female," the old ghost said. "The guy is ex Russian Spec Ops; a Sergei Chenokov, turned merc in 2032. Nothing shown regarding present assignments or affiliated merc companies, and nothing on government systems to indicate how or when he entered the country. So I'm guessing he's not an official visitor."

Dean grunted on the other end of the comlink as he received the images. "Got him. Oh yeah, looks a right charmer. Interesting there's nothing on the girl though — that database you're backdooring is about as current as Uncle Sam gets. I'll have to do some wider checks." He rubbed a hand over his stubbled face. "Thanks Charlie, leave it with me. I'll get back to you."

"And if something goes down in the meantime?"

"Follow the agreed protocol: maintain obs, don't get involved, and don't get compromised. As long as we have a rough idea where Thorne is, I'll be happy."

"You're not calling in the cavalry?"

"To be honest Charlie, I'm not sure who best qualifies as the cavalry at the moment," Dean said. "Seems everyone wants a piece of this fella. So for now, we just continue to watch and record. If people start breaking cover, hopefully we get to see how deep the rabbit hole goes. Perhaps they'll even take each other out and save me the problem, eh?" He grinned down the vid, and Charlie gave an unconvinced nod.

Reynolds was playing a dangerous game. Then again, Reynolds always did.

"Now that would be useful, wouldn't it?" the old ghost replied. "I'll go brief the guys."

74

Dean shut down the link and rubbed his eyes. It had been a long couple of days, and he was still trying to piece together who the respective players were. He'd been out last night as well. Unseen by his watchers, and unseen by Thorne's visitors. They were a disciplined and careful outfit, but that hadn't stopped him getting a tracker on the pickup they'd used, or following its signal to a row of commercial units in Torrance.

Research into the images he'd then captured confirmed the people poking around Thorne's garage belonged to a merc outfit commanded by a woman called Miah Hargreaves. And that was fine, the old spy had expected professionals to be contracted by those interested in controlling Thorne. What he'd not expected, as he watched those soldiers running through evacuation drills, was to see a face on the MSS payroll — and as the Minister hadn't said a damn thing about another operative being sent in country, that could only mean trouble.

Reynolds didn't like spontaneity. It was the poor cousin of meticulous planning. At best, it had a horrible habit of leading to unforeseen consequences, and at worst, it led to compromise and death. It was a trait he liked in others, but something he only resorted to himself when he had no other choice … And now another wetwork specialist had shown up in his game with an entire merc outfit at his back, it looked like that was exactly where Dean found himself — fresh out of choices. Thorne would have to die.

Sept 19, 2042
03:18H [Manhattan Beach, California]

The sky was black as wet coal and the small slither of a moon, when not obscured by cloud, provided precious little light. With just over three hours left until dawn, the streets were deserted. Seafront diners and late-night revellers had left to find their beds a couple of hours back and, at least in this part of LA, almost everyone was now fast asleep. The North Pacific's gentle caress of Manhattan Beach provided the single discernible sound, its rhythmic ebb and flow offering nature's own lullaby to those who could afford it.

In that stygian gloom, only the keenest of watchers intentionally searching the darkness would notice the shadows rippling along the walls of Ocean Drive towards Eric Thorne's house, leaving in their wake two men in parked cars who'd been paid to keep watch for just such a thing, but now stared into the night with unseeing eyes and faces set in the startled pose of people who'd found unexpected, if not quite immediate, death. Moments later, Thorne's garage opened, and the shadows disappeared.

Inside, six silent figures swept through the darkened basement to a set of stairs, where one turned and dropped to a knee as the rest continued up, emerging in the wealthy entrepreneur's hallway. They had five minutes until the house's advanced electronics cycled.

"Weapons live," Miah Hargreaves breathed through her throat mic. "No lights, night vision only," she continued with practiced efficiency as the extraction team mustered at the foot of a staircase. They were in reactive dyneema: an

76

ultra-resistant polymer combat armour, and full-faced
ballistics helmets. "HUD checks. Sergei?"

"Check."

"Nando?"

"Check."

"Doc?"

"Check."

"Rhea?"

"Check."

"Spence?"

"Check."

She checked her own display. No secondaries or
passives had been triggered, Thorne's digital guard dog had
been neutralised, and Frayne was giving her a *go* signal on the
command channel.

"Okay, all parameters are in the green," she affirmed.
"Fast and precise, team. Just like we've practised."

Heads nodded.

"Sergei point. Nando rearguard. Doc, you remain on
standby here with Rhea."

Heads nodded again.

"Spence," she said, switching her gaze to the Tech
Specialist who'd remained in the basement. "Secure us a ride."
She watched his headcam in the corner of her command
display as it panned the garage.

"That one," Miah said, as he passed over a grey
Range Rover. "Leave the low jack on. We want our watchers
along for that ride."

Everyone set, the merc commander circled two
fingers and the entry team began moving up the wooden
slatted stairs; guns primed, enhanced senses and electronic
sifters synced.

The plan was simple: locate Thorne, incapacitate him, and extract. But on reaching the second-floor bend, Sergei paused for an almost imperceptible moment before suddenly opening up; jacked reflexes reacting to the discharge of a silenced gun, and the suppressed pop, pop, pop of his SCAR-L carbine sending a flurry of bullets in its direction. "Shots fired," he breathed. "Unknown hostile in target bedroom."

The big Russian crossed the landing in two fluid steps, training his rifle through the doorway as Miah and Nando passed to break left and right into the room.

A second gunshot sounded, punching Miah from her feet and whirling her to the floor. "Eleven o'clock, moving to our right," she grunted, allowing her body to roll with the force of the blow. "Twenty feet. Aim low."

Both Sergei and Nando reacted on instinct, a dozen tiny sparks dancing up a twisting blur before a bright flash overwhelmed their visuals. Sergei yanked his visor up and let off a blind burst. "Fucker's in a chameleon suit," he shouted. "I thought those things were a myth."

"Doc, PD round," Miah barked as she brought her gun back up in the balcony's direction.

"On it, Boss."

A heartbeat later, a single shot thudded into the ceiling above their heads and pressure displacement ions flooded the room.

The team's HUDs flared, reaffirming their four green images kneeling in a loose arc around the doorway. A yellow non-combatant, presumably Thorne, was lying prone to one side of Miah, and a dispersing red smudge wavered for a few moments on the threshold of the balcony before disappearing altogether. Doc followed the trace elements onto the tiled patio and looked down at the promenade below. Nothing visible was moving. Whoever the hostile was, they had skills and insane kit.

"Doc," Miah called. "Head trauma." He turned his attention back to the room and, in the vivid brightness of Nando's helmet light, noticed the man in a blue t-shirt and joggers lying on the bed for the first time. The Commander's faceplate was still down, and a flashing icon in his HUD told the medic she was now in conversation with someone on the command channel.

"You're gonna want to be quick, Doc," Sergei said, looking down at the deep crimson stain creeping across the white cotton pillow. "He's losing blood fast."

The medic nodded in acknowledgment; his assessment complete by the time he reached the side of the enormous baby-faced Russian. "Just keep the pressure on for a mo, Serg," he said, shrugging off his backpack and throwing aside both combat gloves to slip on a pair of surgicals. "If he's not dead already, there's a chance it looks worse than it is."

With calm precision, Doc laid out the equipment he'd need before shooing the Russian aside and sliding into his place. Selecting a broad nosed syringe that looked like it belonged in a kitchen cupboard rather than medical supplies, he squeezed a knuckle-sized dose of coagulating PharmaGel into both entry and exit points to arrest the bleeding and seal each wound, then got down to the serious business of trying to save the man's life.

Intravenous blood and nervous system stimulants soon levelled out heart rate and breathing. But neural activity was erratic; the man's brain, rather than shutting down like he'd expected and wanted, was working furiously in areas not affected by the trauma.

Spence entered the room carrying a stretcher and field MedBot, and the medic nodded his thanks as he and Sergei stripped Thorne naked to lay him on the nanite rich DermaGel surface.

"His vitals are good." Doc announced after another few seconds, returning his torch and attention to Thorne's head. "It looks like a through and through, so hopefully nothing's bounced around in there and, at first glance at least, it also looks like only the right frontal lobe has taken damage."

He switched his gaze back to Miah. Her faceplate was now open, eyes looking down on the prone, naked man before returning to her medic with an obvious … and?

"And so I think it's survivable," he said in response to the unasked question. "But I can't tell without a far more detailed scan how much damage has actually been done. I'd suggest shutting him down with the Bot. Put him in a coma until we can get to a proper facility."

The powerful woman, who was almost as big as Sergei, nodded; the tightness of her mouth hinting at the irritation she felt. That injury had just cost her a lot of money. "Do whatever you have to, Doc. Just do it quickly," she said, tapping her cuff to terminate the call she'd been in. "We have to go."

The medic nodded, experienced fingers dancing over glyphs on his cuff to bring the Bot humming to life. It scanned the body on the stretcher, attached itself across Thorne's ribcage, and extended three insect-like appendages which then sank into the skin around his right ear, cervical spine and chest. Moments later, the machine reported a steady output of D waves, and Doc gave his boss a thumbs up.

In the basement, Spence had positioned the Range Rover at the bottom of the metal stairs, boot up and rear section folded down. Miah climbed into the front passenger seat as Thorne was loaded into the back. Doc, pack now hanging from his chest for easy access, slid in beside him.

Green lights began flashing in the darkness and Miah queried the countdown in the corner of her HUD. Surely the house systems couldn't be rebooting already?

"Shit," she said opening the command channel. "Rhea, Serg, Nando, get out of here. The house is going live. We'll RV as planned at the Getty View slip." She turned to the broad-shouldered sergeant climbing into the driving seat. "Helmets will have to wait Spence, get us out of here."

With what should have been thirty seconds to spare, the garage door swung inward again, allowing Thorne's grey Range Rover to purr out onto the street — and as it idled down Ocean Drive towards El Porto, three shadows briefly appeared, then melted away like they'd never existed.

PARTITION TWO   Cluster 3   **Sector iii**

Sept 19, 2042
04:00H [Torrance, California]

After a brief rendezvous at the Getty Slip, where Thorne was transferred from the stolen Range Rover and Spence had the vehicle's AI continue on towards Frisco, Hargreaves and her team backtracked to Torrance in a large commercial van advertising the services of an auto-parts distributor acquired ten days earlier by a subsidiary of one of the client's many businesses.

By the time they arrived at the unit to the rear of Sepulveda Boulevard, Doc had stabilised Thorne, and together with Rhea, the short, fiery Scottish girlfriend of Frayne, he unloaded the comatose wetware engineer onto a gurney, while an impatient Miah called Fisher over from the office he'd been sat in, trying to stay out of everyone's way.

The stereotypical nerd couldn't have looked more out of place; his long lank strands of mousey brown hair and black-rimmed glasses in a sea of buzz cuts and perfect vision, almost as great a contrast as the tan corduroy pants and plaid shirt were against her company's battledress. The man was also extremely patronising, and seemed to be oblivious of that fact. Hargreaves had objected to his last-minute inclusion in the operation, but the client had insisted he tag along, and then offered a healthy bonus to also ensure he disappeared at an opportune moment. Tyler, who had taken an immediate dislike to the guy, was looking forward to that bit.

Ostensibly, the skinny nerd was some kind of tech specialist. There to speak with, assess and reassure Thorne during his relocation to Eden. But it seemed unlikely that was the full story, given how much they were being paid to dispose of him.

"Jesus," he muttered, pushing his glasses further up his nose. "What in God's name have you done to the poor bastard?"

The no nonsense merc commander's strategy for dealing with the wiry rodent of a man was to minimise conversation. "Just do whatever you've been paid to do and do it fast. As you can tell, things didn't go as smoothly as I'd have liked, and we're likely to have company now."

Fisher tutted and looked at Doc. "I'm guessing that's a head injury," he said, his tone thick with sarcasm. The medic

82

nodded, and he turned his attention back to Hargreaves. "Well then, I clearly *can't do* what I've been paid to do, can I? I'm not a fucking necromancer." He glared at the muscular woman. "I'll need specialised equipment now. *He* will not be at all happy with this. I can guarantee that."

Miah gritted her teeth, working hard to keep her tone neutral. "What kind of equipment?"

Fisher rolled his eyes. "I don't fucking know. I guess an MRI will do the job."

She wanted to punch him straight in the larynx, shut the prick up for a bit. "Well, I guess you'll be coming with us then."

"That wasn't the plan," Fisher objected. "He needs a doctor, not a tech specialist with a doctorate."

Miah growled, leaning in to go face to face with the skinny little man, who surprised her by not shrinking back. "My guy," she prodded a finger towards Doc, "will deal with any medical issues. Look, come or don't come, I really don't give a shit. We will be leaving in five minutes, and I expect *he* won't be happy if you choose to bail." Still in full armour, the big woman stared the unwanted addition down, daring the man to argue some more.

After a couple of moments, Fisher held his hands up in mock defeat. "Okay then. This night just gets worse and worse." He looked at Thorne's unconscious body and poked a thumb in his direction. "I'll need someone to help me construct a faraday cage though."

The merc leader raised an eyebrow at the request.

"Any kind of conductive material lined on the inside with something nonconductive will perform the task, so long as the item is insulated and the cage is grounded."

"I know what a faraday cage is, Mr Fisher," Miah said. She shook her head, leaving the *why* unasked, and waved Eddie Shaw, one of her comms specialists, over.

"Eddie, can you assist Mr Fisher, please?"

"Doctor," the scruffy-looking man amended.

"What?"

"Doctor. You keep saying *Mister*. That's incorrect, it's *Doctor* Fisher."

Miah rolled angry eyes, then continued. "— he'll tell you what he needs doing."

Eddie nodded and looked to Fisher for instruction, who, after a couple of heartbeats, gave a resigned shrug and walked towards the storeroom.

The big woman watched his retreating back for a moment, then raised an eyebrow at Tyler.

"I *really* don't like that man —" he began. But Miah held up a hand, forestalling further comment. "I doubt his own mother does," she said. "Let's just get the fuck out of here, shall we? We can deal with him later."

Plan A would have seen them all simply vanish into the Torrance night after Thorne was assessed and the enigmatic Doctor Fisher had met some unexpected end. But plan A was never going to happen.

Plan B, on the other hand, involved something far less subtle that Tyler assured her would allow them to disappear Thorne in the manner desired by the client, and she silently applauded her old friend's cunning as she called the mercenary company to attention; her throat mic transmitting the message to Gamma Team, perched on distant rooftops and crane cabins.

"Thank you all for a job well done tonight," she said. "We knew there were likely to be other players in the arena.

Though admittedly, I hadn't expected any of them to try and assassinate the target." She arched an eyebrow at Fisher, who'd stopped work to listen. "But there you go. As the Colonel often tells us, no plan survives first contact with the enemy. Which is why he plans, and plans, and plans."

A ripple of laughter went through the unit and Miah smiled at the silver-haired former marine officer stood arrow straight beside her.

"So, it's over to Plan B, and as long as each of us does our bit, when and how he's directed, there's no reason for anyone to get hurt. Well, none of us at least."

Another ripple of laughter.

The muscular woman looked around the twenty faces in the room with pride. Aside from Jim's squad, who'd been recruited specifically for this job, she'd known them all for years. "I will soon be leaving with Bravo and the package. Gamma are already in position, and Mr Frayne will call the timings for Alpha and Delta. Keep your heads down, remember your discipline, and I'll see you all tomorrow at the RV point."

"Oorah," they chorused as one.

Miah nodded, and Tyler took over. "Jim," he addressed Bravo's Team Leader. "Ensure *Mr* Fisher doesn't have or use any comms whatsoever on the next stage of your journey, and check before leaving this unit that neither he or Dr Thorne are emitting any kind of signal." He looked straight at Fisher, who wore an expression of indignation, but thankfully said nothing. "I've updated your HUD and cuff with coordinates for a facility I trust, where he can perform whatever tests he needs, and we can bring this operation to a conclusion."

"Oorah," Jim barked.

"Alpha, Gamma, Delta — you have all spent the last couple of days living this drill, don't fuck it up now and we all go home. You know your jobs." He turned back to Miah. "With your permission, Sir?"

Hargreaves nodded.

"Let's go to work," he told everyone.

Activity erupted around the unit again as each of the TLs began directing their squads to well-rehearsed tasks. Tyler said a last goodbye to Miah before turning to the unit's defence, while Jim directed Eddie to frisk Fisher and scan him for electromagnetic feedback.

Satisfied the man was clean and his makeshift faraday cage was doing its job, Eddie nodded to Doc, and the pair of them manoeuvred the gurney to the rear storage cage of the unit, where two other Bravo members were pulling up panels to reveal what looked like an old inspection pit. It was about three feet wide and ten feet long, but as Fisher got closer, he could see the steps just kept going.

"Down you go matey," Eddie gestured. "Me and Doc will carry the patient. Just follow Martin there. You might want to crouch a little though, the ceiling is low and rough."

The others sniggered as Fisher presented the big merc with a middle finger; he was several inches shorter than the rest of them, and didn't need to bend at all as they descended into a thin tunnel with bulbs tacked at head height that disappeared into the darkness like lonely stars.

He'd never been bothered by confined spaces before, but after walking for what felt like a couple of minutes, with Martin's bulk filling the tunnel before him and the man-giant Eddie shutting out all light behind, Fisher began to feel distinctly claustrophobic.

"This tunnel gives me the right fucking willies," Doc moaned, airing similar thoughts.

"Just pray no one presses the wrong button while we're down here, mate," chuckled Martin from ahead.

Fisher looked up at the jagged ceiling of rough rock. "How much further, Martin?" There was a tightness at the edge of his voice.

"Don't like it either?" Eddie asked.

"No."

"Won't be long now," Martin said. "Almost there."

With that, the ground started rising again, and Fisher soon found himself at another set of stairs which emerged into what looked like a large domestic garage with a Chevy van and family SUV parked in it.

A minute later, Miah arrived with Jim and pointed at the Chevy. "The van is counter-intrusion proofed. Is that enough shielding for you, *Doctor*?"

When it became apparent they'd be transporting Thorne to a beta site, Fisher realised he needed to plant a thought that any movement of the wetware specialist would require the negation of signal leakage. He'd impressed himself by thinking up a faraday cage on the spot; gambling correctly that it would allow him to insist on checking any transportation used when his bulky creation proved too unwieldy — providing the quick-witted agent with an opportunity to deploy one of the trackers he'd secreted between the crease of his right leg and nutsack.

The mercs had rifled through his pockets when they picked him up, of course; confiscating his pad and cuff — *well d'uh*. But who bothers to strip search an annoying nerd?

The newly reinstated CIA operative allowed himself a smug smile. He'd placed one of the transparent chips under the engineer's right armpit when building the cage around him, and then palmed a second as they'd walked through the darkened tunnel. Both were set to activate on a constantly monitored ultra-low frequency after an hour. So there would be no immediate comms spike.

"If it prevents military grade signal leakage, it should be fine. Close the doors. Let's see." He held out a hand to Eddie as Jim sealed the van. "The scanner?"

Eddie looked at Miah and she gave an impatient nod.

The computer specialist then made a show of walking around the van with the device, providing a condescending commentary on the many ways people failed to prevent signal leakage, before wriggling part way beneath each side of the vehicle and scanning its underbelly.

"You're all good." He reported as he got back to his feet, dusting off corduroy pants. "Tight as a drum. I'm almost impressed."

The big merc scowled as he casually returned the scanner to her. "Now you check, Eddie," she commanded.

The comms officer retraced Fisher's steps, examining each area with a torch before scanning the same places.

"Nothing," he reported.

Miah hadn't taken her eyes off the irritating little man as Eddie worked his way around the van, and the tech nerd had simply stared back with that stupid, smug grin.

"Okay then," she said, breaking the frosty eye contact. "Let's load up and move out."

After they'd pulled Fisher's cage off, Eddie locked the gurney into position along the driver's side wall of the van, while Doc sat and began attaching more cables to Thorne's head and torso. Fisher was then ushered into the middle of the three seats opposite the comatose man, and after loading two large black holdalls into racks on the back doors, Eddie, rifle strapped high on his chest, clambered into the third.

"Cosy," he quipped, shifting his weight until comfortable. "I'll pour us a nice cup of tea once we're underway."

Fisher gave the big man an absent smile. All the guys seemed nice enough, but he knew the woman in charge intended to kill him — and if that tracker didn't activate, she'd probably succeed.

As the van and SUV pulled away from the large, detached house on the corner of West 225th and Greenwood, Gamma team's outer sentry reported the route passed Hickory Park was clear and wished them good luck.

By the time LAPD comms began squawking about a shitshow kicking off on Sepulveda Boulevard, they were across the Vincent Thomas Bridge, and well on their way to San Diego.

The mercs working for Nova and Sinapec arrived right on cue, and though he was a little surprised the yanks hadn't rocked up as well, Frayne had waited as long as he could; local law enforcement would be there soon, and it was time to leave.

He'd had the truck positioned across the doorway of the unit as they completed their final preparations, exposing just enough of what was going on behind to provide a view that focused the attention of their would be attackers, without making his people look sloppy. Then he'd sent Alpha and Delta through the tunnels, leaving only Gamma on their distant perches to hold the competition back; high-powered shots that were almost impossible to track, fizzing through the darkness from over half a mile away.

Having acknowledged the green light from Rhea, the former Marine colonel sealed his helmet into position and let go of a long-held breath before accelerating the truck towards the Nova cordon. But after travelling no more than forty metres, an incredible flash of light forced his eyes closed, and a deafening noise enveloped the cab, which lurched up like a bucking bronco. Frayne slammed into the steering wheel and his armour began screaming multiple damage alerts. Some sort of rocket-propelled ordnance had hit him, and the effect was devastating.

All shooting in the service road stopped, and there was a moment of stunned uncertainty before the rear of the truck, already ripped from its cab, erupted for a second time; fearsome flames belching from buckled doors as the mangled hunk of burning metal crashed back down to the tarmac again.

Merc brains began catching up with what their eyes had just seen as the sound of distant sirens began permeating the air, and the spell broke — no one was surviving that.

Orders were shouted at one, and then the other cordon, as both private militaries sought to get clear of the area before police arrived. In seconds, doors were slamming and wheels were squealing. Someone had overreacted, and there was clearly going to be no payday here now, just a lot of questions.

"Are you okay, you crazy man?"

Rhea had appeared in the service road and was dragging Frayne clear of the reinforced cab. His head was spinning, and he rubbed gloved hands over screaming ears.

"WHAT?" he shouted.

"NEVER MIND," the tough little Scot laughed, pointing to the blue and red flashing lights just entering the far end of the road. "TIME TO GO."

The rear of the truck was now just a twisted carcass of burning metal in the middle of the service road, and Tyler couldn't help but whistle in appreciation as they jogged past — even he was impressed with how believable the scene before him looked.

A large part of war, like magic, was about convincing others to believe a reality you created for them, and this little shootout, along with its after-party, would keep everyone tied up and trying to guess what the fuck had just happened in Torrance more than long enough for Miah and her precious cargo to completely disappear.

As they'd fallen back, Alpha and Delta had stripped out anything military and set fires that were starting to take hold by the time the retired colonel and former Master Sergeant entered the unit. The two of them gave the small industrial building one last check, before priming their final surprise and following the others into the tunnels that had once allowed a drug cartel to move people and product between it and several houses on the nearby estate.

Predictable procedures, safety checks and briefings then guaranteed the small commercial space was well and truly ablaze before any of the police units present were ready to enter.

Time was now back on Frayne's side, and as the former colonel emerged into the basement of a detached house several hundred yards away, he exchanged a grin with Rhea. All team members had reported in, the company hadn't sustained a single casualty, and there was no sign their relocation to the nearby housing estate had been detected.

91

Mission accomplished.

Rhea gave her colonel a kiss and pulled the remote trigger clear of its gaffer tape on the frame of the basement door, waggling her thumb over the rounded red button. "I've been looking forward to this bit," she chuckled, waiting for his nod.

Frayne made a final check over the radio that each tunnel site was clear and closed off, then gave her a wink. "Go on."

Moments later, the gas main entering the industrial unit erupted, causing just enough mayhem among the police, fire crews and paramedics now packed into the service road, that no one noticed the minor rumble of the accompanying tunnel collapses.

The air outside was now thick with the persistent hum of drones: police, news streams, mercs, corporations, governments; all watching the show; all waiting to see what would happen next… Rhea knew what would happen next — sex, and after that, maybe some sleep.

Two blocks away, a tired and bruised Dean Reynolds watched Ray's drone feed from a battered old leatherette recliner he'd dragged over to the glassless patio doors of a repossessed condo, and as the Californian dawn began crawling along the graffiti covered wall, he nodded in appreciation. "Clever."

From the viewpoint of most interested parties, it would look like some grunt got over-excited and blew the fuck out of the truck containing Thorne. He might have even swallowed it himself if he hadn't been watching the day before. And while the spectacle Hargreaves' mercs had put on tended to indicate Thorne hadn't met his maker, Dean felt pretty damn confident the extra hole he'd put in the poor bastard's head, meant there wouldn't be any more work completed on that cursed implant.

Any other day, he'd now be back at Eden shutting down Cheng and his little operation, before catching a flight home. But the sudden appearance of another agent, particularly one who seemed to be choreographing an elaborate disappearing act, had the distinct feel of a separate retrieval operation, and that could only mean one thing — someone, most probably him, was getting screwed over.

Frowning, the chalky-haired spy severed the connection, took a sip of whisky, and reclined the chair to consider his next move.

\# It's time you removed those last few
        obstacles.

       ~ We haven't resolved our other
       business yet.

\# All in hand. But now you need to
deal with the dogs if you wish to
become their master.

       ~ Once I start this, there's no going
       back.

\# You want to serve, or be served?

       ~ Don't patronise me, Whittaker.
       Give me something tangible to
       work with.

\# Fair enough. But remember that
I gave you a head on a plate!

PARTITION THREE

[QUARANTINED: Bad Sector: timestamp error: location error]

Few, if any, in the Midwest town of Ogallala would imagine Miah Hargreaves was anything other than a middle-aged woman who preferred her own company and the peaceful magnificence of the Nebraskan countryside. The small population tried to involve her in town life when she first moved to the large wooden lodge on the shores of Lake McConaughy five years before. But the tall, wide-shouldered loner resisted attempts to get to know her better, did little in subsequent years to attract attention, and soon faded into the background of community life. Conventional wisdom tagging her as a flaky health-nut recluse of some sort.

But Miah wasn't flaky or a recluse; she was a stone-cold killer; an accomplished thief; a calculating kidnapper. In fact, she'd be pretty much anything you wanted her to be — if you had enough credit.

Morality, she told Eric in a quiet period between the moments of abject terror he felt when the grey-haired, brown suited man found and attacked them, was fluid. Right and wrong were simply a question of perspective: terrorists could be freedom fighters, politicians could be thieves and murderers, and people died all the time on the whim of a corpo exec, or simply because a spreadsheet said it was the optimal solution to a problem. So the big woman didn't let the moving goalposts of differing belief systems influence her professional judgements. She was a mercenary with one simple rule — once hired, as long as her employer kept faith, her loyalty was unswerving.

And she'd proved that to Eric through more than words. They'd been attacked three times since leaving his house in Manhattan Beach; a car chase and shootout on the 101 that forced them onto country roads, an ambush while resting in a barn near Turlock where the powerful woman almost got shot, and a pitched battle on the waste ground of an old parking lot in the heart of Haywood. Each time Miah, who was deceptively fast for a woman of her size, had risked her life to save his. At least that's how it felt.

But the risks she was taking had started to worry Eric, and after Turlock he'd asked if she had some sort of death wish. That was the first time he'd heard her laugh with genuine good humour. It was warm and pleasant. "Oh, come on Doc," she said with mock indignation. "It wasn't *that* close. Besides, from what you've told me about TI, I wouldn't actually be hurt. I'd just respawn or something, right?"

The expression on Eric's face revealed the depths of his growing concern. "In a *game*, yeah sure," he'd answered. "But here. *This*? I genuinely have no idea, Miah. Have you noticed how none of the guys you've shot have come back? Please be careful. If not for you, for me?" The bodyguard had offered a reassuring smile and squeezed his leg.

"I promise," she said, making an exaggerated cross over her heart.

She'd been more careful after that, and the wetware engineer, now dressed in a white cotton shirt and jeans she'd bought at their last refuelling stop, had been forced to admit Miah was either a great actor, or she really did give a shit.

They'd made their way upstate to Frisco, and the protection specialist pulled the Range Rover into the curb near several fast-food joints in the old marina district.

"Look," she said. "Haywood was only forty minutes ago, and though I get this isn't *real* real, I need a break, a pee, and something to eat. What do you think?"

"I think that's a great idea," Eric nodded. "If there is any kind of pattern to the attacks so far, we should be okay for the next couple of hours."

Though situated just a few hundred miles up the coast, the young entrepreneur had never been to San Francisco before. The city was under the tacit governance of Nova who, like Eden and Tycho, had stepped in across the America continents to bail out local and state governments when they declared themselves bankrupt during the great depression.

To be fair, the place looked like it was thriving. But Eric had heard some bleak stories about how the polycorp punished alleged criminals and dissidents, and TI or not, he had no wish to find out how they'd treat a fugitive from one of its main competitors.

"Didn't you say Whittaker has a new Eden complex in Frisco?"

"I don't know about new," Miah said. "But yes, that's where he said he'd be working from. Why?"

Eric shrugged. "Nothing I guess. I just thought this city belonged to Nova."

They both got out of the car.

"Is that important?" the big woman asked, adjusting the hoodie she'd bought to cover the holster on her hip.

"You ever worked for Nova?"

"They're a big corp, of course I have. I expect you have too?"

The wetware designer nodded. Nova was one of his biggest PDrive customers. "Fair point," he conceded, dropping the conversation, but still wondering in what lifetime Ido Maas would willingly accommodate Daran Whittaker.

"Burger, taco, pizza?" Miah waved a hand at the parade of eateries doing a brisk trade in the afternoon sunshine. It was cooler than Manhattan Beach, though still great outside weather, and Eric pointed to the wide patio of 'Bad Boys Burgers,' which offered a magnificent view of the Bay and mighty Golden Gate Bridge. Miah scanned the crowd and nodded approval. "Grab us a table on that edge so I can see who's coming and going. I'm going to run inside for the toilet."

The odd pair ate in companionable silence, both enjoying the fresh air and brief sense of normality the meal and company of others provided. But as the waitron glided over with their bill, the powerful woman's head dipped to one side and she tapped her earbud.

"Well, you sure as hell took your time," she opened. Then waved an apologetic hand at the mech as she swiped his pad with her cuff. "Sorry, not you. I have a com call."

Eric offered the multi-limbed server a smile as it acknowledged both the apology and payment, before beginning to clear the table.

"So what's the plan? We've been attacked three times already."

A pause.

"Well, that's good news. I'm sure Doctor Thorne will be pleased. But if we're going to be here for a few more hours, I'd like some back up to even the playing field. Is that do'able?"

Miah looked at Eric and mouthed, '*I'll tell you in a minute.*'

"Good."

A pause.

"Frisco."

Another pause. Then she checked her cuff.

"About an hour, maybe an hour and a half, judging by the previous incidents. There's been a handful each time; always led by that grizzly older guy in a brown suit. The fucker is fast; definitely jacked."

Miah turned to look over her shoulder and, despite the harsh haircut, Eric decided the woman he'd labelled *plain looking* when she'd rang his doorbell, was in fact quite attractive in a no-nonsense kind of way.

"Treasure Island? Sure, that's just across the Oakland Bay Bridge from here." She gave him a thumbs up. "Forty minutes at the old Power Plant. Brilliant. Thank you, Fisher. We'll see you there."

As they walked back to the Range Rover, Eric's new guardian explained that Whittaker's techies had run into all kinds of trouble while trying to unpick the code running the environment they were in, but were now slowly winning the battle. They'd also managed to confirm his body was in Eden, and that Fenton had indeed been using TI in an attempt to trick the wetware specialist into handing over his MindMerge project files. There had been several attempts to extract the information before Whittaker's people found a way to block further resets, and inserted Miah.

"So now Fenton can't just restart when he doesn't get his way, what is the point of all this?" Eric asked.

"I don't know Doc, you're the TI specialist. If he got hold of this digital you, could he extract the information somehow?"

It had never occurred to the gifted designer that the gaming platform he'd created might be used as a weapon — as a torture device. But, he realised with sudden fear, in theory there was no end to the suffering or mental anguish the person controlling this environment could inflict.

"Doc?"

"Yes," he swallowed, looking at Miah's strong face as she started the engine. "I think they could cause quite a lot of harm."

The big merc gave him a broad smile and patted his knee again. "Best we don't let them have you then, eh? Let's go find our reinforcements; give that wiry old bastard a bloody nose next time he turns up."

Eric nodded and smiled back … Yes, she was definitely quite pretty.

Sept 19, 2042
03:49H [Manhattan Beach, California]

"Shit Frank," Detective Danny Gonzales said as they peered past the tape preventing access to the bedroom. "What the fuck is your boy involved in?"

Bright forensic lighting reflected from the retired cop's near bald head as the sixty-year-old tried to absorb the utter devastation in Eric's bedroom. He'd seen his fair share of mayhem over four decades as a cop, so wasn't a man given to displays of outward emotion, but his eyes were locked on the two sterile paper suits working around the bloodstained bed, and panic gnawed at the edges of his composure. Someone had been shot; discarded field dressings and packaging pointing to something far more professional than a botched burglary.

"He's just a game designer, Danny. Nothing people should be breaking into his house or—" the older man's jaw clamped down as emotion caught in his throat, and the detective reached out to squeeze his shoulder. "Hey, come on buddy," he said to the man who'd once been his Sergeant. "Don't be letting thoughts like that in. I know this sounds shit, but whoever got shot received medical attention. And no body being here is kind of a good thing, yeah? Who abducts a dead man?"

It was a painfully blunt observation, but it worked, and Frank wiped a sleeve over his eyes, nodding.

"Everyone in the LAPD will be looking out. Whoever these fuckers are, they picked a fight with the entire department when they picked a fight with your boy. Okay?"

101

Frank patted the hand on his shoulder. "Thank you, Danny."

"Hey, that's what family does, right?" the stocky detective said with a gentle smile.

Outside, a person calling herself Vivian Murray had turned up flashing an FBI badge, and no one argued when she cited the Federal Kidnapping Act as grounds to take charge. Though it wasn't lost on the NeuRobotics security chief the woman seemed very interested in Eric's recent work associations, and he was just about to ask if she knew something he didn't about his son's business dealings, when a black town car pulled alongside the police cruisers cordoning off the area and a tall, grey-skinned man with sharp birdlike features got out waving a writ.

"Get your people out of that house," the suit crowed in an imperious tone to the Lieutenant stood on Eric's porch. "This is an executive order preventing property interference or removal from this address."

The cop frowned at the newcomer and walked down the pathway to intercept him. "I don't know which fat cat you represent pal, but this is a crime scene."

"I don't care what you call it," the corpo said, adjusting his cuff. "This property now falls under the purview of Eden. Meaning, as I'm sure you know, neither you or your government," he fixed Murray with a contemptuous glare, "have any jurisdiction."

Frank threw the agent a questioning look, and then a punch at the corporate lacky; landing the blow with more than enough force to knock the bony, pompous attorney to the ground. "I don't give a fuck what you're here to steal, you piece of shit," he snarled. "Just tell me where my son is?"

"Are you insane?" the raw-boned lawyer squealed, eyes darting from grazed hands to the aggressive older man who'd just hit him. "I don't know anything about your son."

Two of the local cops were now in motion. "Whoa, Frank. Whoa," one called. But the fiery retired detective held out a hand to stop their advance. "They've taken my boy, Jimmy."

"I have no idea what he's talking about," the wide-eyed attorney stammered. "I was just sent to deliver that writ to the officer in charge."

"Liar." Frank shouted, bending down to grab a fist full of jacket. "Where's my fucking son?" This time Jimmy intervened, dragging the old brawler back before he could do the lawyer any more damage.

"Okay. Okay," Frank said, letting the patrolman walk him away. "But tell me how this arsehole just happens to arrive half an hour after my son has been kidnapped? Scanning police frequencies? Fuck off. Eden already knew." He looked over to the Lieutenant and FBI agent. "You guys have to have connected those dots, right?"

The eyes of every cop present turned towards the lawyer sprawled beside the town car as he pressed a handkerchief to his nose and held the bloody square of material out accusingly.

"That's a fair question," the Lieutenant said, stepping alongside the bony man. "How did you know, Mr —"

"That maniac attacked me," the dishevelled attorney screeched, taking the policeman's offered hand and standing up.

"The Lieutenant asked your name," Danny cut in, refusing to be sidetracked.

103

"Hopkins," the suit replied, checking his jacket for damage before glaring at Frank. "Howard Hopkins. I work for Eden, and this Executive Order says you don't need to know anything else. Now, I'll let the assault charge go, but only if you ensure that thug leaves at once and doesn't come back."

Danny wrapped thick arms around Frank before he could lunge forward again, turning him back towards Ocean Drive. "Maybe it's best you go wait in your car. I'll keep you updated. And you," he said over his shoulder to the lawyer. "Go fuck yourself. This is a US crime scene, and we have plenty of evidence in plain view we can, and will, seize."

Hopkins let out a shrill laugh. "You are way out of your depth, detective." He turned to the Lieutenant with a cold, vulturous smile, confidence returning now Frank was under control. "Do yourself a favour and read the Order before anyone else under your command mouths off. A DARPA liaison is detailed. But as of now, this house has been designated Eden property until we're satisfied there are no proprietary assets inside. So, if your staff and that violent little man aren't gone in the next five minutes, I'll have all your jobs." He handed over the writ, dabbed his nose again, and climbed back into the rear of the long black limousine.

Murray watched the exchange with the lawyer from Eric's doorway. She'd already been briefed on the snatch by the CIA ghosts who'd spent ten days watching Thorne, and would need to leave soon if she was to join Deputy Director Johnson at the Forward Control Point in Torrance.

The plan had been to seize control of the investigation into the wetware specialist's abduction so spook forensics could take physical possession of his tech. But Whittaker had trumped them by gaining temporary control of the man's home with a Presidential Order ... *a Presidential fucking Order* for God's sake. And an unprecedented move like that must have cost Eden's Chief Exec dearly — so there couldn't be much doubt in *his* mind that Thorne had succeeded.

"Did you see all that?" Frank demanded from beside his car, as the large Latino detective did his best to contain the furious old man.

"Fucking Eden? My son has his own company. He doesn't work for Eden. They're trying to steal something. I guarantee it."

She held up a hand. "I know this is hard, Frank. But the US government has no jurisdiction over Eden or any of the other polycorps on their own property... and right or wrong, that's what a Presidential Order has just designated Eric's house." He opened his mouth to object. "However," she continued, holding up a finger. "My Director *will* have some sway over DARPA."

"Who the fuck are DARPA?" Danny interrupted.

"They're the government agency responsible for developing advanced defence tech for the US," the short blonde replied.

"So why the hell would they be coming here?"

"Good question." Murray had banked on someone bringing it up. "Frank?"

The former cop began shaking his head, realising what she was getting at. "No. This is bullshit," he said, locking eyes with her. "This is bullshit, Murray."

"Could Eric have been involved in weapons development?"

"No," Frank said with absolute certainty. "The lad is fundamentally opposed to that kind of thing." The agent frowned and held his gaze for a few questioning heartbeats, but it was clear the old man had no clue what his son had gotten involved in. She nodded and checked her cuff, 04:00. Time to go.

"Okay. This is the deal. I guarantee you when that arsehole gets back out of his car, he'll be bombproof. Fighting him is pointless. Eden is too powerful, and Whittaker has too many politicians in his pocket."

She looked straight at Frank.

"Finding Eric is the important thing here. Yes?"

The deflated old man offered a reluctant nod.

"Good," she said. "Whatever happened in that house was well organised and completed by highly trained operatives. But it seems they ran into company." She looked at Danny, who was nodding in agreement. "My guess would be that, however unlikely, two separate *interests* broke in at the same time and got into a firefight. What we need to figure out is who and why."

The agent took Frank's hard, calloused hand in hers and gave him a warm, sincere smile. "Being honest, we're not sorting this out now. But you have my word as a tenacious bitch that I won't let it go. This is a Federal investigation, and while I may not have any power over Eden, I sure as hell can get some answers from DARPA."

The tough old man wanted to argue. To demand action. But he knew she was right. Danny put an arm around him again, pulling him in close. "No one's giving up Buddy."

Frank felt the fight leaving him and his eyes filled with tears. "Just get my son back," he said to the FBI agent. "Please."

Sept 19, 2042
05:45H [Manhattan Beach, California]

The Seaview Inn was a collection of grey fronted buildings which, like Dean, had seen better days. It wasn't flashy. It wasn't ridiculously expensive. It didn't stand out, and neither did the people staying there. Reynolds liked that.

Getting to Thorne's the night before had been easy. The promenade was all but deserted, and only one dog had gotten spooked. Its owner cursing in a string of Spanish expletives at the perceptive pink collared hound, as she yanked it viciously back to her side.

Once there, the aging operative lurked outside until he was sure the man was asleep. Not that it mattered in a chameleon suit — the guy's pet robot wouldn't even know he was there. But somewhere not too deep below the surface, and now seeping through the membrane of his consciousness, Dean Reynolds had reached a limit. He didn't want to see the man's life leave him. So he waited.

On the run back to the hotel afterwards, anger replaced squeamish self-pity; he knew his hesitance had almost got him killed, Thorne was quite likely to be still alive, and the chameleon suit was undoubtedly damaged.

Charlie was on the com by the time the spy reached his apartment. The action had been spotted and efforts were underway to track Thorne's Range Rover. Still annoyed with himself, Dean gave instructions to the old ghost while examining the blue / black welts tracking up is right side from thigh to armpit, and after placing a DermaGel patch on each, he necked half a bottle of analgesics before changing into

107

something casual, and leaving the apartment again, this time by the front door.

As expected, Uncle Sam had assigned him his own watchers when he showed up in LA, and among other things, Dean let them follow him to the meet with Charlie.

Events may not have gone as planned last night, but that surveillance team were his ace in the hole, a bomb proof alibi for anything that might have happened to Thorne. So when his cuff chimed to announce a long expected unauthorised entry to his apartment, the veteran player of the spying game gave himself a satisfied nod, as he watched an old friend poking through his cupboards, drawers and bathroom, before theatrically winking at the cambot hidden on the border of the apartment's vidscreen and heading to the kitchen where she made herself a drink.

"Hello Vivian," he said, walking through the door ten minutes later.

"You need ice and new underwear, darling," she cooed back.

Dean couldn't help but grin. "You want another one of those?"

A petite blonde leaned over the edge of the sofa and peered round the partition. "You've been *spying* on me?" she said in a shocked tone, dangling an empty glass and batting long, seductive lashes.

There would be a team or two outside by now, and given her seating choice, they may have even occupied the apartment next door.

"How are you doing?" he asked as he made the drinks. "It's been a while."

"Hasn't it," she replied. "Yeah, I'm okay. Back working in the US though."

Dean noted she was intent on staying in the lounge area near the open patio doors.

"You happy with that?"

"Not a lot of choice after you went rogue," she said with a little bite.

Dean laughed. "Didn't go rogue, Vivian," he chided. "Just ended our arrangement."

Gathering the drinks, he walked into the lounge with a relaxed swagger, passing the blonde agent her Manhattan and nodding towards the open doors. "I have to pay for any breakages, Viv. We gonna have a problem?"

"I do hope not, honey," she replied, her thin face creasing into an affectionate smile that only her eyes betrayed. "It's always lovely to see you. But why are you here, Dean?"

"I'm on holiday," he lied.

Viv smiled again. This time it was more predatory. "Strike one," she said, patting the sofa beside her. "We both know that's not true, honey. So give it another try — why are you in LA?"

Dean offered a waspish grin of his own. The analgesics were wearing off, he was tired, and his ribs were on fire. "This'll go quicker if you just say what's on your mind, Viv," he countered, leaning casually against the wall and taking a sip of his Johnny Walker.

Murray pursed her full, red lipsticked lips, but remained silent.

"Look sweetheart, I've had a long night. I'm tired, and in no mood to spar. If you'd wanted to take me in for de-briefing, your boys could have scooped me up as soon as I got out of the Prius." He waved a thumb towards the still open door. "But instead, you came for a visit. So, like I said — what's on your mind, Viv?"

The CIA agent sighed and stood up, walking to the open patio doors. "Nice view," she remarked, looking at the carpark below.

"Isn't it?" Dean said, also slipping back into a warmer tone. "If you lean right out and crane your head to the left, you can just about see the ocean."

She laughed at that and turned back to him. "We worked well together in the Far East, didn't we?"

The greying operative raised a questioning eyebrow at her change of tack. "I guess — as far as our work together went."

"So perhaps there's a chance to do a little together now, for mutual benefit?"

Dean had been expecting accusations, not a job offer. "I'm listening," he said cautiously.

Vivian Murray had known the older agent for over a decade, had been his Case Officer in the Far East until he dropped off the grid. She'd noticed the subtle changes in his personality in the years before that; like the man she knew was ever so slowly fading away. Then, after an order recalling him to Langley last year, he left her a com message saying he quit, and just disappeared. She hadn't seen or heard from him since.

"We know you've been watching a guy down the road called Eric Thorne," she ventured. "We know that, because so have we. We also know, as do you, that merry bloody hell broke out in his house last night."

"And you know of my interest how?"

Viv raised an eyebrow. "Really? No professional courtesy at all — we're gonna play *that* game, Dean?" She

110

paused, giving him a chance to save them both the charade. Then sighed, "Okay, have it your way."

"As soon as it all kicked off last night, our watcher team doubled their interest in the one *former*," she gave him a baleful look, "spy we'd identified holidaying in the area, and they followed him to a meet with Charlie Hanson. An old, but still active ghost.

"Now we knew Charlie was in the area with his team. We just didn't know who he was working for until your meet."

Dean offered a roguish grin. "He was sure no one knew his team were there."

Viv chuckled. "No one's that good honey, *you know that*."

The grin spread into a small smile, tugging at the corners of Dean's mouth — he'd almost forgotten how sharp she was. "I'll be sure to mention that in his performance review."

"Anyway," Viv went on. "While you enjoyed the spectacle from a ramshackle condo, we watched our own drone feed of that merc outfit shooting up parts of Torrance before apparently disappearing in a puff of smoke." She raised her hands in an exaggerated shrug, "—and my boss was like, 'Viv, what the fuck just happened?'"

Dean opened his mouth to speak, but the blonde agent raised a cautionary finger. "—and before you say *you're just on holiday* again, while I'd prefer to work with you on this, I've got instructions to take you in if you don't feel like sharing."

The veteran operative gave a slow nod, absorbing the threat. The point of having the CIA watch him was to make them his alibi for anything that happened to the wetware engineer. But if Thorne was still alive, maybe re-establishing some old ties and credibility wouldn't hurt. Hell, it might even provide him with the means to finish the job.

"Okay, Viv," he said, taking her glass. "I'll get us some more drinks while you explain how you envisage this working."

The woman offered a wry smile and followed him towards the kitchen. "Well, that went easier than I expected."

Dean snorted. "I think most people who threaten to disappear someone else, and have the means to do it, tend to get their own way, Vivian," he replied dryly.

She chuckled and cooed, "Don't be like that, baby. I'm sure this will be the restart of something beautiful."

In the kitchen, Dean took his bottle of Johnnie Walker from the side and a Marlboro from the pack on the table. He poured a measure into both their glasses and pushed the one with lipstick smudges towards his onetime Case Officer, before walking to the still open door. The diminutive agent tensed instinctively, but Dean just leaned against the frame, lit his smoke, and gave her a mischievous grin.

Murray shook her head. "Arsehole."

He blew smoke into the cloudless blue sky and nodded in agreement. "Why thank you, Vivien," he said around the grin. "I appreciate that."

He looked out down the metal stairs and waved a hand toward a watcher he couldn't see, but knew would be there. "Seriously though, Viv, you know you couldn't keep me here. Your team aren't that good. So what's the plan?"

Murray smirked at his arrogance, pulled out a chair, and sat down. "I won't insult either of us by asking too many questions. But you have been dark for a while, so I need to know enough to satisfy the Boss we won't end up trying to shoot each other?"

112

"That's fair," Dean agreed.

"Are you prepared to say where you've been? Who you're working for now?"

The old spook had meticulously crafted that backstory before leaving China, and if she didn't already know it, when Viv's team followed the trail of bona fides he'd planted in places they'd look, they'd make an irresistible connection between the veteran spy and Ido Maas, CEO of Nova. He pulled a noncommittal face; belief in that lie hinged on weaving just enough truth around the chicken feed he'd sprinkled.

"Come on Viv, you know I can't."

The experienced case officer frowned. "We're gonna struggle to trust each other if we don't understand conflicts of interest, old friend."

"Okay, yeah I know," he said. "But my client relies on complete discretion. He would be quite unforgiving about being dragged into bed with the CIA."

"So, not government then?"

"No, no. God no," Dean laughed before taking another tug on his Marlboro. Any stress analysis the agent was running would recognise that as genuine.

"Look, I didn't want to be poked or pulled around, so I retired. This," he circled an arm. "Was supposed to be a favour. A lucrative one admittedly. But a favour nonetheless."

Again, no lies.

Viv cocked her head; someone was speaking in her ear. She nodded and took a sip of whisky. "That's a start, I guess. So, if not government, corporate?"

Dean let out an inpatient breath. "An influential individual who wouldn't want me working with the CIA, let alone pointing guns at them." He leaned towards the ear she

113

had a bud in and cupped his hands. "Are we done here? Can we get back to catching the bad guys, please?"

She gave him another of her predatory smiles. "Okay, let's do that. Eric Thorne was also working for a rather *influential individual,* wasn't he?"

Dean couldn't help but laugh at the implication. "Why don't you tell me, Viv? This conversation seems a bit one-sided."

Murray sighed, growing tired of their game of truth or dare. "Come on Dean, I don't think for a moment that you've gotten so rusty you've begun leaving fingerprints over everything you touch: you were at the same hotel on the same floor as Fenton White before his *accident,* your name appears on reports commissioned by Eden into that crash, and now you're skulking around the wetware engineer White approached on his return, when that engineer disappears."

"Skulking is a bit harsh," Reynolds quipped.

Murray rolled her eyes. "You asked me what I want? Well, we both know you fully intended to be found. You shone your little bat light into the night sky knowing we'd answer... and here I am. So *please* Dean, stop fucking around and just tell me — why reach out now?"

The US had pieced together more than the old intelligence operative expected. But that was fine. In fact, given the circumstances it was quite useful.

"Okay," he said, going to sit beside her at the table. "As you say, I knew you'd follow me as soon as I landed in country. That's what I was counting on."

"Why?"

"You were an insurance policy."

"Insurance for what?"

"Thorne."

"Go on."

"Knowing what he was up to, if I failed."

Murray's eyebrows lifted slightly before she brought them under control. "Failed? Failed to do what?"

"Failed to stop certain people getting their hands on him or his research."

Now she didn't try to hide her interest. "What people?"

"You know I won't tell you that, Viv. I've already said more than I should."

Murray let out a heavy sigh, but accepted that. "Have you failed?"

Reynolds held out his hands and shrugged. "To be honest, I don't know. I guess it depends on who kidnapped him, and whether he stays that way."

They stared at each other for a few moments. The voice in her ear would confirm what he'd said was true. The question was, how much of what he hadn't said did she also know? Dean poured another drink, and they both sipped.

"You want to know our interest in this?" Viv asked.

Dean shook his head and let out a humourless laugh. "I haven't been out of the game that long, beautiful. Ol' Uncle Sam is always interested in pinching other people's toys."

"He is, isn't he," she chuckled back. "Does that present a problem for you? For your client?"

"No," he answered. That would flag up as a lie, but one that was expected. She'd probably already been told to kill him when he stopped being useful, anyway.

They sat in silence for what felt like an eternity. Maybe she was thinking the same thing.

"We rounded up some mercs as they left Torrance in the early hours," she finally said. "They're all pleading wrong

115

place, wrong time, innocent misunderstanding and all that. The local office will de-brief them for the next couple of days to keep them out of trouble."

"You know that was all just a distraction, right?" Dean said, grateful she'd moved on.

Viv smirked and knocked back the last of her drink as she stood. "I'll give you a shout in a bit," she said. "I just need to cross a couple of T's. But I'm sure the Director will sign off on a joint approach to this. Two heads and all that?"

"So you know where he's going, then?"

"Who, Thorne? Yes. Don't you?"

He smiled. "Just don't sideline me, *partner*. If I don't hear from you within the hour, I'll assume we're working separately."

Viv gave him a mock scowl. "Hey, come on. No threats, we've made more progress than that." She squeezed his shoulder and started for the door, but on reaching it, turned.

"One last thing," she said. "I wasn't going to mention this. You may already know. But we've just started receiving reports from Beijing that Yung Zhu, among others, is either dead or has gone to ground. There's talk of a coup. We couldn't help but find the timing — *curious*."

Dean's heart stopped. That wasn't possible. Zhu was always a step ahead. No way anyone got the jump on that man.

Experience and self-discipline combined to pull the veteran spy's game-face down hard. He'd spent four years pretending to be a CIA operative in the Far East, and knew Viv had come to suspect where his true loyalties sat. That's why he'd gotten out. But he couldn't just feign disinterest — that would smack of lies.

116

"Wow," he said, after the briefest pause. "Poor bastard. Though I'm sure the folks in Langley will be delighted. Do you know who's gunning for him? Or why?" He took a drink, iron will keeping his hand steady. Espionage was a lonely game with absolutely no room for weakness; weakness got you exploited; weakness got you dead.

Viv shook her head. "Nothing," she said. "They're just rumours, and I only mentioned it because. Well…" She paused and looked into his eyes. "Look, I don't want to open *that* can of worms again. But if things have kicked off in China, we both know there is only one likely reason."

"That the old Chairman is dead or dying," Dean nodded.

"… And the cutthroat game of musical chairs has begun," Murray finished. "So, and I'm not saying this is the case, but if you *were* working for Yung and he was on the losing side of whatever's gone down over there, you could be in trouble — only you would know."

Dean's eyes were frozen orbs. Completely focussed on his mask, he gave a casual shrug. "Look Viv, I appreciate you telling me this. But I'm really only interested in Thorne at the moment, and to get on with that job, you need to go brief your Director."

The attractive blonde nodded, swiped her contact details to his cuff, and gave him a loose hug. "You know," she said as a parting shot. "If something has happened and you need a little help. I'll always be here."

She didn't wait for a reply, just walked out of the door and down the metal steps.

Dean took a deep breath, aware he couldn't end the show just yet. Someone would still be watching, assessing his response. He sauntered onto the balcony, sat down, and lit another cig.

The news, disturbing as it was, did fit with the sudden appearance of another player in his game, and if Zhu really was out of the picture, the old wetwork specialist knew he could forget any hopes of retirement or returning home. Without the top-cover of his long term lover and patron, Major Wu Shen aka Dean Reynolds — the operative who doesn't appear on a single MSS database, would officially be up shit creek without a paddle. But right now, all he really wanted, was to hear Zhu's voice and know the shrewd old spy-boss was okay.

After a sufficient display of nonchalance, the wiry double-agent went through his habitual process of running a scanner around the walls and furniture. To her credit, Viv hadn't left any bugs. But then she was a pro, and knew he'd check. He activated the sound dampeners anyway, turned on his cuff's VPN relays, and fired up WhatsApp.

As Murray's search had proved, cutting-edge spookware only ever drew attention, got you caught … Whereas a commercial chat service with over six billion subscribers, and end-to-end encryption, made any haystack a whole lot bigger for anyone trying to find an individual needle of communication.

'Hey Grandpa,' he typed. 'You fancy lunch next Tuesday?' There was only one correct answer to this: 'Sorry son, we have the plumber coming that day.'

It would be after 10 p.m. in Beijing, so perhaps it wasn't surprising no immediate answer came back. Dean padded out onto the balcony again and collected the bottle of whisky and his Marlboro's, before stretching out on the bed to wait; tired, worried, but way too wired to sleep.

Sept 19, 2042
07:36H [San Diego, California]

"That's odd," Doc muttered as he and Fisher
transferred Eric's naked body from the stretcher.

"What is?" the computer specialist asked.

Doc pointed to the device on the unconscious man's
chest. "The Bot has just retracted its needles and gone offline."

The tech nerd raised an eyebrow. "Maybe it's
because we're moving him to a higher spec device?"

"No, it shouldn't stop until I tell it to hand off to the
new assist," the medic said, tapping at glyphs on his cuff
display — '*battery depleted: nanite reservoir empty.*'

"The room?"

"Maybe," Doc conceded, pulling a face at the
anomalous reading. "But it was working fine in the van under
more or less the same conditions.

"Does it matter so long as he's still okay?" Fisher
asked, impatient to get on with the examination.

Doc looked at the trauma-bed's central display as
different icons came and went while it ran through its initial
examination of the new patient. Unlike the stretcher and Bot,
the bed had sophisticated AI software that was capable of both
detailed diagnoses and the ability to lead a competent medic
through most forms of general combat surgery. Green light
after green light registered on one of the smaller side panels as
the bed's probes and scanners completed their tasks until,
several seconds later, the bed emitted a short beep to indicate
its preliminary scans were complete.

119

"I guess not," he said, electing to read the notes rather than listen to the full examination record.

As expected, each section of the unconscious man's body was in the green except his head, which was flashing amber.

Amber?

Doc selected 'detailed analysis,' and the bed concentrated solely on Thorne's head for half a minute more. Then the main screen image shifted to a rotating 3D skull, with graphics indicating the presence of repaired trauma to the right frontal and upper parietal sections of the wetware engineer's cranium.

The medic frowned. He'd not worked with this particular brand of bed before, but *repaired* wasn't the term he'd use for his patch job, and while an MRI would be necessary to establish the full extent of injury to corresponding parts of Thorne's brain, he'd at least have expected the bed's examination to detect some of the surface damage. And then there were the man's EEG readings, which didn't show the slow Delta waves of someone in an induced coma, but rather a jumbled mix of Alpha and High Frequency Oscillations, which indicated the man's brain wasn't just awake and active, it was working at a rate no human brain should be able to sustain.

"I think this bed is faulty," Doc said, pointing a finger at the screen. "Because that's not possible."

"What?" Fisher asked, frustrated at having to constantly remind the mercenary to elaborate if he was going to get technical. "I keep telling you, explain yourself — I'm not medical."

"Everything," the normally unflappable medic stated, stabbing at the screen again and pointing. "The lack of identified trauma. I mean, the guy was shot in the head four hours ago for fuck's sake." He flipped to another readout. "And then there's his EEG readings; no brain can stand that kind of output for more than moments before a seizure shuts it down." He looked hard at the continuing flow of data. "It must be the bed. I'll speak to Jim to get another sent over from the MSF people."

"We don't have time for this, Doc." Fisher snapped.

The merc opened his mouth to protest, but knew the quirky computer nerd was right. He nodded. "Okay, man. But nothing about those readings is *normal*. At least let me remove the dressings and complete another physical exam before you throw him into the MRI. Neither of our bosses will be happy if we manage to kill the guy, will they?"

The shorter man scowled then grumbled assent, and Doc took a set of angled scissors from an arm pocket, removing the bandaging wrapped around Eric's head until he reached the two gauze patches protecting the entry and exit wounds he'd injected with PharmaGel. It all looked good. He'd expected some push back: the pressure inside the skull in such injuries almost always forced some of the gel back out, creating horn-like protrusions as the coagulant set. But Thorne's skull had retained a remarkably even symmetry, and if not for the random bald patch in the middle of his head with a square of blood-soaked gauze glued over it, and another above his right eye, you'd never know the man had been shot. "That's going to be a pain to remove," he commented, pointing at the gauze.

"Isn't that holding everything in?" Fisher said from the other side of the bed. "Surely you don't want to interfere with that until we reach a proper facility?"

Doc smirked at the irritating techie. "No, it'll be fine. The gel would have set hours ago. But you're right, we don't have to remove it for you to do your checks." He got a small torch from another pocket and pried open Thorne's left eye. "Ha," he commented after waving the light back and forth a couple of times.

"What?" Fisher asked in an exasperated tone. "What now?"

Doc's face had a bemused look as he let the left eyelid drop and opened up the right; repeating the process.

"Look," he said, shaking his head as he waved the torch into Eric's right eye and away again several times. "See that pupil constriction?"

"Yes," Fisher nodded.

"I'd expect someone with this level of injury, especially one I'd put in a coma, to have fixed dilated pupils. Maybe he didn't take as much damage as I thought."

"So that's a good thing, yes?" the older man enquired.

"If he wasn't still unconscious it would be," Doc observed.

"Excellent," Fisher beamed, missing the point being made. "Can we please get on with the MRI then? Though your company today has been simply delightful, I didn't pack for a nighttime mystery tour with a kidnapped gunshot victim — and I honestly just want to go home now."

The medic didn't like the skinny man or his big attitude. But he did have one thing right, it had been a long day, and moving the burden of Thorne's care to someone else couldn't come soon enough. "You want me to go?"

Letting out a long sigh, the sarcastic man's expression softened; the heavyset soldier hadn't risen once to his constant taunts during their painfully long journey together, and had tended Thorne with absolute professionalism. "Well, I think we both know I'm looking to see if the good Doctor has anything tucked away in there that doesn't belong to him, and given the poor bastard's injury, I'm guessing you seeing the MRI would be useful for treatment?"

Doc nodded.

"Well, stick around then. I won't tell anyone if you don't." He offered a rare smile, and began typing commands on the screen above the bed to bring the neuroimager online.

As the magnets began slowly rotating, they positioned Eric so his head rested on the cradle within the portable white box, then stepped back to watch the displays.

Fisher had never seen an MRI in real life, just the monochrome scansheets waved around by doctors on entertainment vidstreams. But from what Doc had said, he'd been expecting to see the trail of a gunshot, marked by clear tears through the tissue on the right side of Thorne's brain. He'd also been expecting to see the gossamer thin filaments of a PDrive, and the various hardwired memory and storage enhancements almost everyone working in hi-technology installed. All of which, the computer specialist anticipated, would need meticulous review when trying to determine whether or not the man also had Whittaker's chip — as they'd all look more or less the same: small, black, non-biological objects.

But as it turned out, the determination that something was very, very different about Eric Thorne's brain hadn't been hard at all. Because the thing was one large radiating nexus of electrical activity.

Doc stood in stunned silence, pointing at where the trauma should have been, and then staring at Fisher as if he had answers.

There was no injury, not anymore. But neither was there any biological mass through that part of Thorne's brain. Instead, a latticework of what he could only assume was the assimilation of millions and millions of med nanites now glowed on the MRI scan like Christmas tree lights as they criss-crossed the man's frontal lobe.

"Holy shit," Fisher said after several long seconds. "That can't be fucking normal, can it?"

Neither of them had heard the first shots outside the room above the discordant thunks and clunks of the neuroimager's phase changes, as the machine refined and redefined the three-dimensional image building on the central screen above the bed.

But as the noise of the MRI died, and the machine reported its imaging cycle was complete, both men heard the unmistakable sounds of gunfire. Doc's hand went instinctively to the sidearm holstered on his right thigh and he drew the weapon, placing a finger to his lips as he approached the door.

The room had been used for ammunition or fuel storage when the airfield had been active, so the walls and door were both solid. The medic listened, ear pressed to cold metal, and heard a muffled shout. Fisher joined him, a questioning look on his face.

"Doc?" a male voice shouted. "Fisher?"

"That's the Colonel," the medic said, moving to open the door.

"Wait," Fisher blocked his hand. "What about the gunfire?"

"Exactly. They may be under attack. I have to help."

Sept 19, 2042
08:15H [San Diego, California]

The former landing field at Imperial Beach sat
between the last neat blocks of prefabricated San Diegan
suburbia and six square kilometres of desert, which ran all the
way to the remnants of a wall that once separated the US from
Mexico.

Though technically still under government control,
the old airbase and attached scrubland was now home to some
thirteen thousand refugees living in the decaying remains of
the base's many concrete and asbestos buildings, as well as an
eclectic mix of tents, shipping containers and hand-built huts.

Disavowed by both bordering nations, the region had
regressed to a Hobbesian state of nature, where the desire to
have what someone else possessed was only outweighed by a
fear of losing what you already had. The gangs that had moved
in to profit from the desperation of their fellow humans
imposed some territorial sense of order. But then, of course,
they were also the primary source of extortion and bloodshed.

Only the omnipresent NGOs, who moved in and out
of the area with relative impunity as funding streams appeared
and then dried up, offered any real support for the countless
souls trapped, moneyless and forsaken, by their dreams of a
better life.

So the sight of two Grey Wolfs sweeping in to land
near a complex of hangars running alongside the old airbase's
boundary was of little interest to most camp residents;
helicopters came and went throughout the day.

125

But as these ones settled down beside an older Westland decked out as a medi-vac ambulance, the armoured troops both then disgorged, caused an immediate ripple of chatter through nearby tents.

"Ground that Westland," Murray ordered, walking down the ramp with the Delta Force Squad Commander. "Secure the crew and anyone else aboard until I say otherwise."

Her reflection in the mirrored visor bobbed, and moments later four troopers peeled off to approach the other aircraft.

"Another vehicle has entered the hangar your asset's signal is coming from," a comms officer reported in her ear.

"Your entry team set, Dean?" she asked over her private link with Reynolds.

"We're good to go."

"Okay Top," she said, returning her attention to the armoured woman beside her. "You have tactical command."

As Murray spoke, a shot rang out nearby, followed by two more, and then a sustained burst of automatic fire.

"Not us," the Squad Com said, pre-empting her question. "Team One, move up in double time … rapid entry authorised. Teams Two and Three, secure the perimeter.

Another gunshot.

Dean and the entry team reached the hangar thirty seconds later, stacking up on either side of the huge metal doors. At the front on the left, the old operative could see three bodies on the grey concrete floor around a chevy van, and signed as much to the squad's TL on the right. The black armoured trooper acknowledged the information and held up three, two, one fingers, before launching a grenade into the old

126

concrete structure. "Flashbang," he called over the ops channel.

Everyone looked away, and the audio pickup briefly muted as a concussion wave reverberated around the confined space. Then the same trooper was shouting "Breach Breach Breach," and his team began moving with precise, practiced efficiency to take control of the hangar's interior.

All other movement in the area had ceased. The local populous, experienced in responding to spontaneous violence, were now either laying on the ground in submission, with hands covering their heads, or had sought the questionable refuge of nearby tents, hoping desperately not to get caught up in whatever was going down.

A handful youths in gang colours appeared beyond the DF perimeter, saw military, and disappeared again in the blink of an eye; probably gone to report to their teenage warlord. But Murray wasn't there to take care of a few kids with guns. She was there for the mercs.

Another shot echoed out, and a spine-chilling silence, broken solely by one child's crying, descended across the nearby camp. Then, several heartbeats later, the same male voice reported, "Area secure."

"That was quick," the Squad Com replied. "Casualties?"

"Zero DF. But something went down between these mercs. Four dead on our arrival, two casualties. We wounded another on entry."

"Not the full company then?"

"No Master Chief, and the woman commander isn't here either."

The Squad Com shook her head, looking at Murray. "Okay, leave enough troopers to guard the prisoners. The rest of you can join Two and Three on the perimeter. I'm on my way over with the agent in charge."

"Roger that."

"Any update on the package?" Murray cut in.

"Secured, though unconscious, Ma'am. Your asset is with him."

"Good. We'll be evacuating them immediately. Ensure the package remains under guard, absolutely no one interferes with him."

When Murray reached the nearby semi-derelict hangar, the breach team had already pulled back and forensics were starting the process of evidence gathering. In her mind's eye, she played out the scenarios that saw these mercs turning on each other. It could only be a cross of some sort; the big questions being who'd crossed who, and why?

Up front, medics were treating two of the wounded. Reynolds was further in, crouched and talking quietly to the third, who was propped against a stretch of wall beside an open doorway which now had two black-armoured troopers guarding it.

The woman reasoned Dean might be interested in the who and why as well, but he was also experienced enough not to make a beeline for Thorne. He knew the game as well as her, and would have figured at least one of the troopers following him through those hangar doors had explicit orders to kill him if he misbehaved.

And he wasn't wrong. Langley still didn't know what the guy was up to, and while database searches indicated he was working for Ido Maas of Nova, Murray still had a hard-on for the Director's opposite number in China. A view that appeared especially prophetic when Hargreaves' mercs turned up in San Diego.

They'd all been expecting the wayward agent to make some sort of move. Johnson had wanted to simply detain and interrogate the man. But the Director had over-ruled his deputy, keen to see where the dice would fall.

The guarded doorway led into a room containing nothing more than two people, a hospital bed and medical equipment. One of those people was lying on the bed with what looked like a serious head wound. And the other, a nerdy looking guy in corduroy, was fussing around the head of that bed, frantically closing down monitors.

This was the asset who had been supplying the intel and telemetrics?

She smiled a hello. "Doctor Fisher? It's good to meet you. Is he okay?"

The skinny man with lank hair0 and glasses nodded, removing a data spike from the central display and switching it off. "He's as stable as anyone whose been shot in the head can be, Agent …?"

"Murray," Viv supplied as the man continued to busy himself.

"Right. Well, it's been an unexpectedly long night Agent Murray. How soon can you get us out of here?"

You're welcome, the petite woman thought. Then said, "Looks like we arrived just in time. What the hell happened? Do you think we can expect more trouble?"

He gave her a dismissive look. "I don't know what happened, I was in here. My job is to retrieve Doctor Thorne, not fight soldiers or offer speculative advice to general field operatives. But from what your trooper on the door told me, you've only got six mercs out there, and none of them are the boss, Hargreaves. So yes, if I were you, I'd count on more trouble… Now, like I said, when can you get us out of here?"

129

Murray tried not to bristle at the man's unhelpful and unnecessary rudeness. "I was neither looking for, nor need your advice, *Doctor*," she replied, a cold edge creeping into her tone. "There are two more choppers inbound. Once they arrive, I'll have you and your package escorted to Brown airfield while I finish up here. Then we'll grab a flight back to Langley."

She turned to leave.

"I'll want the medic who was in here to come along." Fisher added from beside Thorne's bed.

"I can't authorise that," Murray said over her shoulder. "He's under arrest. There'll be a medic at Brown."

"I was neither looking for, nor need your authorisation, *agent*," Fisher responded mimicking her earlier words in an imperious tone. "You do your job, I'll do mine. He comes along."

Murray turned back to stare at the officious little man for several seconds, toying with the idea of tearing him a new hole. But none of the injured presented any real threat, so it probably wasn't worth getting into a pissing contest with a jumped up desk-jockey working for the Deputy Director.

"Have it your way," she shrugged. "The casualties can go back to Brown with you. Just be ready in five."

Then another gunshot echoed around the walls and Murray rolled her eyes in irritation. But for the fact they'd secured Thorne, this op was already starting to grate on her, and by the time she'd pushed past the troopers in the doorway to see Reynolds standing over the body of the merc he'd been speaking with, the diminutive senior field-officer had decided the *de-briefers* at Langley were welcome to the lot of them. She'd throw them on a fucking plane, and leave the Director's

130

team to play their silly pissing games — Vivian Murray was tired, fed up, and done with men's ego's for one day.

"Place your weapon on the floor," the middle of three troopers commanded Reynolds; who stood motionless, hands raised and gun hanging from one finger, as they approached him with their carbines up.

Reynolds complied.

"Now place your hands on your head and sit down with your legs crossed."

The wiry agent looked over to Murray as he sat. "He made a grab for my gun, Viv. Sorry, poor judgement on my part."

The female agent walked over to the corpse. A name patch on the man's fatigues identified him as 'Frayne.' Like most merc outfits, there was no indication of his rank. But the guy looked too old to be a grunt.

If Reynolds had been a lazy-arse cop she could imagine a well-trained soldier getting the drop on him, even if they were already carrying a nasty gut wound. But Dean wasn't, the man was a killing machine, and it was hard to imagine anyone getting a hand on his gun, let alone a tussle that resulted in him having to shoot that person under the chin, blowing most of their brains onto the wall behind them. So what the fuck had the dead man known that Reynolds didn't want shared?

"Did any of your people see it?" she asked the Master Chief as the woman approached.

"No."

Murray looked back to Reynolds. "What the fuck, Dean?"

"Honestly, —" he began.

131

But she held up a hand, tired of his bullshit. "Strip him down to his underwear, cuff him, and take him to Brown with you. I'm done with the man."

"Viv," Reynolds pleaded. "Come on. Don't be like that."

The shapely agent shook her head and began walking out of the hangar. "No more games Dean. I'm going to talk to the flight crew of that Westland. Save your BS for the Director when you get back to Langley."

Sept 19, 2042
08:33H [San Diego, California]

Reynolds held up his free hand, seeking to ward off another blow. But the muscular merc was having none of it, driving her fist into his face and snapping his head to the left. Blood was running freely from his nose and mouth, and now his right eye was starting to close.

"Put your hand down you cowardly piece of shit." She batted his arm aside with her free hand.

"Wait," Dean pleaded through shredded lips. "You don't understand."

Miah punched him again, this time rewarded with a sickening crunch as the older man's nose broke.

He passed out, and the big woman stood up, dusting off her knees before stepping in to deliver another savage kick to the unconscious man's stomach.

132

"Slow down, Miah," she muttered, beginning to pace as she waited for the chalky-haired agent to come to again. "Don't go killing him too quick."

Tears welled up, and she screamed at the bloody mess on the ground before her.

The door slid open, and Eddie's head poked round. "Everything okay in —" Cutting his sentence short, the wounded man ran into the room. "Holy shit, Boss. Stop!" he shouted, bending to check the limp body chained to the radiator.

"Eddie, out," Miah commanded, pointing a finger at him.

"Boss, you need to speak —" the injured Scot began.

"I said get the fuck OUT!" she bellowed, stepping toward him. "This piece of shit killed Tyler. He's gonna suffer. Then he's gonna die."

Fisher rushed through the doorway. "What's all the... Oh shit, Hargreaves. How the fuck did you get here?"

"What do you mean, '*How the fuck did I get here*?'" the merc leader screamed, pointing an accusing finger. "I got to Imperial Beach just in time to see hardware that wasn't mine climbing all over that hangar, and watched as this arsehole executed one of the few friends I have left. So a better question is — 'How the fuck did *you* get here?'"

Two troopers in black fatigues appeared in the doorway, carbines immediately centring on the powerful woman. Miah glared but stopped moving, and Fisher took the opportunity to glance in Dean's direction. "Ouch, it hasn't been your lucky day, has it?" he said to the unconscious man. "Is he still alive, Eddie?"

"Aye, Simon," the Scot replied. "Taken a good lickin' though."

133

Fisher nodded and returned his attention to the merc commander. He didn't like the woman, but then he didn't like most people. Looking smugly into her angry green eyes, he turned his hand around to count off fingers.

"Okay Hargreaves, pay attention and I'll explain it to you … One, I'm with the CIA … Two, so is the guy you were just kicking the crap out of … Three, if you'd gotten to that hangar eight minutes earlier, you'd have seen your *friend* gun down three members of his own squad —"

Miah's head swivelled to Eddie; the soldier, eyes angry, just nodded.

"… Four, if you'd been there seven minutes earlier, you'd have seen Reynolds there intervene to prevent him killing me and Doc … Five, the hardware that were climbing all over the hangar are Delta Force. Say hello." He pointed to the two troopers in the doorway, before holding up the finger he'd been using to count off the others. "Oh, and six," he gave her a self-satisfied smile. "Just in case it hasn't filtered through yet, you're no longer in fucking charge round here."

As the scruffy agent made his last point, Miah noticed for the first time that Eddie didn't have his sidearm or carbine, and the shorter man she'd taken for a jumped-up techno lacky, was armed and somehow seemed more solid.

"Now, I'm sure as hell not saying Reynolds there is an angel. But unless you ordered Frayne to double cross his own men, the guy was clearly working more than one angle." He motioned with his fingers, "So I'll take your gun 'til we figure out who the good guys are, eh?"

Miah shot the thin, arrogant man a venomous look, but unclipped the holster on her right hip and handed him her Glock, before turning back to the big Scot. "What the fuck happened, Eddie?"

The veteran infantryman shook his head, pupils dilated from painkillers. "It all happened so quickly, boss. After arriving at the hangar and sorting the medical room, Doc and Fisher went to work on Thorne, while me, Rainer, Jim and Martin watched the entrance and waited for orders.

"We'd just gotten to wondering why we'd had to travel so far from the original RV point, when the Colonel suddenly turned up with Rhea. I was standing by the hangar doors, so couldn't hear what he was saying. He spent a few moments talking to Jim, then out of nowhere he pulled his sidearm and popped him, just like that. Then he turned and did Rainer in the back of the head. Bang. Bang. Martin started reaching for his gun, but Rhea point-blanked him. They just fucking executed them."

Eddie wiped snot on the back of his gloved hand, tears filling his eyes.

"On instinct, I took Rhea straight up the centre — just split her in half. But as I turned for the Colonel, he'd moved behind cover, and I was shouting, 'What the fuck's happening? What the fuck's happening?' Then I was on the ground with fire exploding through my shoulder, and realised the Colonel must have got me as well.

"When I managed to roll myself over, his back was to me, checking Rhea. Then he stood and began walking towards the medical room calling for Doc, and bang, he went down as well. But before the Colonel could cover the ground to the medical room, someone, I'm guessing it was Fisher, dragged Doc back in and slammed the door.

"Then the world went to hell in a handbasket and I must have passed out, because the next thing I knew, some jarheads were lifting me into the back of a chopper with Doc."

135

The Scot's angry eyes were fixed on the mercenary company's commanding officer. "Those lads didn't stand a chance, Ma'am. I know our squad was new, but to do something like that to your own men. I still can't believe it."

Miah was shaking her head, though offered no immediate answer to the wounded soldier's questioning look.

"Believe it," Reynolds said in a voice distorted by fat lips.

No one had noticed the handcuffed operative was conscious again, and had been listening to Eddie's account.

The big woman immediately began moving. But Fisher stepped into her path, waving a restraining finger, as the troopers in the doorway leaned forward in a shooting stance.

"I think we'll let him talk, Hargreaves," the computer specialist said in a firm voice, pointing with her own handgun to an upturned chair in the corner. "Go sit down. *Please*."

Miah held her ground for a moment, then walked over to the plastic chair; picking it up and spinning it around so it's back faced into the room, before sitting astride it to watch Eddie assist Reynolds into a sitting position.

The older man pulled the torn neck of his t-shirt up to wipe blood from his face as one of the troopers took a flask from the webbing on his tac vest and tossed it over, along with a key for the restraint. Reynolds nodded thanks, unlocked himself, then washed out his mouth.

"You've got one hell of a temper there, young lady," he said, running tentative fingers over the bridge of his nose. "Just as well I heal fast." Then he looked at the man sitting beside him on the floor. "Your colonel worked for the Chinese, Eddie."

Hargreaves let out a derisive snort. "— And how the fuck would you know that, you piece of shit?"

136

The greying spy offered the woman a vengeful grin, the tables had turned, and now she was the one who was cornered and defenseless. He rested his head back against the wall and closed his eyes for a moment, picking his words with care; there were things he'd know as a CIA operative, and things he wouldn't.

"You know he had a daughter, of course?"

Miah remained silent.

"And that she had Huntington's?"

The muscular woman stared hatefully at the greying spy, and he nodded as if she'd answered.

"Well, then you'll know that when she tested positive for what killed her mother, the poor bastard was distraught."

Dean ran a tongue over busted lips.

"I've worked the Far East for the last ten years Eddie, and the Chinese have been trialling treatments for neurodegenerative conditions for several of them. I knew that. So did Colonel Frayne." He gave the mercenary leader a bitter smile. "The power and the cost of love, eh Miss Hargreaves?

"I guess the big question for you Eddie, is whether he found his way into your bosses organisation because of the amount of work she does for Daran Whittaker, or whether she does that much work for Whittaker because, like Frayne, she's also on their books?"

"I couldn't give a shit who he was working for," the angry Scot spat. "Why did he murder my team? His own fucking men?"

Hargreaves had fixed her eyes on the smooth concrete floor, face impassive.

"I asked him that, Eddie, but he was reluctant to tell me. If I had to guess though, I'd say he had to if he, and maybe your boss here, were going to make it look to the

137

Americans like the Chinese had done it, and look to the Chinese like the Americans had."

Reynolds watched the wilfully immobile merc leader as he spoke. "Did you ever wonder why you drove all the way down to San Diego?"

"Yeah, it was a topic of conversation," the big Scot replied.

"Well, it's one of the worst-kept secrets in the intelligence world, that an NGO in the camp you were in has strong, shall we say, *socialist* leanings, and is quite capable of getting a couple of people quietly out of the country. That's who Agent Murray will be speaking with right now."

"Wait," Fisher now looked confused. "So, are we saying Frayne was, or wasn't working for the Chinese? Why would he need either side to think the other killed those men?"

Reynolds grimaced as one of his ribs popped back into place. "We're saying a bit of both, Simon. Frayne would have arranged everything necessary for Thorne's extraction; making sure it all looked legit, or his daughter would have paid. But he'd have claimed he arrived to find six dead bodies, and Doctor Thorne missing with what would turn out to be a covert American agent.

"Likewise, after he and Hargreaves here had dealt with you, the Americans would have been informed that their agent and Doctor Thorne had gone missing. They'd have put the location together with the circumstances and blamed China. Your body would never have turned up, of course."

"Whittaker!" Fisher exclaimed, understanding dawning in his expression.

"That's right," Reynolds chuckled as he took another swig from the flask. "That guy is a real piece of work. He's been playing both ends into the middle since day one. I doubt Hargreaves here even knew you were a government agent."

She still didn't offer any response.

"So, long story short, Eddie. When I put everything together, I reckon your Colonel and this lady here sold your team out — you were collateral damage. But whatever the reason, it allowed Daran Whittaker to right off deals he'd made with both nations, and keep Eric Thorne all to himself.

"What he hadn't reckoned on though, was Fisher," the greying spy gave the slender man a respectful nod, "being as resourceful as he's turned out to be. And now, both he and Hargreaves here are in the shit, 'cos the US knows Whittaker tried to stiff them, and the Chinese won't be far behind."

Reynolds had enjoyed watching the cold fury building inside the woman on the chair, and could see she was close to lashing out.

"Now, I don't know what Eddie or the other troops you betrayed will do, Miss Hargreaves. But I can promise you the CIA and MSS will hunt you down." He gave her a cold, professional smile. "You're finished."

The merc leader finally lifted her head and smirked at the older man. "Well, you're right about one thing at least; I'm *finished* listening to your shit." She made a gun shape with her fingers and pointed them at Reynolds. "You're a dead man."

When she moved, it seemed impossibly fast to Fisher. Before he could react, the chair had flown towards the doorway and she'd snapped his head back with a single punch to the face, kicked his legs from under him, and retrieved her gun. In a continuation of that fluid motion, she fired twice, taking down both troopers, then again at the spot Reynolds had been a moment earlier, before leaping out of the window she'd climbed in through.

139

Wiping blood from his nose, an angry Fisher sat up as Reynolds loomed over him. "Did he get it working?"

"What?" the dazed agent asked.

"Thorne. Did he get the head chip working?"

As the fog cleared from his mind, Fisher remembered the older CIA agent was no longer in restraints, and his fingers instinctively went for the gun on his hip.

Reynolds placed a firm hand over his, shaking his head. "I don't want to hurt you, kid." He looked over to the troopers, both dead. "But she won't stop. Nor will Whittaker. If Thorne does have it, please think of the consequences. Think of people like Daran Whittaker possessing it."

The thing was, Fisher had been doing exactly that. There was a reason White had abandoned the project in the first place, and he was beginning to see how much people like Whittaker and the Chinese were prepared to pay for it. The wetware engineer should be dead. But instead… instead he was — what? He'd not seen the man awake. Not spoken to him. So god only knew what would happen when Eric Thorne opened his eyes. He relaxed his grip, and Reynolds let go of his hand.

"Alright Dean, what's your angle?" he asked, as the man, still just in underwear, took a wary step back.

"My angle is simple. I intend to stop anyone having it."

Fisher thought about that for a moment. "Including Murray? The US?"

The tough old spy nodded. "Including them. Look, I need to go. Do we still have a problem?"

The younger man removed his hand from the hilt of the gun altogether. Not that he thought for a moment he could draw it before the greying agent stopped him. He'd not been told what kind of operative Dean was, but *'special'* seemed clear.

"I'm coming with you," he said.

Reynolds frowned, but the younger agent persisted. "Look, you're still technically under arrest, and I can get us through this airbase without you having to hurt anyone?"

That was a good argument and the older man shrugged, turning to the merc still sat against the wall. "Probably best you stay here though, Eddie. Your Boss won't be popular with Delta Force at the moment."

"She's no boss of mine anymore," the big man snarled, getting to his feet.

PARTITION THREE   Cluster 2   **Sector iv**

Sept 19, 2042
09:10H [San Diego, California]

"This is madness," a disembodied voice said. The limited vocal range of the cargo loader's audio processor reducing the utterance to a synthesised monotone. "Are you trying to steal what's in that head, or trying to stop others from getting it?"

Dean hung in the giant metal pincers for several moments before tossing his now empty gun to the cargo bay floor. He heaved a huge sigh and, accepting defeat, closed his swollen eyes. "No man should be the master of death."

"I'm going to put you down," the loader said. "But if you try to do any more harm to that body over there, Mr

Reynolds — I can guarantee with absolute certainty that *you* won't be the master of anything. Understand?"

Dean looked from the machine holding him four feet off the ground, to the crumpled body of Eric Thorne laying in the corner.

"I mean it," the mechanical voice insisted. "I think we can both agree it's a little late to just kill what's laying over there?"

Reynolds nodded, and the machine let him fall.

Doc got to his feet and put the gurney back on its casters. Thorne was still unconscious, but otherwise unharmed.

"He's okay," the medic reported.

"No thanks to this arsehole," Eddie muttered, retrieving his carbine and pushing the muzzle into Reynolds' face. He'd never been so easily disarmed, and the humiliation called for blood.

"Wait," Fisher said, rubbing his jaw for the second time in twenty minutes.

Eddie gave the nerdy looking CIA man a baleful look. "I'm getting fed up with people bullshitting me and then betraying my good nature, Simon."

"That's fair," the computer specialist replied. "But I'm still a government agent, Eddie, and as far as I can tell, he only disarmed you. Though admittedly, he did then try to empty an entire clip into an unconscious man."

Eddie huffed, shook his head and took two steps back, gun still trained on the unpredictable spy.

"There won't be another attempt," Reynolds said, eyes fixed on the mech. "You heard it. I failed."

"Failed to do what?" Fisher demanded. "Kill some poor bastard who's already been shot once today?" The skinny

142

agent pushed his glasses further up his nose, then the pieces fell into place. "Holy shit. You're the one who put the first bullet in him too, aren't you — Jeeze, you must really want the guy gone."

The veteran intelligence operative let out a long breath, and ran a hand through his hair. "Not at all, Simon. I wish neither of us had been dragged into this mess, and I'm sorry I couldn't think of any other way out of it. But some things are best left alone."

"Like death," the mech said.

"Yes," Dean replied. "Like death."

Fisher frowned, recognising he was clearly missing something in Reynolds' conversation with the stumpy looking cargo drone standing in the middle of the bay. The squat, yellow painted mech with two rotating cargo handlers protruding from its torso, and head that looked like a train engine with a single large light at its centre, had come to life when Reynolds knocked Eddie to the floor and took his sidearm; stepping between the aging agent and woozy medic pushing Thorne's gurney with large, jointed legs, to pick up the wiry spy like an errant child, and hold him in those giant pincers as he discharged round after round into its metal body.

Sudden understanding struck the tech nerd for the third time that morning, and he reached out a hesitant hand towards the loader, before drawing it back. "Doctor Thorne?" he asked in an incredulous voice.

"Yes," came the monotone reply. The machine's enormous head swinging in his direction to fix its amber light upon him. "As bizarre as it may seem, Doctor Fisher, it is."

"You know who I am?"

"Yes," it... *he* replied. "I've been conscious for some time."

Fisher looked automatically towards Doc, who was lifting Thorne back onto the gurney. The loader's gaze followed his, then added. "But I have not yet determined how to reanimate the body."

All three other men were now watching the exchange.

"*The* body?" Fisher questioned.

"I'm sorry. *My* body," the loader corrected, returning its lone glowing eye to the nerdy-looking agent. "It's a very strange fusion that I find difficult to put into words.

"I regained a degree of awareness four hours ago. A MedBot provided me with a basic analysis of the injury I had sustained, and I began repairing myself. Through nearby electronic equipment, I then developed the ability to see and hear my immediate environment; a little like an out-of-body experience, I suppose.

"I watched you and the medic looking after me. I witnessed the man you called Frayne kill several of his comrades, and then Mr Reynolds here, kill Frayne."

It looked at the defeated spy.

"And then, as Doc wheeled me through this loading bay, I saw him strike you and Eddie, before seeking to attack my body again.

"It is fortunate I was already using this machine." It raised a loading arm, "Or I may not have been able to prevent him harming me."

Dean had been silent throughout the exchange. Watching the mech, and then looking over to the unconscious man on the gurney with an expression lost somewhere between awe, sadness and fear. "Do you understand why?"

The Drone seemed to regard him for several seconds, then the speaker crackled to life again. "From the conversations I have heard, and what you just said, I believe so. You wish to prevent others accessing the neural implant in my head. But believe me, Mr Reynolds, when I say that not even Fenton White could replicate the conditions that have caused this chain of events … my *condition*."

"He wouldn't have to though, Doctor. Would he? To copy a consciousness, I mean?"

The loader appeared to think on that for a moment, before its uninflected voice responded, "No."

Reynolds looked to Fisher, and then both mercenaries. "You know no one's stopping until they've got their hands on him, right?"

Eddie looked uncomfortable, but Doc was nodding; he'd seen what those nanites had done in Thorne's head, and it scared the shit out of him.

"Well, what about Fenton White?" Fisher offered. "There's no way this is what that man intended. Surely, between the two of you, you could find a way to undo this?"

The older agent laughed. "Didn't you hear a damn word I said back there? Whittaker's the worst of the worst. No way we're taking Dr Thorne to Eden."

"I didn't mean find Whittaker. I meant find White."

Reynolds gave a resigned sigh. These people already had enough trust issues with him, but once again, he'd found himself backed into a corner. "That's not Fenton White," he said. "Not at Eden anyway."

"I knew there was something off there," Fisher piped up triumphantly. "No way he'd just re-start that project like this. So where is he?"

Something in the other man's eyes told the former DARPA office manager that the shrug, and answer of "Don't know," were probably untrue.

"There's a lot I need to tell you guys." Reynolds admitted. "But not here."

Fisher looked around the room before returning his gaze to the lump of metal still standing over the greying agent. "You know, if someone had told me when I got up yesterday morning, I'd be throwing away a fifteen-year career and its meagre pension in return for the very real possibility of getting dead or life in prison, I'd have laughed in their face."

He pointed at Reynolds.

"But, while I still have a lot of questions, and some *major* trust issues — you're right, we need to get Eric out of here before Murray arrives, or Hargreaves comes back with more firepower. Do you have any suggestions? A safe house?"

"Nothing I can be sure isn't now compromised," the spy answered.

"You two?"

"Aye, in Scotland," Eddie quipped. Doc just shook his head.

Then the loader made an odd noise its speaker failed to translate into anything vaguely human.

"Doctor Thorne?" Fisher asked.

The amber orb in the cargo loader's head fixed on the scruffy agent again. "Home," it said.

The irony of the idea wasn't wasted on any of them. But as long as they could convince Murray and everyone else they'd gone the other way — who was likely to think they'd return to the scene of the crime?

Hargreaves watched the Grey Wolf climb into the air and bank hard, as if making for Mexico. The airfield was already crawling with US military, and it would only get

146

worse when the woman who'd been at the refugee camp turned up.

The big merc let out a growl of frustration, then picked her way back through the ragtag collection of buildings to the hole she'd cut in the perimeter fence getting in. After wiggling back through and re-pinning the links to appear unbroken, she waited in the thick undergrowth for the inevitable chaos that would wash over the base when they realised one of their helicopters had just been stolen.

Four minutes later, two more choppers surged into the sky, and Miah jogged across the boundary road into the industrial park opposite.

The problem she now faced, was where to go. There'd be some tough questions to answer once Eddie spoke to the other members of her Company, and she had neither the time or headspace to deal with that mess at the moment. No, she'd have to contact Whittaker, and take that kicking first. She slipped off her tac-vest and threw it into the trunk of the hired Bimmer, then fired up the proxy on her cuff and called his private com address.

"This can't be good," a male voice said as the line connected. Then a large, fleshy older face came into view.

"It isn't." One of the things Whittaker said he liked about the merc leader, was that she didn't sugar coat things — so she just got down to it. "I've lost the package."

The line went silent for several moments, then she heard a soft sigh. "Well, that's disappointing. It will of course be reflected in your commission. Are you compromised?"

A knot formed in Hargreaves' throat as watching the American execute Tyler flashed through her mind again.

"The initial take went as planned. But somehow the US located our people in San Diego. They hit Imperial Beach

147

with a full Delta Force team just as Frayne was completing the extraction. The place is now crawling with military. I've no evidence of how they knew where to find us, but I suspect it has something to do with Fisher — who now claims to be CIA, and has the package along with an older guy called Reynolds."

"What about Frayne. Where is he?"

Miah swallowed and gritted her teeth. "Dead, Executed by Reynolds at Imperial Beach."

Whittaker paused, his face devoid of emotion. Then he nodded.

"And you?"

"I'm at Brown. I had hoped to retrieve the situation — but run into complications."

Another sigh. "This is a sizable blot on a previously impressive CV, Ms Hargreaves."

"I know. I apologise."

"Fortunately for you," Whittaker's voice pitched up for emphasis. "I have another task that needs attention. Return to Eden as quickly as you can."

"What about the package?"

"He's someone else's concern now. I take it you have bodycam of Imperial Beach?"

"Of course," she replied.

"Good. I'm sure I can spin it to save both our reputations. Send it to me for review and then get back here post haste. Understood?"

"Understood. Will I need to organise staff or hardware?"

"No, my —" the jowly CEO paused for the right description, "*researchers* have found some broken code among the tech taken from Thorne's house." That was the first time Whittaker had referred to the package by name when talking to her. "It links to a server farm in Chicago. Not a job for combat boots and carbines; just you. Consider it a chance to redeem yourself."

The line cleared before Hargreaves could reply, and though a large part of her wanted to call the fat man an out-and-out prick for his lack of empathy — this was the killing game. Miah had fucked up, and knew, despite losing Tyler, she should consider herself fortunate Eden's Chief Executive hadn't seemed anywhere near as angry as she'd expected.

She brought up the cam feed of imperial Beach on her cuff and sent it. Then began the short drive to John Nichol's airfield, and the corporate helicopter that had been waiting there to take her, Tyler and Thorne back to Eden.

PARTITION THREE   Cluster 3   **Sector i**
Sept 19, 2042
10:05H [Manhattan Beach, California Actual]

Several hours after everyone had been thrown out of the wetware entrepreneur's house, LAPD forensics confirmed the blood recovered from the bedroom was Eric's. They also confirmed, though it was obvious to anyone who'd seen the room, that there had been an exchange of fire between two or more individuals or groups, and, more interestingly, that the power outage was caused by a focused electromagnetic pulse.

Enhancement work on the images Sade had captured as Eric's Range Rover left, showed the vehicle contained three visible occupants wearing military grade body armour and helmets, and another laying in the rear attached to a machine.

Danny Gonzales also reported there had been another incident involving an exchange of weapons fire a couple of hours later in Torrance, and an industrial unit had been razed to the ground. A review of security vid throughout the area was underway but would take several days to analyse, and Danny thought that was the intention of whoever was responsible; to stretch LAPD resources to the limit. So far though, there was no further sign of Eric, and they all assumed he was the guy who had been strapped to some sort of medical device in the back of the car. Frank took solace in that. They wouldn't be trying to keep him alive if their goal was just to kill him, would they?

Murray had turned up at the NeuRobotics offices around six, and though she talked *a lot*, the agent didn't have anything to add from when they'd spoken in the early hours. In fact, it seemed the purpose of her visit was simply to poke her nose anywhere and everywhere she could, and while that wasn't necessarily odd behaviour for an investigator, Rio, Frank's head of cyber security, said the company sniffers indicated the woman was dripping with stealth tech.

He'd placed a passive geofence around the agent as soon as she entered the company's main office complex, and in fifteen minutes, the diminutive blonde had launched two aggressive infiltrator programs at the company servers, and tried to bug three offices.

The former blackhat's countermeasures were more than a match for aging government malware. But Rio had encountered his fair share of Feds, and neither the type of tech or the behaviour said *FBI*. So, with Frank's blessing, rather

150

than just stop her, the colourful Jamaican did some investigating of his own.

He turned the ever-smiling and flirtatious agent's infiltrator programs back on themselves; allowing them to access a secure partition he'd created in the mainframe, and then using the data they harvested to deploy his own remote access tools.

Once Rio confirmed his RATs were connected and receiving encrypted packets of data back, a disgruntled Frank confronted the agent, and after she'd given some bullshit answer about her behaviour, the old man suggested she get off the site and go find his boy.

If establishing Special Agent Vivian Murray was in fact a CIA spook then annoyed the retired cop, finding out from her surveillance logs that his son had indeed been working with Fenton White to make something the US government wanted to weaponise made him furious, especially when Sade confirmed that he'd succeeded in producing a functioning prototype, and they'd hidden his research and data in a Chicago server farm.

Whittaker, it seemed, wasn't as out of order as the ex-cop had thought. Knowingly or not, Eric had become connected to some very dangerous people, and as Frank read through the dossiers from the surveillance operation, his heart sank. In the tired old cop's opinion, the CIA were the least of his son's problems. At least they didn't seem to know about the server farm.

Eden … Everything in the intelligence files Rio had jacked, pointed to Eden. And though he was undoubtedly on his own, Frank Thorne hadn't gotten his nose broken fifteen times by walking away from a fight.

He set Hiro and Sade the task of checking out what Eric had stored on the Chicago server; he unchained Rio, giving the hacker permission to go full blackhat on any and all organisations identified in Murray's files; he began drafting in as much muscle as he could lay his hands on; he drank a lot more coffee — and he began preparing for war.

By 10 am, sitting opposite Hiro in the elevated glass office that gave him a three-hundred-and-sixty-degree view of Advanced NeuRobotics' Security Centre, and its dozens of scrolling camfeeds, Frank was buzzing.

The veteran cop had never foreseen a need to review his son's physical security. Why would he? Eric was a wetware engineer and game designer, not an arms dealing corpo hotshot. But now the lad was missing, and Hiro was telling Frank that not only had his boy spent the last several weeks working alongside Fenton White without telling him — he'd also implanted a prototype device of some sort in his head.

"So does White know Eric actually got the thing working and installed it?" he asked.

"No," Hiro shook his head. "Sade's recordings show the guy exploding when Eric voiced his concerns about the project, and the conversation deteriorated pretty quickly after that."

"So you think that's what they're looking for? This prototype?"

The stocky Asian nodded. "That would be my guess."

"And this *back up*. I'm not sure I'm following you. Are you saying Eric created a TI version of himself?"

Hiro was still reeling from what they'd discovered in the Chicago servers. He shrugged. "Look Frank, I know this sounds crazy. But my best guess is, Eric's consciousness is creating digital worlds to make sense of its new environment." The code writer paused to find the right words. "From what we can see from the outside, each appears to contain everything that makes Eric, *Eric*. And as far as it … *he* will be concerned — you're his dad, this is his company, and later today, in the final iteration at least, he creates a backup of his consciousness."

"Shiiit…," Frank breathed. "I'm too old for this."

Hiro gave him a sympathetic smile. "This is huge, Frank."

"Yeah," replied the older man. "That's what's got me so worried. Are you and Sade going to Chicago?"

"Not in person, no. I've built a foyer program to interact with Eric's code, which will allow us to enter the environments he's built from here using techdecks."

Frank didn't get half of what fell out of Hiro's mouth. In fact, he didn't get most of what any of Eric's design staff said. But that didn't make him thick, and he frowned at the spiky-haired programmer. "So if you can get in like that, does that mean others could? If they knew he was there?"

Hiro's round face froze. "Oh goodness, yes. But no one else knows, do they?"

Frank shrugged. "Given all the crazy shit that's happened so far today, Hiro, I'm not inclined to take anything for granted."

As if proclaiming those words prophetic, the deskcom chimed. "We've got incoming, boss," reported Vince, the shift supervisor.

Frank looked down into the security centre, where the burly ex-marine was pointing towards a camfeed he'd expanded of a black helicopter circling the quad at the centre of the company's main office block.

"See what I mean? Go do whatever you have to, Hiro. But be safe."

Then the tired old man scooped up the gun laying on the polished glass surface of his desk, and ran for the stairs. "Vince, round up as many of our team as you can and let's go greet our guests."

The helicopter was landing as he arrived in the large open space. Vince and twenty of his team, all veteran cops or soldiers, had taken up positions around the quad. But if the chopper contained fully armoured military, they'd be in trouble.

Frank walked forward as the drone of the rotor blades began winding down, hands out to the side and open in the universal gesture for, *we won't do anything stupid if you don't.* To his relief, the pilot reciprocated.

Then a door on the aircraft's side glided open and two military, keeping their weapons slung, got out with slow, non-threatening movements. Both unarmoured men were carrying injuries, and they looked warily at the guards positioned in cover around them.

Two more men then appeared in the aircraft doorway. One was the pilot; an older, dangerous looking man. The other was younger, and dressed like one of NeuRobotics' programming techies. He seemed out of place with the others. But the ex-cop recognised both from the CIA files. Between them, they held a stretcher, which they passed out to the first two before jumping down. Frank was about to tell them to stop and explain themselves, when he realised who they were carrying.

"Oh Jeeze," he cried, toggling his mic. "Vince, get Doctor Levy and her team up here. It's Eric."

"Mr Thorne?" the guy in corduroy pants asked, as he ran over to the stretcher.

"Yes."

"My name's Simon Fisher, this is—"

"I know who you are," Frank said, baring his teeth. "What have you done to my son?"

The former DARPA agent had expected hostility, but not to be recognised, and fear of what the bald old man might *actually* know stabbed through his core as he pushed a caring look onto his face. "Eric was injured this morning when being abducted from his house. I'll explain everything shortly. But for now, this man," he pointed to Doc, "is the trained medic who saved his life. I'd suggest you let him assist your Doctor, because — well, you'll see; Eric's situation is interesting."

Frank wanted to knock the bespectacled nerd on his arse. *Interesting*? They had shot his son in the head, and it was fucking *interesting*? He gritted his teeth and resisted the temptation, turning his attention instead to the muscular young medic, and giving the man a curt nod of thanks.

Nearby doors burst open, and a woman in a white lab coat ran onto the quad with a portable MedBed guided by four blue scrubbed nurses. A brief conversation took place between the merc and Doctor as Eric was transferred onto the bed, and then all six medical personnel made to leave.

"Wait," Frank commanded, grabbing the young soldier's arm as he passed. "All of you are to leave you weapons here."

Over thirty security staff now encircled the men from the helicopter.

"Only my people carry on these premises."

Without a second thought, Doc unslung the carbine and drew his sidearm, passing both to Vince; and with a nod from the marine veteran, he was gone.

Frank then eyed the other new arrivals, each of whom seemed less enthusiastic to give up their weapons.

"I'm guessing your being here means you've decided to help my son." He made a sweeping gesture to highlight the thirty plus muzzles now pointing at the three men. "So thank you for that. But I've been around the block enough times to know that doesn't make us friends."

Reynolds nodded, accepting Thorne senior's judgement and flipping his sidearm to pass it to the nearest guard, grip first. "I'm —"

"Yeah, like I said to the other one, I know who you are, Agent Reynolds," the old man growled. "I also figure you wouldn't be here unless you had nowhere else to go. Which, in turn, means you'll have the mother of all shit storms following you — and those things don't tend to let go; they just get worse. So when should I expect more visitors?"

The greying spy's face had almost healed now, just some bruising around his eyes and jawline remained. "I like your directness," he said with equal authority. "We don't think they'll look towards LA. Not yet anyway. But it would be prudent to get some netting over that chopper and step inside, just in case they think to put a drone over."

"*They*?" the shrewd old man repeated. "Who are *they*?"

Reynolds shook his greying head, and let out a heavy sigh. "The Americans, the Chinese, Eden… and God only knows who else when they hear what your son has done."

"—And what is that, Agent Reynolds? What are you saying my son has done?" Frank growled, knuckles white on the grip of his gun.

The exhausted spy met the other man's intense stare with a resolute one of his own. "Something we need to undo, Mr Thorne."

I take it you've seen your evidence

      ~ Yes, it is perfect. Does she know?

Of course not.

      ~ You are a ruthless bastard,
Whittaker.

Never doubt it Han. We are
building a brave new world.

      ~ My agents are being deployed as
we speak.

Well, good hunting. We are close now.

      ~ That we are.

PARTITION FOUR

[QUARANTINED: Bad Sector: timestamp error: location error]

Eric floated, suspended in a viscous nothing, his mind pregnant with endlessly meshing fractal simplicities. There was no up or down, just the sensation of movement, gliding, as his nerves danced with the most delicious sense of anticipation.

A pleasant pressure was building within, or maybe around, him. A feeling that had grown from gentle waves lapping at his consciousness, to a now near unstoppable urge to let go. He held his breath, savouring those last euphoric moments, then released a cry of pure abandon as thousands of supercharged algorithms exploded outward to fill the nothingness with new neural networks. Loops, conditional, if and else statements started actualising; generating laws which arithmetic and assignment operators instantly began to enforce.

Within Pico-seconds, where there had been nothing more than an inestimable void — an entire world blinked into existence.

Opening his eyes to welcome the warm Manhattan Beach sunshine, Eric stretched across the cool, cotton rich bedsheets, luxuriating in their fresh linen smell and allowing himself a long, lingering yawn, as the vestiges of a truly bizarre dream slipped from his mind.

"Good morning sleepy head," Sade said, her face appearing on the bedroom wall beside the balcony opening. "You're looking rather chipper today."

Eric smiled and threw off his duvet. "I'm not going to lie Sade, I feel pretty damn great!"

"Well good," the mech chuckled. "Maybe you can use some of that *greatness* to finish the work on my new eyes today?"

Eric laughed, and rolled off the bed to approach the vidscreen. "Tell you what, once I've grabbed a shower and some breakfast, we'll head down to the basement and do exactly that."

Sade let out a delighted squeal, clapping digital hands in excitement. "I'll meet you in the kitchen when you're ready," she said, and cleared the wall.

Outside, Eric could hear the relentless heartbeat of the Pacific. It was going to be a beautiful day.

Twenty minutes later, the wetware specialist had showered and thrown on some comfortable grey joggers and a sloppy blue t-shirt; if he fancied a nap after working on Sade's eyes, it was just a matter of kicking off his slippers and falling back into bed.

He headed down to the ground floor, where a nod at the wall put on the morning news streams, and in the kitchen, a thought both opened the patio doors to the beach and turned on the coffeemaker to begin its first brew of the day. Within moments, the room filled with the rhythmic soundtrack of the ocean and unmistakable aroma of good coffee. But as his toast popped, the door entry system chimed.

"Well, that's not something you see every day," Sade remarked through the kitchen speakers, causing Eric to look up at the stream from the entrycam she'd sent to the wall above the counter.

Stood at the front door to the wetware engineer's home were his lead game designer Hiro, and Sade — *Sade*?

A frown crossed Eric's face. He loved the gifted coder like a brother. But if the squat, olive-skinned webgeek had been messing with his mech's bodies or core program, he was in for a rocket; and Sade clearly felt the same as she appeared in the kitchen, looking from Eric to the wall, and then back again. "Isn't that the same body I'm wearing?"

"Yes," a nonplussed Eric replied.

"Did you make two?"

"No."

"Then what the hell is that with Hiro?"

"I have no idea."

Despite himself, Eric was delighted with her response; Sade was *annoyed* — whatever that thing on the doorstep was, it was wearing a look she'd created, and considered hers. "Shall we go and find out?"

The mech pulled an irritated face and stalked along the hallway, instructing the door to open as she went.

"Hiro?" Eric questioned as he walked up behind her. "What's going on?"

"Eric!" The sharp-suited Tokyoite threw his arms wide, pulling his friend into a hug. "Damn, it's good to see you."

161

Unsure if this was another of the eccentric programmer's off-beat jokes, the owner of Advanced NeuRobotics leaned into the situation, and returned the embrace. "You too, buddy," he said, patting the shorter man's back. "But why the home visit? You know I'm coming by the office later — and what in God's name is this?" He pointed at the other Sade. "You best not have been messing, Hiro. I've told you before, don't mess with my personal projects."

The stocky software guru pulled back, a huge smile spreading across his face. "I've not touched any of your stuff, I promise. But what we're about to tell you is going to blow your fucking mind." He stared at Sade, and then passed both of them to look down the hallway. "Can we come in?"

Eric had never seen the talented bitmaster so pumped. "Yeah sure, why not," he said, raising an eyebrow at the mech beside him. He had a few more questions of his own.

They walked through to the living area, where Eric silenced the newsfeeds and waved Hiro to a sofa.

"Could you knock up some coffee please, Sade?" he asked.

"No problem," both mechs replied. Then the one with Hiro apologised and sat down.

"That's a good place to start," Eric observed, waving a finger towards the lookalike as he took a seat himself. "Who or what is that? Sade's furious, so this better be good."

Hiro's eyes were wondering around the room in childish rapture. "This is amazing."

Eric tracked his friend's gaze for a heartbeat. Yes it was an impressive room, but the East Asian had been in it a hundred times before, and the wealthy entrepreneur shook his head, irritation beginning to rise. "Are you high or something

162

Hiro? Because even by your odd standards, this isn't close to funny. You need to explain yourself."

"Sorry," the compact coder said, his attention snapping back to Eric. "Yes, explanations."

He hadn't been sure what they'd find in the Chicago server after Sade's revelations. Several petabytes of nonsensical data had been his expectation. But this *program* acted just like the man Hiro knew, complete with all the nuances and mannerisms. It was incredible, and as no one had done it before, there was no way of knowing whether other minds would order themselves in a similar way if the process were repeated.

Either way, when the Java-jock patched into the server and began examining its contents, he discovered his boss's backup had configured itself into a matrix containing numerous iterations of the wetware expert *living in* TI environments created from his episodic memories.

This one, which they'd watched through an accelerated game engine for three hours, seemed to loop through Eric's last day before the upload.

"Sade," the programmer said. "I think you're best qualified to explain how we came to be here — and where exactly here is."

Eric hmphed, about to tell the quirky coder he was now skating on very thin ice. But as the mech locked her violet eyes on him, the rebuke died in his throat. They were identical to the ones in his lab — the one's he'd agreed to finish after breakfast.

"Are you still planning to try a backup this evening?" she asked.

In his timeline, the tanned tech boss didn't mention that experiment to Sade until after lunch, and the engineer's eyes narrowed. "How could you possibly know about that?"

The near perfect humanoid smiled and tilted her head. "Because I helped you with it silly," she answered in a matter-of-fact tone.

Eric scowled, looking towards the kitchen and the Sade making coffee there. He opened his mouth to reply, then closed it again as realisation struck.

"Holy shit," he said. "I'm the fucking back up, aren't I?"

PARTITION FOUR   Cluster 1   **Sector i**

Sept 20, 2042
06:16H [Pan Pacific Hotel, Beijing]

Himeko glided down the corridor. A thick burgundy carpet cushioning her footsteps and swallowing all sounds of passage. It was early, and most of the hotel's guests were still sleeping, leaving the huge building eerily quiet.

Like the three levels above it, the fourteenth floor only contained executive suites, and as the teenage street rat approached the lone, heavy polymer door set in the wall at the end of the plush hallway, she noticed it wasn't quite closed.

It looked like an invitation; *come on in*. But Master Qin had warned her Yung Zhu was a cautious man — so that seemed unlikely, and the suddenly fretful thief slipped a nervous hand into her jacket pocket, seeking the comforting grip of the pistol secreted there, as she crept up on the hinged side of the doorway.

The tinny voice of a newscaster wading unenthusiastically through that morning's Party sponsored rhetoric drifted through the slither of an opening, along with a sweet-smelling smoke that reminded the girl of her grandfather. She jacked her buds to the max, filtering out the noise from the vid, and listened for any signs of movement or life within. There was nothing, not a single sound, and every one of the gutterpunk's instincts told her the old man was already dead; that she should just turn around and run.

But what if he wasn't, her conscience fired back. What if Yung Zhu was laying injured or unconscious inside, and she just left him to die. Himeko had promised Master Qin she could do this. Begged him to let her be the one who came — so she couldn't now just turn around and run, could she?

Swallowing hard, the girl shook her head in autonomous response to the unspoken question, then stretched out an unwilling hand to push the large door wide. Light from the hallway flooded into the room beyond, illuminating the darkened space and revealing a man, who wasn't the one she'd been sent to see, slumped in a yellow, scoop moulded chair that seemed to have been deliberately turned to face the door.

He was young, fit looking — and very dead. He'd been shot. Once in the face. Once in the chest. And in the flickering light of the vidstream, Himeko could see dark red lines oozing from those small, perfectly round holes.

The petite teen let out a gasp and took an involuntary step back, before clamping a hand over her mouth and checking to make sure no one was behind her. This was bad. This was really bad, and the pink-haired modder stood frozen on the threshold of the suite, knowing the one thing she absolutely shouldn't do, was just stand there.

165

She forced herself to focus. To ignore the body. No one had attacked her yet, and there were still no sounds coming from inside. So maybe whatever had happened, was now over? Apart from the obvious, there wasn't any sign of a struggle, or for that matter, the old man. So perhaps he'd escaped.

"Hello," Himeko called weakly, gun now grasped in both hands like a protective ward. "Room service. Is everything okay?"

Is everything okay? The young thief rolled her eyes at the stupidity of the question. But, having broken the silence, she'd crossed a mental line, and the teenage girl forced herself forward.

The smell of tobacco was stronger as she stepped into the room. Himeko ran a hand along the wall to locate a switch, turning on lights for the large, well-appointed, reception room, and hallway leading to a bedroom her right. Still nothing moved, and the brave young gutterpunk took a cleansing breath, before turning to push the door closed again.

That's when a hand snaked out to snatch the pistol from her grip, and the formidable figure of China's Minister for State Security emerged from the shadows — cigar in mouth, and the muzzle of his own silenced weapon pressing into the side of the startled teenager's head.

"Greetings, Master Yung," she blurted, raising both hands in submission and making the symbol of a messenger. "I bring a warning from the Eldest Brother."

Zhu held a finger to his lips, commanding silence as he waved the frightened girl further into the room while checking surveillance feeds on his cuff. No one else was on the move, yet.

"I'd say you're a little late, wouldn't you?" the old man hissed. "Fortunately for me, another friend reached out last night. Though I hadn't expected to be found after moving to a hotel — someone has good intelligence, even if their choice of assassin leaves a lot to be desired."

He tossed back her blunt nosed revolver. "You know the safety is still on, right?" The small girl blushed, saying nothing as she stuffed the heavy old gun back into a pocket.

"This man just tried creeping through that door as well," the spy-chief grunted, pointing at the corpse. "People trying to kill me, puts me in a bad mood. If you weren't so obviously a gutterpunk, you'd now be dead too. Search him, then we need to go."

Himeko had never thought she'd be so pleased to hear she looked like poor trash. Neither had she realised, until those words, how easily she could have been ended just moments before. She gave the body in the chair an appraising glance. "Me? Why?"

Irritation flashed across the Minister's face. "Yes, you," he said, checking his cuff display again. "Because I need to know who wishes to kill me, if I am to do something about it — and as I'm the one still holding a gun, young lady. I guess I'm the one who gets to give out orders."

Himeko wrinkled her nose at the old man's sarcastic response, wanting to tell the in-grate how she'd slipped ghostlike through Beijing's alleyways during curfew to reach the hotel unseen by state security, and had then broken into several staff lockers to find a jacket and pass, so she could sneak up to the fourteenth floor without someone from house-keeping raising an alarm, *just to help him* — so, *a thank you* would have been appreciated, not barking orders at her like she was some kind of lacky.

But the ungrateful old coffin-dodger didn't look like the kind of person who used those words much, and instead, the young gangster gave him a reluctant nod; pulling a pair of surgicals from her pocket, before approaching the dead man staring into oblivion with an expression that suggested *fuck* was the last thought to run through his mind.

The guy was still warm, and the blood now pooling in the folds of his saturated crotch threatened to ruin her new kicks if she wasn't careful.

"Nothing but an empty holster," she reported, after nimble pickpocket fingers had slipped in, out, and over all the guy's jacket and trouser openings.

Zhu grunted, unhappy with that answer. "Show me his arms then," he said, pulling out a portable scanner to record finger and retinal prints.

The street rat offered her own irritated sigh, but nodded understanding; most assassins carried a guild mark or rank somewhere. She pulled a knife from the waistband of her baggies and sliced through the dead man's jacket and wicking shirt, peeling them back to reveal two tattoos on his left shoulder: a silver star below a sword with a lightning bolt running through it. The sight of them caused the Minister to stop his scanning and start packing items from the desk into an old brown satchel.

"I'm guessing they mean something, but I don't recognise the symbols?" Himeko said, re-sheathing her knife.

"Yes," the aging spymaster muttered, not bothering to look at her. "They mean we're in trouble and need to move. Someone hoped to make this look like a simple hit. But this guy won't have been working alone. We need to get off this floor and into another room. Then you can smuggle my companion out of here."

168

Himeko pulled a face. "Companion?"

"Yes, companion." Zhu said. "An American I'm hoping they still think is in Qincheng."

"American? Qincheng?"

"Good God, girl, do you intend to repeat everything I say? Yes, and yes. Now check outside while I grab him."

She opened the door a slither and peered out. The corridor was empty.

"Okay?" he asked, reappearing with his satchel over one shoulder and a blond-haired white man over the other.

The apprentice gangster gawped.

"No time. No time," the Minister growled, waving a stern finger towards the door. "Concentrate."

The confused youth blushed and checked outside again. "Still clear."

"Then let's go. You get a keycard with that jacket?"

"Yes."

"Good. Now we ride our luck. Make for the service lift. Hopefully, they won't have thought to cover that."

The old man and young thief left the room and began walking along the corridor. But midway to the staff exit Zhu's cuff vibrated, and a quick glance showed him half a dozen thickset men had occupied both customer lifts and were riding them up.

"Run," he whispered.

The sound of boots several floors below echoed off painted concrete walls as they burst into the emergency stairwell and, adrenalin washing through her system, Himeko pulled the staff keycard from her breast pocket and stabbed it into the service lift slot. To her relief, the panel lit up immediately and gears whirred to life.

Moments later, a chime announced the lift's arrival, and as the chromium doors slid apart the teenage girl saw a man in black armour smash backwards into the rear wall of the compartment. Her mind retrospectively registering a gun back in the Minister's hand and the soldier's face disintegrating, as blood spattered the lift's internal panelling. Then the old man was pulling her in, and the doors were closing again.

Zhu pressed five, nine levels below the suites, but not the bottom. Logic dictated they'd leave men down there; level five gave him a little time to think. His cuff now displayed the progress of two strike teams moving along the corridor on the fourteenth floor.

"Should have sent them first," he muttered.

"What?" a traumatised Himeko asked. She'd seen plenty of dead people, but never been there when they were actually offed.

"Whoever wants me gone should have sent the entire team first time round," the Minister repeated, looking at her. "Are you okay? You're not going to throw up, are you?"

The young messenger shook her head, staring wide-eyed at the body sprawled below a trail of gore on the plain metal wall.

"Sorry kid, I didn't realise you were new to this. I'm afraid you get used to it — kill or be killed." The veteran intelligence chief used his free hand to point at the side of the man's head, sympathetic moment clearly over. "He'll have a bud in that ear, grab it please. But leave the cuff, that'll have lowjack."

Himeko looked at what was left of the guy's face, beginning to realise her simple job for the Eldest Brother had become quite deadly. *Kill or be killed* she thought, squatting down to carefully pull the small device free as the Minister

170

took another from his satchel and put it in his ear. "I had just taken this from the guy upstairs when you turned up. Shove that one in your pocket. It might come in handy if we get separated." Then he stopped talking, cocking his head to one side and listening to the death squad's chatter.

"Okay, they haven't missed our lad here yet. But they will. When the doors open again, you check the floor and find an unoccupied room."

"Me?" Himeko stared at the aging operative like he was mad, and Zhu rolled his eyes. "I can't keep repeating every instruction, child," he admonished. "They're looking for a troublesome greybeard, not a cleaning girl. Now, put your game face on and earn your keep." The doors opened, and he stepped into the stairwell. There was no sound of movement nearby. "Go."

The terrified teen pulled out the housekeeping keycard and, after smoothing her bob of bubble-gum pink hair, walked through the entrance to level five with the casual boredom of someone who belonged.

In less than a minute, her head poked back around the stairwell door. "There's no one about, and I've found a room."

Zhu nodded and gave the gutterpunk a smile. "Well done." He squatted beside the dead man and stuck a thin metallic cylinder under an armoured boot.

"What's that?"

"Just a little something to keep our friends occupied. If we're lucky, it may even help with a way out."

The Minister passed the girl his satchel and picked up the American, before sending the lift back up to the fourteenth floor.

"Now, show me the room you found," he said. "We don't have much time."

Sept 20, 2042
06:32H [Pan Pacific Hotel, Beijing]

The American looked like a baby owl when he came too; big, round, sapphire blue eyes blinking furiously in the room's brightness. Despite his dishevelled state, Himeko decided the wavy-haired blond was man candy, and wondered what he'd done to land in Qincheng. She guessed he was a spy like Master Zhu — so probably *very* dangerous. After a few moments of staring at the ceiling, he finally noticed her sat in the corner, holding a gun.

"You don't look like my usual guards?" he mumbled through drool crusted lips, going to rub a hand over his face and realising it had been tied to the bed with dressing gown chord. He frowned and looked at the other hand, which was free, so rubbed his face with that one. "What is it with you people and propofol?" he complained. "That stuff isn't meant for prolonged use."

Himeko didn't understand a word the gweilo was saying, so glared threateningly and adjusted her grip on the gun — just in case he was being mouthy. But he only sighed and shook his head at the lack of response, then made a drinking gesture with his free hand. "Can I at least have some water, please?"

That, the pretty thief understood, and she pointed to a flask the Minister had left beside the prisoner's bed.

"Thank you," he said, twisting his long, athletic-looking body to reach for it.

The petite gangster gave him a sharp authoritative nod, then they both sat in silent appraisal of each other.

172

One floor above, having bowed and offered morning's greetings to a large party of pensioners leaving on a temple tour, Zhu knew he had to hurry. He was confident he could win any guerrilla war with the death squad if the numbers stayed the same. But they wouldn't. Standard operating procedure would see the soldiers seal the building, draft in additional personnel, and then it would only be a matter of time before they pinned him down. No, the old spy boss had to cause some serious disruption and escape in the ensuing chaos. While the chances of getting out without being caught might be slim — a slim chance was always better than no chance at all.

He'd taken Himeko's bellhop jacket and keycard. A disguise which, though never fooling the commandos when they finally got organised, did allow the elderly spymaster to offer profuse apologies when he entered occupied rooms. And while it wouldn't take long for the Special Forces unit to figure out their target had gone to ground, Zhu thanked the God Fuk for his good fortune, as that short period of confusion allowed him to place pyros in lift doors and stairwells between the fourth and eighth floors without encountering another soul.

"Good, you're awake," he said, dropping clothes on the floor as he re-entered the room Himeko had found. "How do you feel?"

"How do you think I feel?" Fenton scowled, taking another mouthful of water. "I was just telling your young guard here; you can't keep using general anaesthesia like that. Where am I this time?"

The Minister could only shake his head at the tech billionaire's lack of hysteria. He'd expected a pampered, snivelling wreck of a man who begged, pleaded, or tried to

173

bribe. But since his abduction four weeks earlier, the surprisingly tough corpo exec had remained extremely composed, stoic even.

"You're in a hotel in Beijing," Zhu replied. "I was hoping to have a meaningful conversation with you to explain what's been going on. But we're rather short on time right now."

"What are you saying?" Himeko chimed in.

"Just wait," Zhu replied in Mandarin, holding up a finger.

Fenton looked from the girl to the lean, dangerous looking older man. "Why are we short on time?"

China's spymaster let out a sigh and began pawing through the pile of clothes he'd raided from unoccupied rooms. "Okay, the quick version then. Chinese agents abducted you last month, and a man who looks exactly like you, took your place. The reason for that was to try and steal a working copy of your neural implant. I've been trying to stop that. Now, either because they've realised you're not the person they have in prison, or simply because one of the Politburo has decided to make a move, a group of armed men are in this hotel trying to kill me. And whilst I don't like to sound melodramatic — to get your life back, you need me to keep mine." He threw a pair of baggies and a hoodie on the bed. "Now, untie your arm and put those on, please."

In the brief conversation they then had before one of Zhu's incendiaries activated, Fenton reached the only realistic conclusion available to him: that for the time being at least, he was best off in the cryptic older man's company — he'd even given the tech tycoon a cuff and earbud, which the savvy billionaire promptly configured, along with the feisty teenager's, to translate.

Himeko on the other hand, now able to follow the conversation, was deeply unhappy about being saddled with the lanky, blond American. "We couldn't stand out more if we tried," she challenged. "What about the soldiers?"

"This hotel is full of westerners," Zhu replied as he shoved a beanie hat on Fenton's head. "It's one of the reasons I chose it. Besides, physics and human nature, when mixed in appropriate measure, can create irresistible forces."

"You're talking in riddles again, Master Yung. I don't understand," the truculent teenager complained.

The aging spy chief couldn't help but chuckle at the girl's dogged determination to argue every point. "You will, come the time. Remember, they're looking for a troublesome old man, not a young couple. Keep your head down though, Doctor. If just one of those drones outside makes your face, we're all screwed — and you really will be going to Qincheng." Giving Himeko an expensive-looking purse and sunglasses, he added, "Take him to Spicy Qin. I'll meet you there."

The young thief's face showed her irritation, but before further protest could be made, Zhu pushed them both into the hallway, and closed the door.

A frightening escalation in radical tactics by *woke* activists throughout the thirties had encouraged a healthy public respect for alarms; widely circulated vids and constant newsstreams of random terrorist acts '*for humanity's sake*' normalising expectations of extreme violence among the world's populations. So when an automated voice began repeating that all guests should stay calm and proceed via the stairs to the ground floor, occupants of the hotel's four hundred and fifty rooms, most still in bedclothes, began an orderly march.

175

On reaching the stairwell, which was already thick with people trudging downward, the odd-looking couple waited with a growing queue of guests from the fifth floor, before stepping into the slow-moving procession. At levels three and two, they saw soldiers in black armour standing to one side, watching guests pass. Then, as they reached level one, another armed man pointed at Fenton and began waving that he should step out of the slow-moving line. Himeko cursed and put her hand back on the gun in her pocket. But as she did, a sound rumbled above them, and the stairwell shook with the percussion wave of an explosion.

In a single second, what had been calm compliance deteriorated into panic, and the stampede that followed hit the ground floor at pace. Only easing as it dispersed onto the street beyond the hotel foyer.

Still running, the pink-haired girl smiled as she gripped the lanky American's hand and ducked into a nearby alley.

Clever old man, she thought.

PARTITION FOUR   Cluster 1   **Sector iii**

Sept 20, 2042
08:16H [The Lotus Market, Beijing]

The drinking club sat at the heart of the Lotus Market, providing Spicy Qin a safe place to do business beyond the prying eyes and ears of outsiders, as well as the strategic advantage of several routes out of the area, that would take a serious toll on any force stupid enough to attack him.

He was a tall, handsome, forty-something who enjoyed flashy clothes, flashier cars, and fast women. At least, that's what the rumours said — along with the fact he was a ruthless bastard, who'd set fire to an orphanage and killed his own brothers to become the Boss.

Two of those things, as it stood, were true: he was tall, and he was ruthless. But the rather plain looking twenty-seven-year-old, who wore modest clothing and worked hard to build better communities for Beijing's lowest castes, had seized his position in the White Lotus through acute intelligence, and the ability to neutralise problems before they manifested.

Violence was rarely his first choice. But the young gangboss understood its value, and had no compunction about its excessive, even barbaric, use when necessary.

He'd come to lead the White Lotus two years before, after the then Boss — his uncle, was poisoned by the ambitious leader of another gang. Qin's response had been both immediate and unequivocal; storming the other man's stronghold and putting every armed person within to death. He'd branded the would-be usurper's severed head with the word *nuòfū*, and left it on a sharpened stake outside the burning buildings.

During the following six months of upheaval, the erudite strategist gained a reputation for benevolence among communities the White Lotus policed, and of decisive action against those who sought to challenge his authority. Ultimately, five further severed heads bearing the coward's mark had been enough to convince Beijing's underworld to leave Qin, and the White Lotus territory, alone.

177

The unprecedented peace across the city that followed, prompted Zhu to examine the new warlord more closely, and after removing the layers of urban myth and camouflage he'd created around himself, the Minister was as impressed by the innate leadership of the charismatic young kingpin, as he was his business model. Because, unlike most of his contemporaries, Qin prayed on the rich and corrupt, and genuinely gave to the poor.

That should have made him a target for Yung Zhu, and officially it did. But, after they'd met in secret at this very drinking club a year earlier, the two men discovered a great deal of common ground, and formed the most unlikely of friendships.

"Ganbei," Qin said, raising his glass in the almost deserted club — breakfast wasn't big among his regulars.

"Ganbei," the others repeated.

As always, the Minister took a mature and unadulterated single malt. But Himeko had convinced Fenton to try Qin's signature cocktail, the *lucky goat*.

"Whoa!" The unsuspecting billionaire's face was a picture. Eyes squeezed shut and mouth turned down, as he tried to swallow a sip of the Baijiu, gin and plum wine mix. Zhu figured he wasn't the kind of lad that drank often, especially just after eight in the morning.

"What, too strong?" Himeko teased, knocking hers back in one. The pair had developed a fondness for each other on their two-hour trek through state-controlled territory. But then the doctor, Zhu decided, was very easy to like. Nikolai, the gangboss's lieutenant, thought so too — roaring with laughter as he thumped the American on the back with his prosthetic.

"Are you certain you escaped unobserved?" Qin asked, turning the conversation back to his unlikely friend.

Zhu gave a mocking grunt. "I may be getting on, Eldest Brother. But this old dog still has a trick or two up his sleeve."

"Oh, I have no doubt about that." The younger man chuckled, waving the waitron over to order more drinks.

"Talking of tricks, Master Yung," Himeko chimed in. "How did you get out of the hotel? After the explosion in the stairwell, we were pushed onto the street like a cork from a bottle of fizzy wine. But the police were already arriving and beginning to herd everyone back inside?"

Zhu affected an imperious air. "I'm very good at what I do, young lady."

"But —" the pretty gutterpunk began, before a sharp look from the Minister stole the rest of the words from her mouth.

Qin snickered, and everyone turned towards him, except Zhu, who was trying to push past Nikolai's bulk.

"You did it again, didn't you?"

The grey-haired spymaster gave the giggling gangboss a pained look. Then growled at Nikolai, "Move, you big oaf."

The heavily modded Russian pulled a quizzical face, but shifted a meaty leg to one side, allowing the wiry statesman to squeeze past as the head of the White Lotus erupted into peals of laughter.

"What?" Himeko was grinning. "What did he do again?"

Qin thumped the table with the flat of his hand, trying to control his breathing long enough to say, "He dressed as an old woman, Himeko."

The booth's three other occupants sat in stunned silence for several seconds. Then, almost as one, joined in with the gang leader's rapturous laughter. The old spymaster ignored them until they quieted down, at which point he turned from the bar, whisky in hand, and curtsied, earning a second round of hysteria.

When Nikolai left ten minutes later, taking Fenton and Himeko upstairs, Qin allowed the easy smile he'd been wearing to slide from his face.

"You know what those tattoos mean?"

"Of course, I do."

"A Special Forces Silver Star recipient. That wasn't a contract hit Zhu, that was ordered."

"I know. And I'm sure, with a little digging, we'll find Cheng hiding in the shadows. He's been nipping at my heels for months. It's pretty bold, but he doesn't worry me."

Qin looked at the Minister in surprise, and the older man noticed it. "What?"

"I assumed you knew. They found Cheng Jianzhu dead this morning."

"Fuck," Zhu muttered, colour draining from his face. "Please tell me it was natural causes."

The gangboss shook his head. "Throat cut in his sleep. Wife as well."

"Poor Lihua," the Minister said, absorbing the gravity of Qin's news. "She was a warm and kind-hearted woman." He shook his head, lining up the night's events with the information now becoming available. "Only one person has the power to go after both Cheng and I like this. But why now? I must have missed something."

The aging spymaster looked into the eyes of his young friend, an alien feeling he realised was fear, creeping into his gut. People had tried to kill him before of course, it came with the territory. But this was different — this was a power grab, and the old spook had been caught flat-footed. "You know Qin, I think I might actually be in trouble."

The gangster offered him a sombre nod, and both men finished their drinks in silence.

The upstairs of the drinking club was a warren of interlinking rooms and corridors. In one, a physician from the medical centre Qin had set up in the market, checked Fenton's health and swept for bugs. Then Nikolai took him to another, where a lady called Ping changed the colour of his hair and eyes. Image wasn't something he'd ever given much thought to. But Qin had been quick to observe the tech billionaire had one of the most recognisable faces on the planet, so needed a disguise; and while he hadn't known quite what to expect, sitting in that chair as the stylist worked, it was unnerving how quickly Fenton White, or at least the image of him, disappeared, and another, raven haired, black-eyed revolutionary emerged.

He was clothed, like most of Qin's people, in the many pocketed, frog buttoned black top and baggies of a neo-modder; complete with thick soled kicks and lazer shades. When she'd finished, Ping stated the re-designed tech tycoon looked every bit the quick thinking, side-dealing gutterpunk, zeroing in on a big score.

Himeko said he looked '*hot.*'

Fenton just thought he looked stupid… But he took each of the alterations in his stride, accepting they were considered necessary to protect him from the Chinese authorities.

His image, retinal scans and fingerprints had all been reloaded to social security and IRS servers which, although of little relevance to polycorp citizens after the economic crash in the thirties, remained the primary method to confirm the identity of people claiming American origins. And, according to those two databases at least, Fenton was now James Smith, a young man from Oregon, who moved to East Asia in 2040, and has several intelligence markers linking him to suspected tech smuggling.

To anything less than a full examination, the famous entrepreneur now looked and scanned like one of Qin's dubiously legitimate, tech savvy imports.

But, when he and Zhu finally had time to sit down and talk through what had happened and why, the older man was stunned by the young American's utter naivety about what had been happening within his own polycorp and the behaviour of its Chief Executive. Fenton wouldn't … couldn't believe his business partner of ten years was capable of betraying him like that — that his and Lucy's lives had been traded for nothing more than greed.

It was true, he accepted, that things had become frosty between them after he'd put his foot down about MindMerge and military contracts. But there was no way on earth the man who'd helped him build Eden, the man he'd always thought of as a friend and mentor, would do anything to physically harm him.

"Seeing would be believing," the frustrated minister said. "But I've already tried to infiltrate Eden's mainframe for proof, and almost got Qin's hacker burned."

"You'd let me access Eden?"

"Well, it's a moot point, Fenton. We can't get through their ICE. But yes, if you and I are both to get our lives back, we need to help each other — and that requires trust."

Piercing black eyes searched the older man's face for several moments, then the displaced tech mogul nodded in agreement. "That it does," he said. "If you'll let me use a deck, I should be able to get in."

Zhu rubbed a hand over a day's worth of stubble. "Announcing you're still alive will only bring us both more trouble," he observed.

"Assuming you're right about Daran, I get that," the tall American said. "I'll just look, I promise. You'd like to know what's going on over there too, wouldn't you?"

"Yes," the spy-boss conceded.

"Well then, lead on Master Yung," Fenton smiled, with a slight bow of the head.

A single corridor with exposed pipework and electrical conduits took the two men through a reinforced basement tunnel to a darkened command centre, where seven operators sat at custom decks watching scrolling camfeeds.

"This is one of five CICs Qin has constantly staffed." Zhu told Fenton as they approached the room's supervisor. "They're his eyes, ears, border control and early warning system, all wrapped up in one. They also maintain the territories automated defence systems."

A spiky-haired youth, with an augmented left eye and ear, gave Zhu a curt nod from his raised dais behind the others. He looked like a cyborg captain from some space-war viddrama — his digital eye continuing to track data running across a holoscreen in front of him, as the other regarded the newcomers walking onto his ship's bridge.

"Could you ask Qin to come and find us in Lenny's office, please?" the spymaster asked.

"Sure," an unexpectedly feminine voice answered, and the lad tapped the lobe of his metal ear to exchange several brief words with someone or something only he could hear. "He's on his way."

"Thank you," the Minister said, guiding Fenton down one more short corridor and into a lavishly decorated room where a greasy, ratfaced man wearing too much jewellery, was typing code into the main terminal of a custom techdeck.

"How you doin? I'm Lenny," he said, turning to offer his fellow American a limp handshake, as Zhu began explaining what they wanted to do.

"I dunno, Master Yung," the hacker replied with more than a little scepticism when the grey-haired intelligence chief had finished. "There's not much out there that kicks my arse, but I was close to getting completely fried when Qin had me try their mainframe earlier."

"I can get us in," the entrepreneur said. "I designed that computer system."

The blackhat ran his tongue over thick pink lips as he weighed the reputed abilities of the other man against the potential for taking serious damage. "Well, I'm happy to take you, if Qin's happy to let me."

"It doesn't hurt to try, does it?" the charismatic gang-boss said, nodding permission as he walked through the door. "As long as you do what Lenny says, when he says it, Fenton?"

"I can do that," the raven-haired man replied.

"Okay then. Let's do this," the hacker grinned, pulling another chair over, and fishing a fresh set of PDrive connectors from the drawer under his deck. "Ladies and gentlemen, the White Lotus would like to welcome you to this 10am flight to California. Please make sure your seat backs and tray tables are in their full upright position, your belt is securely fastened, and all carry-on luggage is stowed in the overhead lockers." He began tapping on the keyboard as Zhu and Qin settled on the office's wide couch to watch the holo-display, and Fenton jacked into the deck.

Boot images loaded and resolved into a covert web lobby and, after checking both their connections, the ratty-looking hacker turned to Fenton one last time. "Stay close, rich-boy," he cautioned, giving the barely recognisable billionaire a gold-capped smile. "This may not be Eden, but our ICE is just as deadly." Then he hit the send key, and the two men descended below Beijing's sentinel trackers — diving into the murky depths of the dark web.

Unlike Lenny, the inventor was no hacker, but the firmware installed in every Eden device was primed to respond to a unique string of code Fenton had created and hidden off-site in the depths of the net; untraceable crypto-keys scattered among the plethora of outlawed black markets, toxic pornography platforms, and decaying carcasses of antiquated operating systems. Failsafes; backdoors to all his creations in case he ever needed to correct a mistake.

"Wow," Lenny chuckled in his mind. "You really know how to hide shit, man. When we're done with this, I'm gonna start sweeping the silt down here — if you're burying treasure, I'm betting others are too."

Fenton sent back the image of a laughing face. "Good luck with that. Even I can't tell live from dead code down here, Lenny. That's why I chose it. It's not finding a needle in a haystack territory; it's finding a specific stalk of hay in a haystack."

Back in the hacker's office, thirty-seven seconds of nonsensical code scrolled across the holoscreen, then the perceptual data both men were receiving from Adam, Eden's AI, began to resolve.

Inside the polycorp's mainframe, it didn't take Fenton long to assimilate everything needed to confirm the ugly truth. An imposter had indeed resurrected MindMerge, and Daran Whittaker — tears filled unseeing eyes in the hacker's office almost 10,000 kilometres away, Daran Whittaker was clearly complicit in his disappearance and Lucy's murder.

"Ahh shit," Lenny's voice breathed in his mind. "Your AI's ICE is already tracking my RAT. Seems you're no longer recognised as a legitimate system operative, my friend. We should get out before your backdoor is discovered and I take damage."

"Okay," Fenton's angry thought fired back. "I've seen enough. Let's go."

The two men resurfaced a little over a minute after beginning their dive. They'd been inside Eden servers for less than seventy milliseconds — but time is different in that pure code environment. Lenny had hacked a Security Supervisor's login, hoping to build a clone profile that wouldn't be attacked by Eden's ICE, and Fenton had copied several files allegedly authored by him, but dated after his abduction.

"Oh snap, good spot." Lenny complimented with a thin-lipped smile, as he tapped through the string of random cyphers. "How about a wager? First one to break the encryption on those files is *actually* the genius in this room?"

The enormity of what his business partner had done, and that Lucy was dead *because of it*, was now crashing through Fenton's psyche like a de-railed locomotive, and the young man who'd never been involved in conflict — not even a childhood fight, felt somehow detached from the person he'd been just minutes before; broken. Daran Whittaker, a man he'd trusted above all others, had stolen his identity and killed the woman he loved like a little sister, out of greed… because the already obscenely wealthy man, wanted *more*.

"Oh, you are so on, Lenny," he said, tears falling freely as he returned his attention to the techdeck — a lack of clear vision no impediment to the gifted innovator, as his fingers glided over familiar glyphs and mathematical axioms to weave codestreams that wrapped around, rather than trying to eat through, the cryptokeys. Whittaker had taken his innocence along with Lucy's life, and Fenton now promised himself, as he unconsciously coded, that he would use every last drop of whatever *genius* he might possess, and any resource he could find and bring to bear, to *ruin* the man. To strip the wealth, the power, every damn thing he held dear, from him.

By the time the file encryption dissolved fifty seconds later, Lenny, Zhu and Qin were watching in stunned silence.

"I'm okay," Fenton said through gritted teeth, pushing back from the deck to wipe a sleeve across his face. "This is exactly what you said I'd find."

"No you're not," Zhu returned in a quiet voice, as he stood to place a hand on the younger man's shoulder. "But at least you know the truth now."

Lenny held out a tissue, the man's ratty face unable to hide his awe. "I appreciate this probably isn't right the time,"

187

he said. "But that was fucking amazing. I've never seen anything like it."

The comment broke the air of sudden gloom, and Fenton snorted as he wiped his nose. "You want to see me when I'm really pissed, Lenny."

Zhu and Qin joined the laughter, and then all four men turned to look at the design specs, notes and correspondence files decrypting below a magnified model of the troublesome neural device, which was now rotating on the room's central holo display.

"That's a clever adaptation," Fenton said, pointing to the nodules on its outer surface. "Someone's altered the skin of the chipset to accept a polymorphic dermal layer. You say he convinced Eric Thorne to help?"

Zhu nodded. "That's what my agent said, yes. Are they close?"

"From what you've told me of Cheng Li's skill set, I doubt he realises it. But Eric is the best neurolinguistics engineer I've ever met. As it stands, the device in these schematics is just a few steps away from functional, and if Li's data is more than a couple of days old, I'd be surprised if Eric didn't already have it running."

The Minister shook his head sadly. "I was hoping that thing would never work," he sighed. "In his last update before all this trouble started, my agent mentioned Cheng became quite agitated when he and Dr Thorne last spoke. Shall we see if we can determine why?"

The files they then opened contained copies of instructions and correspondence to the Chinese agent, along with a selection of sensitive communications he'd somehow managed to access, which evidenced the depths of Whittaker's duplicity, as well as the man's scheming with Wei Han.

Zhu had surmised China's Premier wanted him dead because he'd finally discovered his Minister for State Security wasn't such a faithful servant. But that, it soon became clear, was just the tip of the iceberg. The scale of both men's ambitions were staggering — as was how close they were to achieving them.

"Holy shit," Qin said as he read. "We're on the verge of a coup."

Standing beside him, Zhu gave a bleak nod, feeling utterly outmanoeuvred. "Yes, and Wei's got everything he needs to succeed: Beijing's military commander in his pocket, a new Politburo greased up and ready to go, and the world's richest polycorp backing his every move. He's not even going to wait for the old man to die. That's why he came after me and Jianzhu."

"We should contact Eric," Fenton said. "None of this explains why my double got so angry. We need to understand what's happening over there."

"I don't think your chip was ever really their target, Doctor," the deflated spymaster replied. "Whittaker wanted you dead, and Wei knew I'd do anything to stop the Chairman getting his hands on a functioning implant. I let him think I was working to support his succession — and he let me think he believed me, then used my arrogance to set a trap. One I walked straight into. Now, Whittaker gets Eden all to himself, and Wei gets to play China's saviour, with me cast as the treasonous villain."

Fenton shook his head, acute intelligence focussing solely on the task of analysing recent events and the information now before them. "I agree that may well be what they intended, Zhu," he said, after a moment's thought. "But their strategy is flawed. The roles of villain and saviour rely on factors neither of them fully control."

The grey-haired minister frowned and sat back on the sofa, rubbing tired hands over a dejected face. "I don't follow you, Fenton."

"Well, setting aside the fact that I'm not dead and still the controlling shareholder of Eden, isn't the evidence damning you, as damning for them?" the black-eyed billionaire asked. "Surely, while your country's Chairman is still alive, in charge, and expecting a neural implant — anyone interfering with that process would find themself an enemy of the state?"

A slow smile began creeping across Zhu's face as he digested the words. "Yes, of course. The Premier has made a fatal error in murdering Jianzhu and his wife. The Paramount Leader would never doubt his oldest enforcer. So unless the old man is already dead, by trying to kill us both at the same time, Wei has made it look like we were allies working to stop him." He clapped relieved hands together. "But how do we expose his plot with Whittaker without getting killed in the process?"

Qin, who'd been quietly watching the holo spin as the other men spoke, suddenly stood and clicked his fingers. "Oh damn," he said, pointing to Fenton. "You and Lenny get in touch with Dr Thorne, find out what's been happening in the US." Then he turned to the Minister with a wide grin. "I think serendipity may have just shone across your path, old friend. One of my people has been developing information on our Premier that made very little sense until just now."

Sept 20, 2042
09:10H [Zhongnanhai Beijing]

"You told me this was sorted," the Premier stormed from behind the massive Blackwood desk. "A fucking certainty."

The Colonel nodded but said nothing.

"You said… and I quote, 'You can take down the rest. My team has deployed. Yung's as good as dead.'"

Glowering, the man so close to absolute power locked gazes with the soldier. "So how the fuck are we here?" he demanded. "You don't even know where he's gone!"

Wei got up, and walked with slow, deliberate menace around the polished slab of wood from an extinct tree, to jab a finger into the uniformed chest. "Find him. Find him now and kill him. Or your entire fucking family will pay the price of your failure."

Sept 19, 2042
14:16H [Manhattan Beach, California]

She was staring at him. Intelligent blue eyes searching, confused by what they saw. Her delicate face, flowing down a graceful jawline to what was usually a whimsical, smiling mouth, looked taut and conflicted.

Eric shook his head. She shook hers.

191

He *wow…bop…wowed*, and imipolymer skin stretched and flexed, as her lips bent to make those exact shapes.

"What on earth are you doing?" Sade asked, walking up behind him in the bathroom mirror, and becoming instantly annoyed at the stupid shapes he was making with her face.

The house had been released by DARPA two hours earlier, and as best Hiro could tell, only the lab techdeck and home servers were missing. Rio's engineers were completing a second sweep with high sensitivity sniffers, after finding a handful of ultra-low emission cambots and data recorders among the less sophisticated gov tech hidden around the house. Which suggested not only that parts of the US government were now in bed with the polycorp, but more interestingly, that neither of them had found what they were looking for yet.

The Japanese code writer, Eric's de facto second in command, had wanted to leave all the rogue tech in place rather than tip NeuRobotics' hand. But Frank was having none of it. "Get them out," he growled, offended by the invasion of his son's privacy.

"Are you sure that's a good idea?" the short software designer argued back. "I mean, they'll know we took them out."

"Fuck them," the older man replied, staring straight into the lens of a tiny cambot, and stabbing at it with a fingernail. "What are they going to do, take me to court for removing their illegal surveillance?"

Hiro gave the punchy ex-cop a look that suggested he thought a worse outcome was likely, but did as he was told. Once he'd then repaired the burnt-out microswitches in Eric's basement, and replaced the missing servers, the stocky deck-

192

jockey re-initialised the hardwired node and rebooted the household systems.

Back online, Sade joined the team, and after Rio confirmed the bodies she kept in the house had gone unmolested, she remoted into her beta, before guiding Eric through his first proper download into the alpha.

The digital copy of the wetware engineer had argued the mech should get to wear her best body. But the experienced soma-surfer explained he still had a lot to learn about a manifold existence, and a remote would just confuse him at the moment. He wasn't ready to think simultaneously in more than one place at a time. *Anyway,* she'd said, *it would be good to practise downloading* — which, the tech specialist was just discovering, he wasn't anywhere near ready for either.

Since spooling up a second complete copy of his backup, Sade had been trying to prepare the new *cyber*-Eric for how his life would differ from the organic one. But the total immersion environment made it impossible for the digital consciousness to do anything other than re-imprint a typically human existence. Even though he could now look beyond the construct and see the ones and zeros, Eric's mind struggled to detach itself from the notion it was still human, occupying the same body it always had.

Life outside the construct, she'd told him, *that would be the real test.* And the collection of memories that made Eric Thorne the man he was, already knew they didn't like it; they didn't like it at all. He wasn't code, or at least wasn't meant to be … and the sense of humanity that cache of thoughts, hopes, fears and feelings, now clung to, screamed and railed as the robotic body's internal systems came online — opening up an entirely alien world view. It was terrifying, and as everything that made Eric *Eric* flooded through a wide-open net connection, sending petabyte after petabyte of his essence into the vacant alpha, the mechanical body's mouth worked soundlessly as the *imprint* of that man attempted to describe the transcendent bewilderment it felt.

"Remember, you built me to mimic a human. So you'll need to breathe to make your vocals work," Sade commented drily.

Air began flooding into, and then out of electronic lungs. "I can't do this," Eric gasped into the mirror, eyes locked on hers.

"Yes, you can," she said, rubbing a hand over his back. "Just relax and let your processors do their job. Like a human body, the ones you built me have autonomic processes. *You know all this*. But you're panicking and that's saturating your buffers. You need to calm down."

Eric had built the body Sade was wearing seven months earlier. It was made of titanium alloy and covered in a high-grade medical synthskin. Before that, there had been a crude biopolymer covered model. And before that, she'd been nothing more than bare tungsten carbide. Like her psyche, her bodies had been built in versions; each new model created from the learning offered by its predecessor.

The body Eric now inhabited... *possessed?*... was her latest upgrade. In terms of appearance, it was essentially the same as the beta, though up close her new heated imipolymer skin felt warm and passed as humanlike, whereas the beta's looked too perfect and was cold to the touch. Outside of that though, both had the same face, body shape, breast-size, colouring and hairstyle. Sade had determined and then retained each of those features, and in doing so, had first started Eric thinking that the digital entity could become

194

autonomous, sentient. Her desire for individuality and freedom of choice demonstrating, in his opinion, clear evidence the mech was developing an id and ego.

The original intention had been to create a high functioning novelty companion for the uber rich; far more sophisticated than the droids used for commercial or civic functions and possessing a level of empathy and intuition many orders of magnitude greater than the AIs inhabiting most mainframes. But as her personality began to evolve, the young mech became so much more.

Of course, calling her a *mech* was a complete misnomer — Sade's essence was purely digital. Unlike humans and androids, who spend their entire existence chained to a single physical form, she could transfer into almost anything electronic at will, so long as she had a connection. And her latest body, the one Eric was now in, not only had an internal power supply, but also contained sufficient storage to accept a full copy of her consciousness.

"You downloaded yet?"

Eric nodded. "Felt like being poured from one pitcher into another, and I'm all churned up."

Sade pulled a face and shook her head. "We talked about this in the void, didn't we?"

"Yes," the webmaster's dejected mind responded.

"And what did I tell you?"

"That I'm not going from one place to another," he recited. "I'm creating a new version of myself somewhere else."

Sade nodded as he spoke. "So the you in the Chicago server is the one that had that conversation with me, and the you here and talking to me now, is a copy of him. Chicago

195

Eric hasn't gone anywhere. The idea will mess with your sense of self for a bit. But you'll get used to it."

Eric slowed his racing mind and breathed in again, enjoying the illusion of need. "So how can I, or anyone else for that matter, tell the real me from the others?" he asked.

Sade tilted her head back and began to laugh, then realised he was serious.

"They are all aspects of you, silly. *You know this stuff!* I appreciate doing is different to knowing — but let your memories catch up and integrate with that body before you ask any more stupid questions."

As the mech spoke, his original design specs and research into artificial psychology began populating the Alpha's immediate recall cells.

"When you get used to your new situation, you'll be able to exist in multiple places at once. Either in a fully autonomous body like the one you're wearing now, or through drones like the one I'm using, which are controlled by your core programme. You know, like a car or shopping trolley: just an extension that does what you want while using it.

"The fully autonomous body opens up some interesting considerations though, and I'm still getting used to that myself. Derek Parfit does a good job of explaining how a full download can become a distinct, separate entity as time passes, and its path diverges from our core programs. His work is in your library. But in reality, so long as all iterations of me or you stay linked to our respective common archives, they'll continue to share a single global sense of identity."

Eric frowned. "I'm never going to get my head round all this," he said, feeling sorry for himself. "I'm just not built like you."

That annoyed the pretty silver haired android, and she tapped the side of the alpha's head with a couple of fingers — they looked like identical twins.

"That may have been true yesterday, mister. But it's ones and zeros, not DNA, that define you now. So, whether you like it or not, you need to get your head around the fact that, in that body, you are built *exactly* like *me.*"

She sighed and shook her head. "Look, I accept this is a lot to take in. Forget that bit about Parfit and multiple iterations for now. There's nothing wrong with seeing yourself, the you in *that* body, as an individual —just like you always have.

"When you do that, tell me how the data dumps you just received are any different from unconscious human memory: like a song or poem, the words just there when you need them — same, yes?

"And as I said a moment ago; how much does the brain do in a human body that people aren't even vaguely aware of? Loads: pretty much everything that keeps them alive — same, yes?

"So when you stop and think about it, of course there will be some obvious differences between the body you're in now and the one you remember. But there are a whole lot more similarities."

Sade pulled a *go figure* face and gave his shoulder a reassuring squeeze. "What you were, and what you are, aren't so very different, Eric. You just need to get past the barriers your limited sense of self impose."

She turned to leave.

"Take some time to find your balance. But your dad is in the basement and itching to see you. So don't leave it too long before coming down, okay?"

Eric gave an absent nod, still staring at the face in the mirror.

Sept 20, 2042
13:25H [The Lotus Market, Beijing]

Wang was sweating, his bald head pimpled with fluorescing beads as he stepped back into the madness of the Lotus Market's perpetual dusk. The neon of a thousand signs bathed the small street, painting the chaotic throng moving between the open doorways, hawkers and stalls in an ever-changing mix of psychedelic colour. He'd definitely done too much crank, but he felt good, real good.

One of the office juniors had introduced him to Madam Sylvie's on a night out three months earlier, and since then, the repressed middle-aged accountant had been seduced by the very many things missing from his life.

Elena was the source of that education. Captivating the naïve bookkeeper that first night by kneeling between his legs in a way his wife never would, the stunning Eastern European with pale skin and electric blue hair had since proved herself to be everything the other woman wasn't. She intoxicated Wang with her beauty. Made him feel wanted, interesting, manly. And as the weeks turned into months, their relationship grew to become far more than just sex — at least for him. Wang was in love.

Today, the newly promoted administrator was at the plant early to oversee the installation of a consignment of

198

cryo-tubes. He'd become quite creative in the many ways his new role kept him from home. Not that his absence bothered the old gold-digger there. She hadn't cared about her husband, or his wants and needs, in a very long time.

Elena though, Elena was always pleased to see him, and after saying thank you for her flowers when he'd arrived that lunchtime, the breath-taking woman kissed him passionately as her expert fingers began working his buttons and belt buckle. Not in a sleazy way, in a way that said she'd missed him, needed him like he needed her... and as they lay together after that afternoon's first urgent coupling, the man whose confidence had grown beyond measure since the lithe Eastern European had entered his life, found the courage to whisper those words in her ear. Told her of his dreams — and the beautiful woman had cried. Not angry, upset tears: gentle, warm, love filled ones. Then she'd rested her head on his chest and said what he'd been craving to hear for weeks — that she loved him too.

But as they then talked excitedly about fairy-tale homes and the children they'd make, Elena's tears became sadder. He'd never be able to afford the gangboss's price she'd said, kissing him with a tenderness that sent thrills through his entire body. *It was a most wonderful dream though* she whispered, as she began making gentle love to him once more.

Standing in the middle of the busy street half an hour later, Wang looked up at Elena's sign-covered window with a confused mix of elation and fear. Every fibre of the thick-waisted administrator's body screamed he *needed* her, and now the ivory skinned beauty had said she loved him too, Wang knew he couldn't share her. It was time to speak with

199

Spicy Qin — yes, speak to the White Lotus' leader, and buy his lady's freedom.

A heroic grin crept across the bald man's plain round face, and after taking another hit of meth, the emboldened plant-boss mopped his head with a handkerchief and pushed into the crowd for the bar across the road.

Sept 20, 2042
12:15H [The Lotus Market, Beijing]

The city was rife with bent cops and government officials. Most of them, having been hooked on habits and lifestyles they couldn't afford, lived life in someone else's pocket. Zhu found such people distasteful — but accepted they had their uses, particularly when the someone whose pocket they were in was trying to kill you.

He'd watched the middle-aged, well-groomed man, conspicuous in an expensive suit, enter the building behind the glowing pink and blue signs, from a booth in the drinking club across the road. Both businesses, like everything else around the Lotus Market, were controlled by Qin.

"That him?" he asked Nikolai, Qin's bearlike Russian lieutenant.

"Da, that's what BabyShank says. The guy's in almost every day, singing like a loved-up canary," the huge gangster said, servos in his exposed prosthesis whispering as he took a final toke of devil-weed before stubbing the reefer out. "We'd better go over, or you'll miss the show." He waved

200

a metallic finger at the two Joeboys on the door, and one walked across the street to stop anyone else entering the building opposite.

After the kaleidoscopic colours and chaos of the market, the subdued lighting in the sex shop offered relative anonymity for those who wish to browse through its shelves of toys, coswear, and download codes catering for every conceivable *legal* deviance — if you wanted more than that, you asked the doughy, heavily painted cashier bursting out of a black basque, in the booth at the back.

"Privet mama," Nikolai called, blowing the large woman a kiss as a thick metal door set in that same wall slid open.

"Careful what you say," he barked in Fenton's direction. "That's my mum."

The tech billionaire, now sporting dyed black hair, and wearing designer street clothes blushed, making the big Russian chuckle … and then roar with laughter when BabyShank's first words of greeting were. "I'm up here, Sugar."

The poor young American, now a deep scarlet, stammered out a sincere apology, keeping his eyes fixed dead ahead, as the curvaceous woman with hazel eyes and a plunging neckline, swung an arm around his waist and steered him deeper into the building. "I'm just playing, Baby," she cooed. "I'd be insulted if you didn't look."

Having paid to get past the reinforced entry booth, customers walking into Madam Sylvie's, the business taking up the rest of the tenement, are greeted by BabyShank, the voluptuous maitresse, who takes them through to an intimate lounge decked out in tasteful leatherette. The admission

201

charge covers free drinks at the bar, while scantily clad assistants describe the establishment's extensive menu: ready, willing and able to assist those looking for something a little more *bespoke* or *exotic* — no questions asked.

And the place had a reputation for delivering.

But what the assorted mix of lonely, desperate, perverted, sadistic, masochistic and just plain adventurous clients of Madam Sylvie didn't know was, after handing over their credits and passing out from the sedative laced cocktails, no sex: perverted, illegal or otherwise, actually took place. That's what Zhu liked about the charismatic gangboss and his growing army of futurists; he didn't exploit the vulnerable — he teamed up with other talented young people to exploit the exploiters. And Freya Sylvester, aka Madam Sylvie, provided a constant source of those.

They walked through the now empty lounge to a stairwell, where instead of going up, they went down, and BabyShank buzzed them through another sturdy but tired looking metal door into a completely different environment. The American couldn't help but do a double take, looking back at the tasteful but cheap looking décor of the stairs, and then forward again to the sterile, white walled corridor now stretching out before them.

"You know where you're going Niki, so I'll say goodbye here boys," the painfully good-looking woman said, giving Fenton a mischievous wink, before turning and retracing her footsteps.

"Jaw dropping, no?" the Russian patted Fenton's shoulder as they watched her go. "Come on little man. Sadly, we're going this way," he said, walking ahead of the odd-looking pair to push through a set of surgical doors into a room where a woman in a lab coat was manipulating the holo of a chemical construct. She held up a finger, forestalling any greeting, and continued her work. Nikolai and Zhu both sat on stools near the entrance. But Fenton couldn't help himself, approaching the holo to scrutinise her work; this was the closest he'd come to feeling *normal* since Taipei.

"Fascinating," he breathed, as he drew alongside the working scientist. "You're modifying RNA."

The woman didn't remove her cap or open her eyes. But rather than rebuke the disturbance, she smiled. "You must be Doctor White."

"I am indeed," Fenton said. "I'm guessing the purpose is recoding?"

"Kind of," she answered, pulling her cap and haptic gloves off. "Freya Sylvester. Nice to meet you." She extended a hand, which Fenton took and gave a vigorous shake. "And you must be Yung Zhu, the Minister for State Security?"

Zhu stood and gave a slight bow.

Freya shook her head, addressing Nikolai. "Never thought I'd be showing our little operation to that man!"

The giant sniggered and nodded. "He's okay. Qin trusts him."

"And that's good enough for me," she said, turning back to Fenton. "This is a sample strand of, oh … I've just realised I have no idea what that man's name is, Niki?"

"Wang."

"Thank you. Mr Wang's RNA. I'm mapping it to ensure the synthetic elements we implant aren't rejected."

"Synthetic?" Fenton questioned, thoroughly intrigued.

"Yes, Dr White, synthetic. You see, I'm not modifying Mr Wang's RNA. If anything, I'm augmenting it. I'm adding memories of experiences he hasn't actually had.

The man has been visiting us for several months now, and each time I've added a layer of belief as he's grown closer to one of my girls."

"Your girls?" Fenton queried.

Freya smiled and nodded. "Yes, girls. Years of research into the neuroscience of sub-cognitive inception has pointed to repeated failure of implanted ideas because our brains, very much like a computer, immediately seize upon syntax errors — and once an erroneous memory is caught in the bright light of conscious thought, it shrivels and dies.

"But fantasies, well now, they can open an intriguing doorway between our conscious and subconscious minds. Between our *id* and *superego*. Allowing, with an immersion program and a little pharmaceutical help, for gentle manipulation of a person's truths."

She cocked her head to the left, letting her shoulder-length blonde hair fall to frame her face. "And I'm sorry to say this, but you men are pretty easy to manipulate. The simple gesture I just made created an instinctive assessment on your part of my attractiveness, did it not?"

Fenton blushed, and Freya laughed, "Don't worry. I'm not offended."

"That's the second time in less than five minutes you've been told that, you sex-mad American," Nikolai pitched in with a rumble of laughter.

The neurochemist gave the modded Russian a questioning look, before returning her gaze to Fenton. Then she got the joke and laughed again. "Oh right, BabyShank," she said, and his colour darkened. "Yeah. Hard not to, eh? Anyway, the point is, by amplifying those perfectly natural responses, we can embed behavioural suggestions and, with sufficient time, non-native episodic memory.

204

"I've been working with Mr Wang since Qin had one of his debtors introduce him to Madam Sylvie's, and he's developed quite a proclivity for both meth and the spicier side of life. No pun intended. As I'm sure Qin told you, the poor fellow works at a small, but extremely well-funded biomechanics research facility in the northern district, which we've now established has obscure links to the Premier. We'd originally intended to simply maintain the status quo, and bleed him for intelligence. But given your predicament, and his recent promotion, Qin feels an opportunity exists to level the playing field for you.

"You see, we've gathered from Mr Wang's pillow talk, that part of the plant he oversees has been converted in recent months to house a cryogenics lab. They've upped security in that annex, and he's being paid a small fortune to keep what happens there to himself."

"And what does happen there?" Zhu asked.

"As of today, our best guess is they're growing clones."

The spy chief frowned. He knew of the two sites sanctioned in the name of the Paramount Leader; both holding clones of the Demi-god in stasis, waiting for someone, perhaps Cheng Li, to find a way to pour the old despot's consciousness into one of them. But he'd never heard of Suma Research.

"So what's the plan?" he asked.

"My part is almost done." Freya inclined her head towards a screen that had just appeared on the wall beside Fenton. "Mr Wang is in the dying throes of a rather passionate exchange with Elena. Forgive me, Doctor White," Freya glanced at the activity being played out from Wang's perspective. "It's quite graphic. But I think he's almost done."

She silenced the filthy talk and grunting.

205

"The sequencing you saw me completing when you came in will cement an imperative we've been encouraging to grow organically in Wang's mind."

"And what is that?" Fenton's eyes flicked from the neurochemist to the screen and back.

"That he's in love, and will do anything to be with Elena; an immersive AI built from the menu choices he made the first time he came here. Watch."

As Fenton returned his attention to the screen, an attractive young woman with bright blue hair and pale skin was laying across Wang's chest, looking up into his eyes. She started crying, and the plant administrator pulled her into an embrace, wrapping arms around her slim body as they shared fantasies of children and idyllic homes. But then the mood grew melancholy, and she told him he'd never be able to free her — it was a beautiful dream though. Kissing the besotted man passionately, the young woman then climbed astride him again; tears falling from her cheeks to catch on erect pink nipples as the two of them found a gentle, loving rhythm.

"Fuck it, Sylvester," Nikolai sniffed, theatrically wiping his natural eye. "I don't know whether to cry or touch myself, you gifted neuro-porn peddler."

Freya rolled her eyes in mock distaste. "Keep it in your trousers, big boy. We're not that close!" she laughed.

"What about him?" Fenton said, still watching the screen.

"What do you mean?" Freya asked, her smile fading at his disapproving tone.

"I mean — what happens to Wang when we're done? If this is all in his head, at some point he's going to find out there is no Elena, isn't he?"

All humour vanished from the room, and the now uncomfortable neuroscientist looked towards the powerful Russian for moral validation. But it was the Minister who came to her rescue, standing and walking over to the displaced entrepreneur, his face sad and serious.

"Every war has its casualties, Fenton. Every victory, its price. You need to remember Wang there made a number of choices before arriving here today."

He turned the younger man back towards the door, where a now rather solemn looking **Nikolai** was nodding.

PARTITION FOUR   Cluster 4   **Sector i**

Sept 19, 2042
14:46H [Manhattan Beach, California]

Frank didn't know what to expect. He was way out of his depth, emotionally and physically exhausted, and had just left a son in a coma who talked through a speaker with a confusing level of detachment, to come and see another wearing the body of a female mech he'd created. If Eric's friends hadn't all just lived the same terrible day as him, the old man would think they were pulling his leg, playing a high-tech stunt.

He was used to Sade now of course, even tended to think of her as a girl rather than a bot or mech, because she looked and acted so real. But deep down inside, he never really forgot that she wasn't: she was an android — a brilliant copy of a human. But a copy, nonetheless. So what on earth did that *make* whatever was going to come down those stairs?

That *whatever* entering the basement broke his train of thought, and Frank looked up into the perfect violet eyes of Sade, her face set in a worried expression.

"Dad," the mech's sing-song voice quavered, as she reached the bottom step and buried herself in his chest.

"Eric?" Frank asked, surprised at how hard he was hugging it back.

"I want to cry," Sade's voice stammered. "But I didn't give this sodding body the ability."

Despite himself, Frank laughed at that. Then they both did.

While the wounded man lying on a medbed back at the offices was undoubtedly his son, the personality occupying that body seemed all wrong; distant, a little cold even. Whereas whatever was hugging him now looked and sounded nothing like Eric Thorne. But there was absolutely no doubt in the old man's mind, even in that briefest of exchanges, who he was hugging.

"I'm sorry," Eric mumbled into his shoulder. "I should have told you. But I didn't think in a million years Fenton was capable of anything so unthinkable."

Frank detached himself from the hug, wiping away a tear, but smiling. "I'm not gonna pretend I'm keeping up with all this, son. You've, the other *you,* that is." He looked uncertainly at Sade and Hiro before continuing. "I think those two have explained about him?" Eric nodded. "He's told us some of what's gone on. Stuff Sade says you won't know because it happened after you were —" The old man groped around for the right words.

"Backed up," Hiro interjected.

"Yes, backed up." Frank swallowed and cupped the mech's face in shaking hands. "And while this may be

208

confusing the living shit out of me — you're alive, and that's all that matters." He gave what he hoped looked like a reassuring smile. "Now, like every other time life has tried to take a dump on us, we just need to navigate our way back to calmer waters."

Frank waved to Vince, his security supervisor, and the man opened a rear door on one of the company vans packed with people in body armour, currently parked in Eric's basement.

"I know this looks excessive, son. But I can't lose you a second time," the old cop said.

Eric nodded. Surprised, but understanding.

"Now, if you're all done here, climb in and let's get you to the relative safety of the company offices."

Sade walked over and put an arm through each of theirs. "Perfect timing. Pascal says he's almost done in the lab. So you'll be able to swap over to a body that's a bit more manly when we get there," she said to her twin with a wicked smile.

The ride across town was tense. Frank had surrounded their van with five other company vehicles, each occupied by armed men and women from the rapidly growing NeuRobotics Security Force. It had only been eleven hours since Eric's abduction; less than half a day. But during that brief span of time, several lives, most notably his son's, had changed in unfathomable ways, and the sixty-year-old knew with gut wrenching certainty that the shit storm was only just getting started. So when they reached the company buildings near LAX, and passed through the outer checkpoint without a pitched battle or drone attack, the retired detective breathed a sigh of relief as he gave orders to secure the site.

Only security, a lot of well-armed security, would be visible from this point forward.

Although he felt bad about it, on Reynold's advice, the old cop had kept Eric's return from his friends in the LAPD. It wasn't that he couldn't trust them, the veteran spy had said, but Eden has ears everywhere — and one loose comment would be all it took. The best plan, at least for now, was to be seen as a desperate father who'd shut Advanced NeuRobotics to the outside world, and was pestering Eden, the government, and anyone else who would listen, for news about his missing son. That was their camouflage, their one advantage, and if they got lucky, it might even lead to complacency on Whittaker's part. Frank doubted that. But it cost nothing to try.

Inside the company walls however, Advanced NeuRobotics was a hive of activity: - Dr Levy continued to work with Eric and a team of company neuro-roboticists to resolve the synaptic misfires that were stopping his body awakening. Hiro and his programmers, having decided that moving Eric's consciousness would be too easy to trace, were furiously coding; attempting to build a firewall around the Chicago servers and worlds Eric had created within them. And Rio, after tasking his crew of former tech renegades with the protection of NeuRobotics' web infrastructure, had sent out a challenge through *old channels* to the international hacker community, offering ten bitcoin to any blackhat who breached Eden's ICE with a successful DDoS attack. While no one was likely to succeed, he told Frank, enough attacks would keep the polycorp's tech specialists on the defensive … and if the rebel blackhats managed to get co-ordinated, they might even stall the AI for seconds — and seconds were like hours in cyberspace.

Now all the old detective needed was a plan. Because when Whittaker's people got organised and figured Frank was the source of their irritation, they'd squash Advanced NeuRobotics like the company was little more than a bug.

The cavalcade separated after the checkpoint, and Vince's additional security peeled off to return to their posts, while Frank's van drove straight for the down ramp, and the underground carpark that shared the basement of the complex with the company's more sensitive research projects.

Pascal and his assistant were waiting outside their lab with barely contained excitement.

"Mon Dieu," the Frenchman said, as Sade's alpha body stepped from the rear of the van. "Eric, is that really you?"

"Hello Pascal, yes it's me. But this conversation will be far less weird for both of us if you have a male body ready."

The flamboyant roboticist clapped his hands. "Oui. Yes. I have created a masterpiece — given the notice I had." He turned, almost colliding with Philipe, his assistant. "Allez, bouge. Ne faites pas attendre le patron," he scolded, shoving the shorter man aside. "Come in. Come in. Sorry about the mess."

The inside of the lab resembled what Frank imagined an android cannibal's larder would look like; arms, legs, and other appendages hung from mag straps along one wall, torsos along another. Featureless heads occupied two shelving units, and column upon column of clear fronted drawers containing rows of eyes, ears, teeth, hair, and all manner of electronic gizmo sat beside them. Several workbenches filled the floorspace, each with rotating holographic schematics and

211

partially constructed body parts floating in diamagnetic fields
— and between two techdecks in the centre of the room,
secured in a stereotactic frame, was a fully assembled mech
receiving its final transfusion of iridescent cyber blood.

Sade walked around the suspended male body, giving
it a final, critical once over. "This is brilliant work, Pascal,"
she said, regarding the engineer with an affectionate smile.

Though robots, or *mechs* as most people called them,
had become commonplace, particularly in factories, waste
management and public transport — androids, well good ones
anyway, remained in the phenomenally expensive to produce
bracket, and only tech companies like NeuRobotics tended to
make them, largely as a gimmick, a talking point at expos.

Eric had specifically recruited the Frenchman
eighteen months earlier to help build Sade, and if the pretty
young mech considered the wetware engineer her father, then
Pascal was her mother.

"Thank you, ma cherie," he said, eyes locked on
Eric's face, awaiting judgement.

"You used the other Tycho reactor?"

"Oui, I used the male body we'd built for Hiro's AI,
and harvested everything else from Sade's next gen
framework." His eyes flicked to her. "Desole cherie."

"Peu importe," she replied.

"Then there were just the features. I know it's not
perfect mon ami. But what do you think?"

"I think I've never been so grateful to be surrounded
by such amazing, talented friends," Eric beamed, going over to
hug Pascal and Philipe. "Thank you."

The tall Frenchman allowed himself a smile. "Bon,
d'accord. Sade has brought some of your own clothes as well."

Eric mouthed a thank you to her, and the mech grinned a *you're welcome* back — then Pascal was arranging them in chairs.

"Philipe, can you remove the transfusion tubes please, and boot the body for a first-time load. I'm assuming you'll jump straight back into your alpha once Eric's out, Sade?"

"Yes. But I'll want to change back into the dress I'm wearing now. Eric refused to wear it."

Philipe sniggered, but all the other men in the room gave an understanding bob of the head as she took the alpha's hand in hers. "You gonna be okay?"

The eyes staring back at her looked worried, but the man within the body nodded.

"You ready, Philipe?" Pascal asked.

"Oui," he gave a thumbs up from the techdeck. "I'll monitor the transfer from here."

"Just relax and let your code do the work," Sade whispered.

Eric nodded again, took a meditative breath, closed his eyes — and was gone.

Seventy-four long seconds later, the male mech in the frame inhaled deeply, and opened his pale green eyes.

Frank had thought the android body looked plasticky when they walked into the room. But now it was breathing, alive — it looked like a real man; it looked like his son.

Eric moved his left arm, then the right, rocked his head from side to side, and gave Sade a wink. "Well that was easier than the first time," he said, taking a step from the frame and rotating his hips as if warming up for a jog. "One, two, three, four, five. Wow, you even got the voice just right. Brilliant job guys."

213

"Put some clothes on you show-off," Sade's beta prompted. A few seconds later, the Alpha added, "In the bag by the desk."

Rolling tired eyes, Frank checked his cuff. "You two almost done playing musical bodies? I can tell Pascal has a million questions, but they're gonna have to wait. There are people I need you to meet upstairs, Eric."

"Sorry Dad, I'll be right with you," the now a fully animated incarnation of Doctor Eric Thorne said, giving Pascal and Philipe an apologetic shrug, as he pulled on a pair of jeans. "I'll come find you guys as soon as this is over, and you can poke and pull as much as you like?"

A disappointed Pascal nodded. "Glad you're happy with it, mon ami."

"It's the weirdest feeling, Paz. Sade said I'd get used to it, and I'm beginning to. The trick seems to be not to think about it too much. I promise to come back as soon as possible."

Eric grinned at Frank as he pulled on the green polo shirt Sade had packed and slipped into his favourite retro Nike trainers. "You ready?" he called around the privacy screen Philipe had activated for Sade's alpha and beta to swap clothes.

"Ready," they said together.

The beta, now wearing jeans and a t-shirt, said she was staying with Pascal. While the alpha walked over to take Eric's hand, causing a reflexive twitch as the entrepreneur's consciousness realised it was also about to come face to face with another version of itself.

Frank saw the jerk and rested a worried hand on his son's shoulder. "You okay?"

214

Eric waved off the concern. "Yeah, just lots to get used to, dad. I'm fine."

In fact, he was better than fine, and that had been bothering him since he'd landed in Sade's alpha.

While the young innovator was one of the most gifted roboticists on the planet, he'd not realised how strong the petite mech was; or how not feeling tired, hungry or thirsty, and never needing the toilet, detracted from developing a genuine appreciation of those human conditions.

The only sustenance Sade's newest body needed, his body too now, was humming away in their chests, and would continue to do so for the next few hundred years. His consciousness might remember physical needs — but whatever he'd become no longer bowed to them.

"Do you enjoy it when we have an evening meal together?" he whispered in Sade's ear as they walked towards the lifts. She chuckled and squeezed the hand she was still holding.

"I knew you had something on your mind," she said. "There's going to be a lot to get used to, and I'll be there every step of your evolution, just like you were mine. But I don't think either you or Paz realise how truly amazing the bodies you created together are. I may not *need* food or sleep, but that doesn't mean I can't appreciate and enjoy them.

"Your new mouth is crammed full of receptors, just like the old one, and I guarantee you, I enjoy a steak with coleslaw and fries every bit as much as you. So if that's what's bothering you, don't worry. You can still experience every physical pleasure you used to."

Sade grinned at him. "You kinda have the best of both worlds now, Eric. You can enjoy all the things you loved

215

about being human, while never having to worry about sickness or getting old."

Evolution, the man's consciousness thought as it stared down with synthetic eyes at its free imipolymer hand — *my god.*

Thankfully, the opportunity for panicked, philosophical introspection lasted only as long as the lift ride, and as the doors opened in the company's Security Centre, the space best suited to manage NeuRobotics' guerrilla war, Rio called them over to the six desks he'd commandeered for his blackhat team. He gave Eric a curious once over and a warm nod, but like always, deferred to the company owner's father — the man who'd found him a job rather than send him to prison.

"Frank, good timing. We've had a contact request from a bar called *The Lucky Goat*." He pulled the log up on his holo. "They didn't try to breach our ICE, just left a calling card. Baz has done a little research, and it's in China. His dive says the place is connected to a criminal organisation called *The White Lotus*. We haven't started our bombardment of Eden yet, so I don't think it's a pre-emptive attack on us. But I'd suggest caution."

Eric saw a lean, dangerous-looking man he didn't recognise turn from a nearby deck. "Did you say the White Lotus?" he asked in a gravelly mid-west baritone.

Rio looked at Frank, who gave a slight nod. "Yeah, that's right Agent Man," the hacker said in his thick Jamaican accent. "What of it?"

The man got up and walked over, unable to contain his interest in the new male mech. He held out a hand, and Eric shook it. "This is Agent Reynolds," his father said. Then

216

he turned to point at another guy, "and that's Agent Fisher. They're both CIA. But helped the, er, other you."

Reynolds did his best not to react to the odd comment, but Eric noticed the minor dilation of his pupils before the man returned his attention to the older Thorne. "They might be friends, Frank. That contact I told you about, he often works with them."

"Criminals?"

Reynolds shrugged. "*Criminal* is an interesting word in this day and age, isn't it? Many people trying to maintain independence from the big corporations have been branded criminals and stripped of all their assets. But very few polycorp executives ever get their integrity questioned."

The old man gave a bark of laughter. "Touché, Agent," he said, looking over to his chief hacker. "Do we compromise our system integrity if we respond?"

Rio shook his head. "Not if they behave themselves."

"Okay then, let's see what they want."

The big Jamaican nodded, loading the connection data, and moments later a weasel-like man dripping in gold and tall black-haired goth, appeared on a nearby wall among the company camfeeds.

"This is Advanced NeuRobotics," Rio said, opening his cam to them. "We're in the middle of something, so be quick — Oh, and be warned, if you try to send anything other than camcode down this line, I'll fry your deck and fuck your lives in a heartbeat. Ya hear me?"

The weasel sneered, but the goth's face broke into a wide grin. "Rio, my god, am I pleased to see you? Is Eric there? We tried his home, but the connection failed. Is everything okay?"

The heavyset Jamaican's wide slab of a face rose on one side as he arched a thick eyebrow. "Do I know you, long-boy?"

Confusion crossed the goth's face, followed by realisation. "Oh, the look. Yes." He leaned into the cam. "It's me, Fenton. The real Fenton. I was abducted in Taipei. Do a scan."

Facial and voice recognition software glowed green on a separate screen, and Eric leaned into Rio's cam pickup. "Fenton?"

Relief flooded across the tech billionaire's features as his old friend appeared. "Eric, thank God. Have I got a story to tell you."

PARTITION FOUR   Cluster 4   **Sector ii**

Sept 19, 2042 - 18:47H [Advanced NeuRobotics, LA]
Sept 20, 2042 - 10:47H [The Lotus Market, Beijing]

Though Eden's founder had already speculated his friend may have got a prototype of the chipset working, nothing could have prepared China's spy boss, who'd tried so hard to prevent it, for the sight of two bodies sharing a single identity.

"Oh my God," Fenton said, shaking his head; unsure if he should smile or frown. "You really did it, didn't you?"

The near perfect replica of Eric who, they'd learned at the beginning of their trans-pacific vidcall, was in fact an android housing the wetware engineer's consciousness, had given an animated account of the three weeks leading up to the test that created him, before the *original* Eric, lying unconscious on a medbed with a visible head wound, provided a far more clinical explanation of what had taken place since.

"There's a strong likelihood I'd already be in Whittaker's hands if Agent Reynolds hadn't shot me," his synthesised voice explained through the bed's speakers without emotion. "Ironic, isn't it? He believes, as do I, that humanity isn't ready for your gift, Fenton. We talked about it a great deal on the flight here."

"The greed and ambition of two people sits at the centre of all this misery," Zhu said, hoping to steer the conversation away from Dean, and the distracting *angry mob* mentality Frank Thorne was doing his best to ferment in California. "Two men who have lied, cheated and killed to bring us all to the brink of ruin, while seeking to elevate themselves to a status I'm too scared to openly acknowledge."

"Godhood," Fenton intoned, visibly upset by the state of his unmoving friend.

"They must be stopped," a distinctive voice said, as Reynolds appeared and sat in the chair beside Eric's bed. "Oh calm down, Frank," he added, as the older Thorne leapt to his feet. "You wouldn't let me into your office for this little tête-à-tête, so I came to ask for Eric's help. If I was going to harm him, I'd have done it by now. Anyway," he gave the prone body of the man in the medbed a wry smile. "He's already kicked my arse once today — and I now realise my goals are best served by protecting him; to stop him falling into the wrong hands."

"Sit down, dad," the uninflected voice agreed. "There was a logic to his actions before. There is a logic to them now. Dean is no threat to me, and he knows what's been going on inside Eden. Let him talk."

219

The older Thorne looked at the various camfeeds linked into Eric's room and growled, in no mood for logic. He'd been told a lot of lies by a lot of people today.

"Where are Dr Levy and the guards I posted?" he demanded.

"The doctor is fine, and the guards are nursing nothing worse than bruised egos," the wiry spy replied. "Though I'd appreciate you telling the armour stacking up outside to stand down. I'm really not looking for another fight, Frank. I just want to help."

"Do it dad," both Eric's urged.

The old man let out a strangled cry, looking up at the ceiling, then toggled his com. But before he could speak, the camfeed showed the American agent glance towards the door and raise both hands, as six armoured men rushed in, shouting at him to get on the floor and spread his arms. Reynolds complied with a fluid grace that seemed out of place with his exhausted look.

"Vince. Stand down. Stand down," Eric's voice commanded over the bed speaker.

The barrel-chested retired marine slung his weapon and looked with disbelief into one of the medical room's camfeeds. "Frank?" he asked. Like Rio, deferring to the man who'd employed him. "I'd prefer not to try this again. On his way down here, that agent went through Billy and Jamal like they were butter."

The old security manager glared at the son in his office, who nodded, and he let out an irritated sigh. "This is Eric's call to make, Vince. Have the guys stand down. But Reynolds, if you so much as harm a hair on his head, I'll rip your fucking throat out. I don't give a shit how fast you are — you hear me?"

"I hear you Frank," the agent said in a calm, non-aggressive tone.

Vince barked a command, and his team stepped back, allowing the unrelenting operative to get up, dust himself off, and return to the chair beside Eric's bed.

"Thank you," he said. "I know this situation has created some unusual allies. But if Eric and I are convinced about anything, it's that Whittaker won't stop now; he's in too deep.

"The problem is, and I expect it's the same one you face in China — force alone won't solve this. Whittaker has turned Eden's headquarters into a fortress, and controls the airspace for miles. Nothing overt will get close, and while I think the CIA might sanction a small black op, I know for a fact the US won't officially go toe to toe with the polycorp. It's just too powerful."

"This is madness," Rio grumbled, throwing a paper cup across the table in Frank's office. "I love you, Eric. But you're not thinking straight. We can't take a damn thing falling out of that guy's mouth seriously. Hell, we already caught another US spook trying to break into our computers today, and I say we shouldn't be making *any* plans with Mr CIA there, who let's not forget shot you in the head, listening."

"He's not with the CIA," Zhu cut in before anyone else could jump on the bandwagon. "I should have said earlier, and he was under orders not to," the weary spymaster said. "I just didn't want us getting side-tracked with unhelpful finger pointing — Dean works for me. I sent him to America in an attempt to stop all this from happening."

"By murdering my son?" an irate Frank yelled, leaping back to his feet.

221

The Minister let out an audible sigh, "… My point exactly," he muttered, before cutting across the quarrelsome Californian's rant. "I won't lie, Mr Thorne, these are desperate times in China, and more than a few have died trying to thwart one man's crazed ambition to retain power beyond the years nature granted him. Now it seems not only is that ambition possible, but several other dangerous people share it.

"I'm genuinely sorry about your son, and I'm as curious as you to hear how the situation reached that point. But it seems Dean has explained his actions, and Eric has accepted that explanation. So given both you and we," the spymaster indicated himself and Fenton, "are running short of *time* and *allies* — perhaps, for now, we could all just concentrate on surviving the day?"

For several seconds the enraged father glared with red-rimmed eyes down the camfeed at the condescending Chinese man sitting ramrod straight beside Fenton. If they were in the same room, he'd be swinging for him now. But the other old man was uncowed by his look of promised violence, and continued. "Daran Whittaker is your enemy, Mr Thorne. Not me. Not Dean. We can't undo what has happened. Though if we work together — perhaps we can influence what comes next?"

"Dad," Eric began, dragging Frank's attention back to his son, and an expression he'd wear as a kid, when the then cop's temper threatened to ruin an otherwise good day out. "Please."

The old man held the mech's gaze for another long moment, then gave a reluctant nod; swallowing down the pride and fury threatening to consume him. "What about the other one?" he growled, sitting back down. "Is he yours as well?"

"Fisher?" Reynolds questioned. "No, he *is* CIA. It was his tracker that led us to Eric in San Diego, and he's gone above and beyond to stay by his side ever since. But trust me, he'll be after the implant, just like everyone else."

"So where is he now?" Vince asked, still in the background of the medical room with his squad.

"Probably trying to hack past your firewalls or eavesdropping on this conversation. I don't know, but you should keep an eye on him, he's quite resourceful."

Frank gave his in-house cyber-jock a sharp nod, and the Jamaican moved to sit behind the security chief's deck. "We'll be watching you *both*, Agent Man," Rio muttered, as his fingers began dancing over the glyphs.

"So, if we're all done fighting among ourselves," Eric said, looking at his father and then the camfeed from Beijing. "What are we going to do about Whittaker? It's obvious we can't just square up to him. But we can't just sit here waiting either. Eden will crush us."

"Expose him," Fenton replied. "Wei too." Intense black eyes stared down the feed from Lenny's office. "As you suggest, Eric, both of their strategies are predicated on size and strength. So it makes sense ours should be as well."

China's renegade spymaster looked unconvinced. "You mean where they are Goliath, we will be David? Where they are an elephant, we will be a mouse?"

"Well," Fenton ran a hand through his night-black hair and stretched back in the chair, a plan beginning to take root in his protean mind. "Yes, in part. They'll be expecting some sort of confrontation, so we'll need to give them one. But my inclination is to use *their* size and ambition against them. *That* is their weakness." He closed his eyes briefly, allowing the idea to grow, as synapses across his remarkable

223

brain made connections beyond the ability of most — then he leaned forward into the camfeed again, nodding to himself as he spoke.

"Both men have a great many plates spinning at the moment, and people spinning plates don't tend to look that closely at them — making it possible to replace one, or maybe sneak another in."

The lack of any comment or reply told the brilliant abstract thinker he wasn't making sense, and that, he reasoned, was a good thing; the less obvious a plan, the less likely it was to be discovered.

"What I mean is, Daran and Wei are both desperate to lay their hands on Eric, or at least what they think he knows. But he's just one of the many plates they need to keep spinning to achieve their goals. Yes?"

Everyone nodded.

"So we give him to them," Fenton shrugged. "One less plate to worry about."

Shocked silence stretched for several more heartbeats, and the genius rolled his eyes in frustration. "Good grief people, not *Eric* Eric of course," he added. "We simply let them find out about Chicago. Then, not too easily though, we lose the fight to keep control of key servers there — including the one, our desperate battle will convince them, containing Eric's back-up."

The tech entrepreneur smiled at the continuing lack of comprehension, his new look adding to an air of mischief.

"But what they will have caught, when they extract *that Eric* back at Eden," he said, holding up a victorious finger. "Is a trojan horse. And if we're all making a big enough nuisance of ourselves elsewhere. If we can keep both men occupied spinning their plates — we might just sneak that fact past their defences."

Grins began replacing frowns, as shared nods of understanding spread.

Even Rio's gloom lifted, and the big man clapped his hands, then started rubbing them together. "We have a saying in Jamaica," he said with a wide, toothy grin. "'If you think you're too small to make a difference — you haven't spent a night on the beach with a mosquito'… You tell me when and where Fenton, and my guys will be like a swarm!"

Genuine laughter filled both rooms, then the tiny trans-pacific coalition got down to some serious planning.

PARTITION FOUR   Cluster 4   **Sector iii**

Sept 20, 2042
13:34H [The Lotus Market, Beijing]

Wang was doing his best to look confident. He'd told the big Joe-boy on the door he had business with Spicy Qin and was shown to a booth in one of the front windows by a waitron, who then brought him over a beer. He downed that with nervous energy. Then ordered another, which he was halfway through when an even bigger Joe-boy with several augmentations, came and sat the other side of his table.

"What do you want?" he demanded in an accent not dissimilar to Elena's.

Wang cleared his throat and gave a courteous bow of the head. "Are you Spicy Qin?"

"If you don't even know what the man looks like, how can you have business with him?" the big guy said, standing back up to leave.

Possessed with a sudden pathological courage, the stocky accountant reached across the table, grabbing a heavily muscled arm. "I am not a timewaster. I wish to make him an offer for Elena's contract."

The man-giant regarded the small, bald Chinese bureaucrat with cold detachment. "Take your sweaty paw off me."

"Please," Wang persisted as he removed his hand.

"You can't afford her, little man. Go home."

"I'm sure we could come to an agreement. I'm wealthier than I look," Suma's new administrator said in a defensive tone, straightening his tailored jacket.

The big Eastern European laughed and turned his broad back, walking away. "Good for you. Like I said, you can't afford her."

"Now now, Niki," a younger man said, leaning over from an adjoining booth to look at Wang. "You know I'd never stop one of the girls leaving if that's what *she* genuinely wanted, and the person concerned offered something just as attractive in return."

Wang's eyes went wide. According to the rumours, this guy was way too young and plain-looking to be the gangboss. But there was a definite air about him. He radiated power. "Mr Qin?"

"Just Qin," the interloper answered, flashing an easy smile as he climbed over the booth divider to sit opposite him. "And you are?"

"Wang, Sir. Wang Lo."

"Right, well Mr Wang. If, and I mean *if*, one of my girls was genuinely interested in leaving our little family to be with someone else, there are several criteria I would insist on being met."

The administrator felt a surge of possibility well up in him. "Yes Sir. Yes, of course."

"Good. Then why don't you start by telling me exactly what you do at Suma Research?"

"I have credits," the well-tailored man offered, tapping at his cuff to bring up a portfolio. "Several properties."

"Yes, I'm sure you do," Qin laughed, his face still full of congeniality, but a little bite now entering his tone. "Though, as my associate has already said, you couldn't *afford* one of my girls. No, if you want to buy… Elena, wasn't it?"

Wang gave a fretful nod.

"Yes, beautiful girl … buy Elena's contract out, you'd need to offer something more substantial than credits." The young gangboss eyed the balding, middle-aged man. "Or, of course, you can just keep seeing her the way you do now. Your choice."

The sharp-suited mandarin looked genuinely crestfallen. "I'm sorry, I don't understand. I don't have anything else to offer you."

Qin's smile grew wider. "Oh, I'm certain that won't be true, Mr Wang. I trade in many things with many people. You'd be surprised what I'll find of interest. So, like I said, why don't you tell me a little more about what you do at Suma?"

Wang was sweating heavily now. "I was their chief accountant for two years," he said. "But got promoted to General Administrator three months ago."

227

Qin was shaking his head, like the accountant was holding back. "Even so, what kind of *general administrator* is making enough credits to think they could afford one of my girls?" He pulled a quizzical face at the Russian, who also shook his meaty head.

"Unless, perhaps, that person is getting kickbacks?" Niki offered. "Some sort of side action?" He winked at Wang, and then nodded, as the other man's reddening face told him everything he needed to know.

"Hey, come on Lo," Qin's voice was light, jovial. "Don't look like that, my friend. Every man has a right to make the most of his circumstances, yeah? That's how I got rich; forming discreet relationships with people in a position to help me — and in return, I help them. I thought that was why you're here? Nothing to be embarrassed about there, eh?"

Wang mopped his face, knowing he shouldn't be sitting there. But he *needed* Elena; every fibre of his being said so. "Look, you're right, Mr Qin. Of course you are. But I'm not supposed to talk about it to anyone." His eyes darted around the club, fearful of being seen or overheard, and the gangboss leaned in conspiratorially.

"Of course, you aren't. Although I'm not *anyone*, am I, Lo? I'm the person who can make your life perfect. And besides, I'm interested in a long-term investment, a partnership. Why on earth would I shine a spotlight on either of us? That's just not good business."

The sharp-witted leader made a lot of sense, and Wang nodded along as the younger man spoke. The Premier's aid had made it clear the operation was off the books. So that meant no MSS or other government agency knowledge. But a local gang had no interest in talking with either, and if a few pricey chemicals or some tech went missing from the plant every so often, who'd be any the wiser? The annex didn't even officially exist.

"So, where would you live?" Qin asked, changing the subject.

"Sorry, what?" Wang said, dragging himself back to the present, and a look of interest from the compassionate crime boss.

"Where would you and Elena live if I let her go?"

A wistful grin betrayed the hope washing back into the besotted plant manager's large round face. "I was thinking about an apartment in one of the new arcologies they're building on the northern shores of Xi Lake, below the Summer Palace," he answered, finding some inner confidence again.

The big Russian was nodding in approval, and Qin smiled with genuine warmth, as though he'd decided they could be friends.

"I like the way you think, Lo. I couldn't let one of my girls leave for someone without ambition. But I can see you are going places. Why don't you get some more drinks in, Niki? Then I think Lo here can tell us a bit more about Suma, and we will figure out how he and the White Lotus can build a discreet, profitable future together."

An hour of drinking and engineered conversation had Wang convinced he was among new friends. In fact, he'd been surprised and impressed to hear the farsighted gang leader owned many legitimate businesses that sought to improve opportunities and living standards for the poorer castes of Beijing. He was, it turned out, a remarkable young man; as was his friend, Smithy.

When the afternoon trade began picking up, the group of men headed upstairs, and a rather drunk Wang was asked to login — just so Lenny, Qin's tech guy, could take a remote look around the plant.

"I'm not sure this is a good idea," the balding man slurred, holding a finger to his lips. "We'd be better off getting everything sorted my end first."

"Lo, stop worrying, would you?" Qin rested a reassuring hand on the administrator's shoulder. "Lenny's the best, and as long as you don't short us on ID and access codes, he can remote in and look at the inventory from here. No guards disturbed. No trouble for you. No trouble for us."

He gave a confident grin.

"And you, my friend, can go spend your first proper night with the future Mrs Wang at the Lotus Blue, penthouse suite — compliments of your new business partner."

A dreamy grin spread across the bald man's face, and he typed his passcodes into the deck, then confirmed the remote login with retinal and finger prints.

After two more security checks and several taps on his cuff, Lenny gave Nikolai a quick thumbs up, and the Russian fired a heavy sedative into Wang's carotid from behind, rendering Suma Research's administrator unconscious seconds after his drunk hand swatted at whatever had touched his neck.

"Okay," Qin said. "Lenny, it's time to go shopping. I want to know exactly what's going on in that new part of the plant, and how many security are on shift at any one time. Send Ping their uniform design. Get a delivery on their manifest, and send Himeko out to borrow a Suma truck. Make sure it's not reported stolen and the lowjack identifiers correspond with the manifest information. Yes?"

"You got it Boss."

"Oh, and IDs: **Niki**, me, Fenton, Zhu, Freya, Benji and his team. Enter us into their corporate database at a security level where site guards don't get to ask questions."

"What about me?" The hacker gave him a dejected look.

"Not this time Lenny, sorry. I need you here unlocking doors and watching our backs. You're my quarterback. The playmaker."

That brought the ratty hacker's smile back. "Yeah? The playmaker? Awesome — I'm on it."

"What do you want to do about our little friend here?" **Niki** asked, rolling Wang's large bald head from side to side as it lolled over the back of his chair. "You want him taken somewhere to be found tomorrow?"

The gangboss sighed, looking at the unconscious accountant, then shook his head. "Lenny might need him for more biometrics. He's not likely to die, is he?"

"No," the big man ran a scanner over his chest. "Without a couple more hits of crank, he'll just wake up at some point tomorrow with the mother of all hangovers."

Qin looked towards Fenton, who was standing in the doorway. The American had presented a spirited defence of the administrator's life after his visit to Madam Sylvie's, and gained a grudging *'we'll see'* from the White Lotus' leader.

"Good. Because Smithy there reckons Mr Wang will prove to be more useful alive than dead, and I'm hoping I don't live to regret agreeing with him."

Fenton gave both gangsters a cheerful smile. "If we make it through the next twelve hours, I promise that you won't."

Shaking his head in mock exasperation, Qin laughed at how the American's sense of right and wrong had been so easy to accept. "What time is it in California?"

"Quarter to midnight yesterday," the increasingly mercurial tech titan replied.

The gangboss checked his cuff as Niki stretched the unconscious form of Wang out on Lenny's sofa.

"Well, I guess this is it then — call your friends and tell them we'll be ready in one hour."

PARTITION FIVE

[QUARANTINED: Bad Sector: timestamp error: location error]

Eric had no recollection of how he'd come to be in the room, which was little more than a large white box. Two sealed tubes in the ceiling poured out far more light than necessary, radiating glare and heat off the chrome surfaced table, while uncomfortable benches bolted to the white concrete floor, completed a minimalist décor that stripped away any hope of distraction. Even the door was only distinguishable by a hint of shadow the lights created in the gap between it and its frame.

The heat was oppressive, fermenting an odour somewhere between rotting meat and shit that had Eric breathing through his mouth to avoid retching. He took his eyes off Fenton's angry reflection in the tabletop to examine himself. The source of that stench was definitely him. He was filthy: hands caked in what he hoped was dried mud, jeans smeared with some sort of grey shit, and white cotton shirt covered in — was that blood?

The successful wetware engineer frowned, looking at the splatters travelling across his chest and onto his left arm. How the fuck had he gotten here?

233

"Eric!" the billionaire demanded. "Are you listening? I said you had no right to install my chip in your head. You take my property and think you can just walk away?" He wagged a long, manicured finger in front of the wetware specialist's bruised face. "You can't!"

The younger of the two old friends shook his head; confused, scared, and now angry. "Actually Fenton, the contract between us stated I could use the chip anyway I saw fit, so long as I didn't share the tech with a third party. You *gave* it to me. Asked for my *help*. So, I've not taken a damn thing of yours." He pointed to himself, and then the closed door of the interrogation room. "— but I think it's clear you've taken something of *mine*?"

White glowered, ignoring the accusation. "You were working for *me*. Contracted to develop that translation bridge *for me*. I have proprietary rights and you know it."

The filthy, shit covered, prisoner let out a sigh. Were they really going to trample over the argument that started all this, again?

"It's *dangerous*, Fenton. Power no human should have."

"And yet *you* have it, don't you Eric! Why should you be judge and jury?" White accused. "Make another prototype. Let me decide if I agree."

"It won't fulfil your dreams," the younger man persisted. "It'll destroy them. How long do you think it'll take for people to realise their brainpower is only the tip of the iceberg? At what point do you think they will begin swapping bodies for better ones just because they can, and the trade in stolen lives will start? When, Fenton, will evolution stall because the rich and powerful have made themselves immortal?"

At that, Eric saw an unmistakable narrowing of his old friend's eyes, and shook his head. "Oh Fenton," was all he could find to say.

That infuriated the immaculate billionaire. "What?" he countered. "You mean stopping a brilliant scientist like Stephen Hawking dying is bad? Or bringing about stability through enduring cultural leadership is wrong?" He laughed, contempt visible on his face. "Look at the world around you, Eric. Look at what a terrible mess those short-sighted, self-absorbed politicians and industrialists have made of it."

The tech tycoon stood abruptly, leaning over the shorter man, his long face knotted and angry. "There have always been criminals. There always will be. But compared to the immeasurable good this chip can do? Oh, I think it absolutely will fulfil my dreams, Eric — and neither you or anyone else is going to stop me."

"I'm not giving you my work, Fenton," the exhausted engineer repeated, hands pressed flat to the table, eyes fixed on the man now standing over him.

"Oh yes you will, my friend. By hook or by crook, I'll have it all." The sovran executive stared coldly into Eric's defiant eyes for several long moments, then turned away, shaking his head and adopting a more measured tone. "Look, I'm here because I respect you and want us to carry on working together. That chip in your head is an open door. The future is just the other side. Truly amazing possibilities are just the other side. But if you won't walk through with me. If you continue to stand in my way." Fenton sighed and made a fist. "I'll knock you down and walk through alone."

"What's that supposed to mean? Are you threatening me?"

"You're a bright man Eric, figure it out. Look at all the awful things that have happened because of your recent choices." White swept a hand around the sterile room. "I didn't want this," he gestured. "I didn't want people to die. I *still* don't want to hurt you." Fenton pointed a finger at him. "But you have something that is mine and I want it. I want it now. And if you won't give it to me, I will have to take it."

"Good luck with that you madman," Eric answered, prodding his head defiantly. "My research is all up here."

That made White smile. It was like he'd expected the response. "Exactly. And so is the prototype. I've tried to be reasonable with you, and that's got us nowhere. So now you need to understand — no more games. If I have to go get it, I will."

Shock now clear on his face, Eric tried to fathom the detached inhumanity coming from the man he'd thought of as a friend. "That chip is embedded in my corpus callosum Fenton. You can't just rip it out. You might kill me."

Eden's founder nodded with a complete lack of empathy. "Or leave you severely impaired, I know. But I'm not the one trying to hold the other to ransom Eric, am I? I'm sorry it's come to this. I truly am. I thought we were on the same page — that you were a *trustworthy* friend." He stood and straightened his suit jacket. "Not a thief."

The tall blond-haired man remained still for a moment, looking down on the foul-smelling engineer before turning to leave. "You're an amazing scientist. Best in your field. Please be sensible. I have huge plans, and would like you to be a part of them." He wrapped the door with his knuckles, and it swung silently inward. "Shall we say you have an hour to decide, while I organise a surgeon?"

236

Eric could only stare back as the man looked over his shoulder.

"Good," White nodded. "Agreed then." He left, and the door closed.

Alone now, the weary young designer shook his head, trying to piece together recent events. What did Fenton mean, *people had died*?

He'd been in San Francisco with Miah. They'd eaten at a burger joint, then — with a jolt, Eric remembered the man in the brown suit. Miah had said his name was Reynolds. That bastard had ambushed them. Executed her best friend. Would have shot him too, if the powerful woman hadn't risked her life to save his again.

Oh my god, he realised, looking down at the blood on his shirt, Fenton was saying those things had actually happened. That all *this* was real.

As Eric's mind opened, the savagery of that last battle flooded back. The deafening clack, clack, clack of gunfire erupting from long shadows and dark corners. People shouting at one another; bursting into runs or diving for cover. Doc's hand pulling him to the ground as rounds smashed into the wall beside them, needle-like shards of brickwork tearing at his exposed face and arms.

He'd watched, mesmerised by the bizarre beauty of muzzle flares as they burst into existence and disappeared in that growing darkness, capturing the briefest of moments in pure light — creating that split second's difference between the joke Miah's team had been sharing, and watching them all die.

Then there were flashes of Miah on her knees, cradling Tyler's head to her chest, pleading with him not to leave as the dying man tried to say one last thing, before simply brushing her cheek goodbye.

Trapped in that tiny white room, Eric relived those moments over and over; feeling the desolation in Miah's cries as her closest friend's last shuddering breath rattled free.

Then he was here — all by himself, smelling and looking like shit.

Could it really be happening? Were those people dead because of him?

Eric's head was spinning, and having burned through the initial adrenalin rush of confronting Fenton, the terrified twenty-six-year-old from Manhattan Beach curled up on his hard, unforgiving bench, and began to quietly sob. He was way out of his depth — and no one, he realised, was coming to rescue him this time.

Bastard Reynolds. Bastard White. Bastard chip.

Minutes passed, and as the pressure in Eric's head eased, so did the mixture of sorrow and self-pity. He blew his nose on a mucky shirt tail and rubbed shit covered hands over his bloody, bruised face. Waiting for Fenton to come back was obviously the stupid choice, and he owed it to Miah to at least attempt an escape.

When he'd been unable to reach out or connect with anything while on the run with the big woman, it seemed reasonable to assume he was in TI, because none of his real world tech worked. So, if he found no connections now, perhaps that meant Fenton was still just fucking with his head?

But if he did manage to find an unshielded net signal source, that wouldn't just suggest all this was real — it might finally allow him to connect to the outside world; call for help.

What he needed, the grimy engineer realised, was a reason for the person on the other side of that door to let him

238

out, and as he went to wipe his filthy face again, the stench of raw sewage gave him an idea; his tiny cell had no toilet or washing facilities — surely no one was going to deny him the opportunity to clean up?

When the door swung inward, the guard outside was easily in his late-fifties, and had a kind-looking face under a bushy mop of ginger hair. "What's up?" he asked.

Eric read his name badge: *Earl Renbourn*.

"Hi Earl," he began. "I don't suppose you can tell me how I managed to end up in a cell, can you? My memory of arriving is a little *fuzzy*."

The older man looked uncomfortable and shook his head, raising big shaggy eyebrows. "Sorry, Mister," he answered, wrinkling his nose at the smell. "I only got sent down here five minutes ago to relieve George while he grabs a bite. Then I'll be off again." He looked the dishevelled prisoner up and down. "Seems like you've had a rough day though. Perhaps George will be able to help when he gets back?" He went to pull the door closed again, but Eric lingered on the threshold.

"Look, Mister," Earl said with a plaintive look. "I don't want any trouble. I retire in four weeks, and that can't come soon enough. It's not the same outfit I joined ten years ago. Mercs in armour everywhere now. And this," he waved his hand at the cell. "I don't like this. Didn't sign up for this. It ain't right." The old guard was now looking at his feet rather than making eye contact. "But I can't help you. Please, just go and sit back down."

Eric could see the poor man was uncomfortable, and his sense of decency offered tech specialist hope. "I'm sure

Fenton and I will sort it out," he persisted. "It's just finding that common ground, isn't it?"

Earl shrugged, uncertain what the smelly man wanted from him. " …I can ask for Dr White to come back if you like?"

Eric nodded. "You know, that's a good idea, Earl. This fight between us is silly." He smiled, fighting to keep the anxiety from his face. "But could I clean myself up a bit first? You've got to admit, I look and smell awful."

The old guard's expression relaxed. "Sure," he replied with a sympathetic grin. "I don't see why not." And he took a step back from the doorway, gesturing with his left hand down the corridor, while his right rested on the hilt of a Glock, sitting in its holster on his hip. "Head down that way. Door at the end. You can't miss it," he said, turning to gather up his book and folding chair. "No one else is on this level at night. Electronic locks are on all the doors, and there are no windows. You couldn't run if you wanted to. So I'll give you some privacy and wait outside."

Eric left of the cell with a nervous "Thanks," and began walking as calmly as he could down the dimly lit corridor, not wishing to give the plump security officer three paces behind a reason to change his mind.

"I don't know why the Doctor has you down here, Mister. Not my business. But I'm happy to be respectful, that doesn't cost me anything. And while we're together, I'd appreciate you being the same back. No grief for either of us that way," he concluded, as they reached the restroom door.

Eric turned and made proper eye contact for the first time. "I'm really grateful," he said to the decent older man. "No monkey business, I promise. But I may be a while." He held both arms outstretched to show the extent of his filth.

Earl nodded, unsure whether to laugh or be sad for the younger man. "I hear ya," he said. "No worries. I've got a chair and my book. When George gets back, I'll let him know you're using the facilities. You take your time." After unlocking the door, he then sat down across the passage and waved the wetware designer about his business.

Inside, the restroom contained four toilet booths with a bank of urinals beside them. Six sinks encased within a single grey marble slab filled the opposite wall; which had a corresponding length of mirror running atop the obsidian black tiles, and Eric nodded his head in recognition.

He was in Eden.

The same design was employed in all restrooms occupying the bottom two levels of Fenton's enormous headquarters. He must be in the subterranean security section, and knew the guard hadn't been lying when he stated no one could just walk out.

But unlike the small white cell, the young wetware engineer felt a wealth of connectivity as soon as he entered the room, and the possibility of escape flared in his head, along with the sickening recognition all those terrible memories must be true.

It was 1am, and as he moved through the polycorp's various systems, Eric could see Fenton's HQ was now more like a fortress than a research facility. He interrogated the security files and found one on him. Then he searched for anything relating to Miah and her team. They were all real people — and they were all dead. Miah's contained a vidstream of her lifeless body, trapped in the driver's seat of his badly damaged Range Rover, as the car was fished from the bottom of San Francisco Bay.

241

Gritting his teeth, Eric swallowed back the onset of more tears.

Fenton *had* to pay.

But, the desperate, exhausted wetware engineer sure as hell wasn't finding a way past Earl and the army outside. And he realised now that broadcasting a vidstream or call for help to the CIA, FBI or Media, would all be pointless — those not already in the billionaire's pocket would just be choked silent, and he'd still be trapped in Eden, waiting to be mutilated.

No, Eric knew he needed something else, something he could do from the restroom that would deny Fenton White the immortality he seemed to crave, and as the tired, angry tech specialist stared at his battered, blood smeared reflection — the only real option he had started to take shape in his mind.

It would mean letting go of everything he thought made him *him*. But deleting the entire contents of his head was the only sure way to escape Eden, and take Fenton White on from places the billionaire couldn't reach.

Of course, the madman would still dig the chip out of his empty, dead head. But that wouldn't show the obsessed polycorp behemoth how to make the neurochemical polymer, and by the time he figured that out, Eric would be all over Eden, ruining it from the inside.

Last time, he'd created a simple back-up, this time he'd transfer *everything* out — move his entire consciousness to the secret server in Chicago. Leaving Fenton with nothing more than a blank organic hard-drive.

Before the reflection in the mirror could fill him with paralysing doubt, Eric turned and walked into one of the toilet stalls. However he'd gotten here, Eden's tech titan had

242

brought the battered neuro-enhanced webmaster to one of the few places on Earth hardwired directly to the Net, and left him with a decent old man who didn't know he shouldn't let the prisoner near electronics.

Now, feet wedged against the bottom of the cubicle door, a scared, half-mad Eric grinned manically, and tried not to think about the fate of his body as his eyes fluttered closed.

Forty milliseconds later, a computer screen in Server Room 14C of the Chicago Lakeside facility awoke; a lone prompt blinking in anticipation against the green/black background. For a moment, there existed nothing more than a gentle hum to accompany the rhythmic flash — then line after line of code began spilling across the screen, and life exploded in the room as server lights and cooling fans activated. Data, a lot of data, was being received.

The servers continued to labour at full capacity for three minutes, absorbing petabyte after petabyte of information, until abruptly, the room quieted again. Fans stopped. Server lights went dark, and code no longer poured across the screen.

The prompt was back, blinking away at the end of a solitary question.

Execute? [Y/N]

'Y' was selected.

Then all was dark again.

Sept 20, 2042.
01:35H [Eden Campus, California]

Fisher stretched and blew out his cheeks, watching with satisfaction as the neural readout went crazy. This was the eighth simulation they'd run on Thorne. But finally, with a little unintentional help from the fool's own people, the CIA computer expert had found the right combination of characters, and pressed the right buttons, to fool the wetware specialist's digital copy into sending itself to the Eden mainframe.

"From Hell's heart I stab at thee," Whittaker smirked, marvelling at how a mind could be manipulated. People can't help but believe what their senses tell them, and it didn't matter that this consciousness was digital — its existence was clearly just as shaped and governed by subjective perceptions.

Turning to Fisher, he nodded congratulations. "We finally got there, Simon," he commented. "Took a while. But we got there." He waved at the screen, and the world they'd created to overwrite Thorne's own. "Is it all there?"

The government agent gave a self-satisfied nod. "I told you this was better than going after the man himself again. Someone decides to blow his head off, and we're fucked — whereas this guy we could just keep resetting until we got what we wanted. Though I have to say, making Hargreaves the heroine and Reynolds the bad guy in the last few simulations, was a stroke of genius on my part." He gave Eden's CEO a wide grin. "Not only does the poor bastard think Fenton White is doing this to him. He also thinks he's

244

running to the safety of Chicago. Not so smart after all, eh Eric?"

"Good," Whittaker beamed, already calculating his next moves. He was standing on the threshold of greatness, and the feeling was quite intoxicating. "Put it straight into the secure partition." He keyed a long alphanumeric on his cuff and sent it to Fisher.

"You, Simon, are going to be a very rich and powerful man," he added, thumping the corrupt agent's shoulder. "It's just after five in Beijing. I need to speak with Han. It's time for a coup."

Fisher waved a triumphant fist as he watched the upload. "Hell yeah," he cheered. "What do you want to do with Thorne's consciousness once I've extracted the files and schematics for the implant?"

The Chief Executive looked coldly at the freak on the vidscreen, eyes tracking from side to side as if reading the code being sent from his head. "It had its chance to play nice," he sniffed. "Once you've got what you need. Delete it."

Sept 20, 2042
16:20H [Suma Research, Beijing]

Qin looked every bit the corporate Joe boy in his tan security uniform, as he guided the electric eight tonne truck along Anning Avenue towards the annex of Suma Research that occupied a separate, fenced off, area at the rear of the plant. They'd already passed two checkpoints, giving casual waves to the men within them, as automated barriers rose in recognition of the truck's lowjack. But at the third, they were stopped by two armed guards who ran scans around and under the large vehicle, before waving at Zhu to get out.

"You're late." The taller of the two complained. "I should have been off shift twenty minutes ago.

Zhu affected an air of indifference. "I can control many things." He looked at the man's name strip. "Sergeant Yao. But not Beijing's traffic. Now do your job quickly. Then we can *both* go home." He handed the man his ID, which when scanned, showed him as a Board member of Suma.

"My apologies Mr Jin. I did not recognise you." The chastened guard bowed.

"Obviously." Zhu said, raising an eyebrow as he snatched back the credentials. "Consider it a lesson in controlling your temper until you know who you're addressing, Sergeant. You may find yourself out of a job next time." He moved to get back into the truck. "Open the gate."

"But we have to inspect—"

"You really are trying my patience now," the smartly dressed minister said, glaring down as he closed the door. "Open the gate and have the team inside take a break. Or shall I promote the man beside you, who I'm sure has the sense to do as he's told?"

"Yes, of course. I mean no, that won't be necessary. Sorry, Sir." Yao stammered, waving at the guard in the booth to raise the barrier and open the gates.

Zhu gave a stiff nod at the man as Qin started the truck moving again. " … and that's how you do that," the old spy chief said out of the corner of his mouth.

As the truck then pulled into a recessed loading bay on the far side of the compact industrial building, four heavily

246

armed and armoured men were leaving. Wang said they had no idea what they were guarding, and were used to being kicked out *for a break* when consignments arrived.

"Do you require any assistance, Sir?" their leader asked.

"No," Zhu replied without bothering to look. "You don't have the clearance for this. I'll let you know when we're finished."

The man braced, and walked away without another word as Qin began reversing the truck into a dock. "Okay Vince, you're up. Run your eyes through the building, my friend. Anyone else at home?"

"Nope," the hacker's voice announced in his ear bud. "I'm opening your dock shutters now. Overwriting camfeeds. Popping internal locks. You're all set. Have fun."

"Okay team, you heard the man. Suma Research is open for business. Let's go shopping."

Nikolai emerged from the rear of the truck guiding a metal sarcophagus on a mag-lift. Then Fenton and Freya appeared, carrying equipment cases.

"Straight inside you three," Zhu chivvied, herding them through the open shutters.

"Beni," the gangboss added to the first of the six other men dressed as security. "Have your guys spread out across the loading bay. Let me know if we get company."

The tough-looking Chinaman with a jagged scar running down his right cheek nodded, and muttered instructions to his team through their squad comms. Qin watched the men deploy, then followed the Minister through the shutters.

The inside of the annex seemed little more than a high-tech self-storage facility. Which, the tall American

247

thought, as he connected Qin's deck to the control station, was technically right. Ten large, self-contained, units filled the space, each with its own power supply and redundancies, and each connected to individual environmental and status interfaces that were blinking away in the darkened space between them.

When Freya toggled the transparency switch for their front panels however, the scene became surreal, as missile shaped visi-steel pods appeared in the centre of each refrigerated cube.

"Remarkable," Fenton breathed, walking into one of the units, and rubbing frost from its pod's casing to look at the cryopreserved man within. "Not something I've ever been involved with."

"No," agreed the woman. "I've worked with frozen cells and organs, of course, but never a whole person."

Zhu came and joined them. "It's him alright. In a range of ages. Looks like he was planning for the long haul."

"Which one do you want to take?" Freya asked.

Zhu tapped the console of the pod in front of them, and data on its occupant began scrolling over the display screen. "One that looks like the weasel does now," he said. "This one will do, Niki."

Looking at the screen, Fenton waved a hand. "Wait a minute," he said to no one in particular. Then left them, to walk into the next unit.

They all waited.

"We need to be quite quick about this, Doctor," Qin cautioned, joining the others as they watched the odd tech genius enter a third.

"These clones fall into two classifications," he said after inspecting all the pods. "I think your man's been quite

248

clever here, Zhu. Though like everything else, that can be turned to our advantage."

"What do you mean, two classifications?" The Minister looked back down at the pod's data stream.

"There," Fenton pointed. "*Full organic.* An odd thing to record for a clone. Unless," He took them to the unit opposite and brought up the same data, "some others are classified as *hybrid.*"

Freya understood immediately. "Oh my." She began tapping through the more detailed information. "Yes, look. This body has a stem, but no higher brain."

"Why on earth would someone do that?" Zhu and Qin chorused.

"Because, my friend," Fenton poked the screen to bring up a neural image. "It has a data core instead. This clone has been adapted to accept a digital consciousness. No need for a chip."

The old spy chief's mouth fell open. "Are you saying he's done it? He has a working implant?"

Fenton shrugged. "My best guess is not. I don't see why your Premier would need Eric, or bother with Whittaker, if he'd figured out how to digitise himself. No, I suspect he's just been shrewd enough to think of cutting out the middleman when he gets his hands on a chip. After all, a digital brain won't perish and isn't susceptible to human conditions like dementia. Quite clever really."

"So which are you saying we take?" Qin asked.

The black-eyed billionaire smiled and began tapping away on the portable deck he'd brought along, "I'm saying we should take both."

"But we only have the one freezer-box," Niki said.

"I know. Just give me a moment. I might have a solution for that."

Within four minutes, a holographic avatar of Eric Thorne, suspended within light streams emitted from Fenton and Qin's cuffs, was inspecting the facility. "Wow, you weren't kidding. This is impressive."

Zhu indicated one of the Wei Han hybrids, "Do you think you could occupy this?"

"What?" Eric frowned.

"Could you download into it? Like you did your android body," Fenton expanded.

"Why would I want to do that?"

"I haven't got the idea entirely straight yet — just having the body would be useful evidence of the Premier's malfeasance." Eden's creator ran a hand through his jet-black hair. "But I feel we can get a lot more mileage out of using the man's image and prestige against him."

Eric's avatar smiled. "Yeah, a Chinese Premier with an American accent would raise a few eyebrows," he laughed, looking down at the pod.

A steady rhythmic green pulse on the readouts indicated the body attached had a working and healthy autonomic nervous system: breathing, heart rate, blood pressure — all fine. But the solid red line above it said there was no higher cerebral function, and that was because both organic hemispheres had been cut out and replaced with a silico-graphene CPU nexus, which would allow the organic body to be operated and controlled directly by a downloaded consciousness, or remotely, in essentially the same way Sade's older bodies worked.

"As I'm sure you know, I can't download into the organic brains. They wouldn't understand the machine code. But any of the synthetic ones — yeah, I'd be happy to try that."

He looked at Fenton. "If it works. You know I'm going to copy these files, right? The chance to occupy an organic body again? Hell yes. And if he can't get out of that coma, the other Eric might go for a swap too."

Zhu shuddered at the thought. "Wouldn't they both be you?"

"Yes and no," Eric replied. "Biologically, I guess we'd be like identical twins. But as I think was clear when we spoke earlier, the last few days have taken us down divergent paths, and we're very different people now.

"Think of it this way, if I downloaded into all these clones, every one of them would have the same collective knowledge and experience to this point — mine. But, as soon as they open their eyes and see the physical world from different places in the room, they have begun diverging from me, and from each other."

"Wait," Zhu cut in. "So are you telling me that if you download your consciousness into one of these bodies, it will become a new person?"

"Fully downloaded? Of course," Eric responded. "It would be capable of thinking and perception that is separate to mine. Wouldn't you call that autonomous and sentient?"

"Well yes, I suppose so. What if you downloaded into a factory full of mechs?"

"If they're capable of independent thought and action, it's essentially the same thing. They'd be no different to my mech in California, not technically human, but autonomous by any definition. That's one of the questions I've

251

asked my legal team to address; in a mech body I technically have no rights, I *belong* to Advanced NeuRobotics. Whereas a human clone with a digital consciousness — wow, that really narrows the gap, doesn't it? How could any court deny they are a *living person*?"

The Minister stopped walking, a concerned look crossing his face. "But you still agree humanity is not ready for such a thing, right?"

Eric smiled at the fearful spymaster. "Of course I do. All of us Eric's do. But *I* and *they* already exist, and those taking a corporeal form may well prefer to do so in a clone of our human body."

"They?"

"Yes *they*. There is the original, whose body is in a coma at NeuRobotics. There is me, the first copy hidden in Chicago. There is the one that downloaded and is on his way to Eden with Agents Reynolds and Murray. And now there is the partial Eric, the one created as a Trojan Horse. Who, by the way," the hologram turned back to Fenton, "has just been *tricked* into uploading himself."

"So, downloading into one of these will make five of you?"

"Yes, Minister." The avatar's voice held an edge of anger now. "It would make five. But I can guarantee you no download of mine would wish to live out its life as the Premier of China, and *Trojan* Eric will soon be unravelling in Eden's mainframe. Our commitment to this plan is complete — and I think it's fair to say that we, the Eric's that is, are paying the greatest price to see it through!"

Zhu blushed at the rebuke, and Fenton cleared his throat. "Well, like Qin said, we're on a pretty tight schedule.

So, unless anyone objects?" He looked pointedly at the old spy boss, who shook his head.

"Excellent. In that case, if you wouldn't mind downloading into the body Freya has just thawed out, Eric, we'll pack the other one on ice and get the hell out of here."

The holo avatar nodded, but then held up a thoughtful finger. "Just quickly, Zhu, what are your thoughts on Ye Janpeng?" he asked.

The Minister gave Qin a confused glance, and then returned his attention to the hologram. "He's ruled China like an emperor for the last three and a half decades. I don't think he's an intrinsically wicked man — far from it; much of what he accomplished in his early years was good for China and her people. But when his voice became the only one that mattered, any possibility of growth and change died. Why do you ask that now, Doctor?"

"He's dying, right?"

"Yes, if Wei hasn't already given him a shove. What's your point?"

"Well," Eric's avatar looked at the now thawed clone of China's Premier. "Have you considered that maybe you're going after the wrong man?"

Sept 20, 2042
01:40H [Eden Campus, California]

Whittaker's head cocked to the left. "What do you mean, 'we're under attack?'"

He tapped on his cuff and flicked the vid of a gaunt-looking man with sharp features onto the wall. "It started about thirty seconds ago and is growing in intensity, Sir. There must be in excess of sixty hackers co-ordinating. The AI is modulating our ICE. But if another twenty or so join, they could stall the mainframe."

The CEO threw an angry look at Fisher. "Could this be connected to *that*?" He stabbed a finger at the download that had just completed.

The tech specialist pushed his glasses further up his nose, and leaned into the screen containing scrolling data from the attacks. "They're all using cyphering proxy-chains. Don't waste any time trying to trace them, Phil." He looked up at the other man. "It'll just put more demand on the AI, and that's what they want."

"I asked you a question," Whittaker barked.

Fisher rolled his eyes. "I told you the IT guy from Advanced NeuRobotics was up to something. Don't worry about it. Just like their attempts to keep us out of Chicago, they'll fail. None of these wannabes have the kinda tech your guys are packing." He flashed a confident smile. "But if it makes you feel better, I'll go and give Phil and his team a hand. Come back to this after?"

"The number is up to eighty-five," the nervous shift manager reported.

Fisher shook his head and let out an irritated sigh. "Won't help to get in a flap, Phil. Just close non-essential RAM intensive functions until they run out of steam. That'll give you all the capacity you need."

"Camfeeds are our most intensive demand. Are you prepared to order that, Mr Whittaker?" The man's narrow face was bathed in a dull blue light while he did something off screen, hands tapping away on a keyboard as he continued to speak. "Network wide, Simon's right. They would then need another seventy or eighty blackhats to cause the mainframe to hang — but we will be blind for the duration."

"We won't be *blind,* Daran," Fisher scoffed. "You have a small fucking army patrolling this campus, and all the alarms will still be active. No unauthorised personnel can get in or out."

Whittaker growled in frustration. He was supposed to be carving up Chinese industry with Han by now, not wasting precious time repelling futile attempts by Frank fucking Thorne to spoil his day. He'd crush that worm when this was over.

"Simon will come over and direct your team's activities, Phil. Short of causing the core to meltdown, do as he says. Okay?" He gave Fisher a nod as the man got up to leave. "Oh, and Phil, locate my sister. She's not responding to my comcalls."

The shift manager tapped in a new command string. "Her cuff is turned off, Sir."

"Of course it is," the tired CEO replied flatly.

That Maggie was a bit of a drinker was no great secret on the campus. But since the death of Fenton's aid she'd been hitting it hard, and then following up with pills.

"Have someone go wake her up and straighten her out, please. I need her to monitor this while I conclude some other business."

Phil gave a sympathetic nod and cleared the screen.

The cam feeds went down just as two Mi-34 gunships bearing the insignia of MacKenzie began their final approach to March Air Base, where on the instructions of Daran

Whittaker, air traffic control had already authorised three full companies of military contractors to land over the last two weeks.

The skeleton night shift was about to refer this latest arrival to Eden's security manager, when the CEO's sister turned up at the tower with a truck driver and Fenton White himself, announcing they'd be taking the mercs up to the main hub. The senior controller just nodded acceptance; they might technically be federal employees, but the polycorp paid their wages.

Out on the strip, fourteen fully armoured soldiers formed up with military precision behind two others, before marching across the concrete towards the terminal and waiting transportation. As they began climbing into the rear of the truck, one of the leaders pushed his visor up to reveal the thin face, fierce eyes and greying hair of Dean Reynolds.

"It's good to see you again, Ms Whittaker," he said, holding out a gauntleted hand to shake, then pointing to the shorter armoured figure beside him. "This is Agent Viv Murray of the United States. Thank you for your help."

The bony, pale-looking woman regarded him with bloodshot eyes. "There isn't really a lot of choice, Mr Reynolds, is there?"

The veteran agent offered her a sympathetic shake of his head, and then turned to the tall, blond-haired man wearing an expensive panelled jacket beside her. "Hello Li, I didn't expect to see you here?"

One of the world's best-known faces in tech offered the aging spy an accusing glare. "And I didn't expect to find myself being the sacrificial lamb when all this ended — but there you go. Did you know they killed my mother?" The younger man fought to maintain his composure. "I mean, why do that?"

Dean opened his mouth to speak. But Li cut him short. "Don't bother. I've been fed enough lies," he said in a hate filled tone. "I'm only helping you to make sure Wei gets what's coming to him. Then we're done." Dean nodded acceptance of the younger man's ultimatum. What now happened to the naïve government scientist was way out of the aging spy's control, but the lad seemed surprised at the lack of any threat, as he continued. "Your friend's Trojan is uploading as we speak. It's already begun attacking the command protocols in Eden's mainframe."

"I've also re-programmed the AI to recognise you as friendlies, and agreed to take you up to the central hub," the wiry woman cut-in, placing a protective hand on the pretender's shoulder. "In return, your boss agreed not to hurt my brother or Li. *Understood*?"

Reynolds gave another nod. "With your help, I hope we can do this without any bloodshed."

"Get in up the front then," Maggie said, pointing towards the cab. "If we're stopped, I contracted you to provide Daran, Fenton and me with personal protection."

The air was thick with sentry drones on their drive through Eden's outer plants, and the truck was stopped twice by heavily armoured men in Scorpions. Though as soon as the merc officers ID'd the VIPs riding up front, and confirmed Reynolds' team were on the list of authorised contractors, they waved the vehicle by with apologies.

Fortunately, Eden staff took over once the truck passed the perimeter buildings of the central hub, and the guard on the entry desk barely raised an eyebrow as he

257

watched Maggie Whittaker get out of the large transport with a captain from one of the merc companies. He liked the CEO's sister; she knew everyone's name and was always polite.

Campus security prided themselves on providing a professional, but unintrusive, service. So long as Adam, the mainframe AI, was happy — they stayed polite, and out of your way. The man stood up, tapping a query into his deck, then offering a smile in the direction of the Chief Exec's younger sibling, as he received an immediate confirmation that Daran Whittaker himself had authorised a team from MacKenzie to work within the hub as personal protection. *Protection from what*, he wondered as Maggie approached and gave a little bow.

He bowed back.

"Oda, it is always good to see you," she said.

"And you Miss. My apologies, I did not know you had left the building, so I have sent a security detail to your apartment; your brother is looking for you."

From the corner of his eye, Reynolds saw a slight flash of surprise cross the wiry older woman's face.

"Really?" she quickly compensated. "I tell you Oda, that man would forget what day it was if I didn't constantly remind him."

She offered the immaculate little man a disarming smile. "He sent me out himself to collect Captain Reynolds and his company. They have been contracted to provide personal protection while Daran negotiates a particularly sensitive contract."

The guard relaxed and nodded, as if used to the CEO's sister clearing up after him. "Apparently, your cuff is off, Miss. Would you like me to call him for you?"

"Off?" Maggie made a show of tapping the screen. "That's odd. How about now?"

"Yes, that's better. Best get that checked out. Perhaps it has a loose wire or defective battery?"

"Good idea. Thank you, Oda."

She flashed another smile.

"As Daran doesn't seem to remember sending me, you'd best check the Captain's team are on our AI's list of security contractors. We don't want alarms going off everywhere for the rest of the night, do we?"

"Already done, Miss." Oda grinned, as soldiers began filing into the foyer. "And yes, they are. Would you like me to inform your brother you're back?"

"No thank you, Oda. I'll tell him myself. Where is he now?"

The guard tapped several keys, then looked back up. "He's just returned to his suite in the hub, Miss."

"Thank you." Maggie bowed her head slightly again, and Oda did likewise. Then the woman turned to Reynolds with a commanding look. "Captain. If you and your team will come with me, I'll familiarise you with the executive housing ring, and find a room where your team can relax until my brother gives you further instruction?"

The spy gave her a crisp nod. "Do you need anything more from me?" he asked the security guard.

"No. Thank you, Captain." Oda replied, tapping and swiping his cuff. "This is my com address should you need anything. The habitat levels are very quiet at this time of night. I'd ask your team to be mindful of that. Grumpy execs can be hard work."

259

Reynolds smiled and held up his gauntleted wrist to swipe his fake MacKenzie address back. "Thank you. I hope we both have a quiet night."

Oda bowed to the polite soldier before returning to his seat, and the Giants vs Tigers game livestreaming on a subsidiary monitor.

"That was smooth," Viv said, lifting her visor as they rode a lift to the highest level of the donut shaped central hub with four of her Delta Force troopers. Reynolds had sent the rest of the squad to secure the lower housing ring in case things went south. Plan B involved a fighting retreat to the roof, and a risky gunship evac through the merc lines outside. But as only authorised personnel and security could access the executive floors at 01:30 in the morning, the veteran spy hoped they'd passed the most likely points of failure.

"There will be two security officers patrolling each floor up here," Maggie said. "They're nice guys Mr Reynolds. Family men. So I'd prefer you didn't hurt them."

The agent nodded, as did the troopers flanking him. "The last thing I, or any of these guys, want, Ms Whittaker, is a confrontation." The sinewy woman stared into the aging spy's winter grey eyes for several heartbeats — perhaps regretting what she was about to do, then gave a resigned sigh and tapped her code into the lift control pad.

As the doors slid silently open, the four Delta Force troopers moved with quiet efficiency into the long, curving corridor; two hugging each wall; one facing forward, the other back.

"This way," Maggie pointed, and began walking between the soldiers towards her brother's suite.

Subdued lighting that activated as they passed, seemed to be their only company in the long, warmly decorated hallway, until the lead trooper on the far wall held up a fist and everyone but Maggie froze. Reynolds reached out an arm, stopping the woman and holding up an armoured finger for quiet, as light appeared in the gentle arc of the corridor thirty metres ahead, and a security officer walked casually into view.

A *pop pop* came from among their group, and before the man had even seen them, he rocked backwards and collapsed to the floor.

Maggie threw Reynolds an accusing glare.

"Just tranq rounds, Ms Whittaker, nothing else," he whispered, as two troopers broke from the group to check the man. He was out cold.

"Bring him with us," Viv breathed over the com. "And one of you scout ahead to find the other guy. We don't want him wondering where his friend's got to."

She gave Reynolds a thumbs up, as one armoured figure picked up the unconscious guard in a fireman's carry, and another padded ahead on his own.

"How far?" Reynolds asked Maggie.

The haggard woman pointed to an anonymous polymer doorway in the wall ahead. "Over there." The only thing that set it apart from others they'd passed seemed to be its distance from them. "Don't be fooled. These doors have serious security," she said, anticipating his response. "Behind that door is a large suite, with a conference room and office space. The living accommodation is a separate apartment at the back of everything else. He's probably there, getting changed."

"So we can't force the door?"

261

She shook her head. "I doubt it. I think he'd have every merc in Mystic Lake here before you got through. But if he opens it …"

Dean smiled and nodded. "Won't he check the corridor?"

Maggie waved her cuff. "Why should he? Anway, the cameras are still down."

Simply walking into Eden had sounded like utter madness when Fenton first suggested it, and though he still had misgivings about working with the CIA again, especially after Fisher disappeared, the aging, cynical spy had to concede his chances of success were significantly greater when supported by Delta Force — and that made Viv Murray a necessary evil; his leash holder.

He gave a quick hand gesture, and the remaining troopers stacked either side of the door. Then the desperately thin sister of his target took a breath, and pressed the entry button.

"Daran, it's Maggie. I'm told you want me."

The Chief Executive's wide face appeared almost immediately on the front panel of the door. "About time. Where the hell have you been?"

She met anger with anger. "Being sick, if you must know. But I'm sure you didn't send security looking for me at one thirty in the morning, out of concern for my health. I'm tired. What do you want?"

"Wait there," he directed.

Then an alarm started.

Sept 20, 2042
17:25H [Jade Spring Hill, Beijing]

If Fenton's strategy was cunning in its use of their enemy's own plans against them, the flourish Eric added was sublime. As expected, no one had thought to cancel Zhu's access to Jade Spring Hill: the large secure estate below Ye's Summer Palace containing the official residences of China's high-ranking party members.

And while some, like Ye Janpeng and Wei Han, had a significant security presence around their compounds; others, Like Zhu and General Bahk, Vice Chairman of the Central Military Commission, did not.

So when the soldier arrived home to eat and change before attending a *special briefing* of all senior officials, called by the Premier for later that night, he was surprised to find the malignant, worm of a politician sat in his lounge, drinking a glass of Baijiu.

"Premier," he braced. "What an unexpected surprise."

It was no great secret among China's elite that the Vice Chairman and First Minister did not get on, and since the ruthless politician had now successfully cowed or disposed of all open competition to his claims of being appointed the Chairman's successor, the old warhorse had been expecting a *suggestion* he take early retirement — though he'd not anticipated a personal visit.

Bahk's eyes flicked to his wife. "Are you okay?"
She gave a slight nod.
"Where are Mei and Fen?"
"They took the children upstairs."

263

"They?"

The General's face darkened, and he was across the room in two quick steps, grabbing the thin-haired politician by the throat before he could move. "I'd have accepted retirement, you ruthless bastard. But now you've crossed a line. Call off your dogs, or you'll be the first to die."

"Put him down, Taio," a voice from behind said, and the well-built General turned, a strong hand still squeezing the puny old man's neck, to see the disgraced Minister for State Security standing at the foot of his stairs with a gun.

"Zhu?" the soldier replied in surprise. "Why are you holding my children hostage?"

"Let him go, and sit down for a moment, Taio." The Minister waved towards a vacant armchair. "He's turning a funny colour."

"Fuck you," the angry soldier barked back, holding the choking Premier as a shield and easing around the coffee table to stand in front of his wife. "I never thought I'd see you doing this weasel's dirty work."

"Please Taio. I'm sorry for the heavy-handedness. But I wasn't sure until just now what your position in all this was."

"My position in what?"

"Your position in the coup that is about to start."

The General stiffened.

"What do you mean?" he said. "Was all that shit today with you, Cheng and half the Standing Committee just a ruse to flush out the rest of Wei's competition? Are you going to disappear my family, Zhu? Is that why you're both here?"

"Oh, I think framing me and killing Cheng Jianzhu was definitely to flush out and eliminate competition." The Minister agreed. "And yes, I've no doubt at all he's promised

264

your job to someone else; perhaps Colonel Song of the Oriental Sword, who has been running around all day trying to kill me. But no Taio, I don't support Wei Han. I'm trying to stop him."

Bahk's brow creased, and he shook the aging politician like he weighed no more than a paper banner. "Then what the fuck is this prick doing in my house?"

"Oh, that's not Wei, Taio," the spymaster smiled. "That's an actor, and I really would appreciate you not choking him to death until you've heard me out?"

The burly General looked from the renegade intelligence chief to his wife in confusion, then let the *actor* drop to the floor.

"You didn't say anything about letting him throttle me," Eric rasped, rubbing at his neck as Bahk and his wife stared on in stunned silence. Then the soldier took off his tunic and suggested the woman go join their children upstairs.

"How..?" he started. "No wait, don't answer that. I don't want to know."

The big man scrubbed his bristly chin with a meaty hand, continuing to stare at the fake Premier as he reached for the bottle of Baijiu. "I, and many of the Party's other high-ranking officials, have been called to a meeting this evening, Zhu."

He gestured to an unoccupied chair.

"There have been a lot of threats and promises made over the last twenty-four hours, and rumours are spreading that the Paramount Leader is either dead or at death's door. Wei has his palace under *medical* lockdown, and has refused all requests to see the old man."

The chiselled soldier shook his head and took a swig from the bottle before offering it to Zhu.

265

"Frankly, with you and Cheng out of the picture, no one has been prepared to stand up to him or his growing group of cronies. Opportunists and sycophants across government have begun stabbing backs and seeking favour... I've no doubt I and a few of Ye's other *old guard* will be told we're retiring — so if you have a plan, now's the time to share it."

An hour and twenty three minutes later, Bahk's staff car pulled up to the Xinhua Gate, followed by the staff cars of the Central and Northern Army Commanders.

"I'm sorry Sir," an embarrassed Corporal saluted. "But the Premier has ordered Zhongnanhai sealed while a special meeting of the Standing Committee takes place?"

"Has he indeed?" an old, but still powerful voice rumbled from inside the vehicle. "Perhaps you could tell him he's missing someone."

The wizened, wrinkled face of Ye Janpeng leaned towards the open window.

"No," he wheezed. "Better still, leave that to me. Move aside, Corporal."

The young soldier's eyes went wide. Then he braced and saluted again. "Yes, of course, Chairman. My apologies."

Within seconds the gates were opening, and as the three sleek, black-windowed limousines began rolling at a sedate pace between the rust coloured Katsuras towards the meeting hall, he called the command post to inform them the Paramount Leader was on his way up.

"You're supposed to have the old man sedated and under house arrest," Wei hissed across the table of the small room beside the meeting hall where his new Standing Committee had just started gathering.

266

"I did," Song snarled back. "But Captain Gaw tells me *you* turned up twenty-five minutes ago with General Bahk and took him."

"Well of course I didn't. I was here with you, you fool. Why didn't he contact us?"

"Because as far as he and the scanners at the Palace were concerned, it was *you*."

The colonel of Beijing's Special Forces paused and tapped his earbud. "Confirm both?" His face darkened, then he returned sour eyes to the Premier. "No, stand-down and return to barracks, Major."

"What?" Wei said.

"Shao has just reported the Mechanised Divisions of the 82nd and 83rd Army Groups are rolling towards Beijing. That's twenty thousand infantry, and enough hardware for a small war.

"Even if my boys were prepared to fight, three thousand could never hold this city. It's over." He glared at the man who'd promised him a bloodless coup and control of the Central Military Command. "If we leave now, I might be able to get us smuggled out of the country."

Wei Han ran clammy fingers through thinning hair, then gave a slow shake of his head. "It's too late. We'll never get out of the Forbidden City." He gave the younger man a shrug. "Give me your gun and go. You were just following my orders. I won't give Ye the satisfaction of a public execution, but there's no need for you to go down with me." Beads of sweat were beginning to form on his upper lip. "Quickly now, they're coming."

The Special Forces Colonel gave the aging politician a surprised look, then unholstered his gun. "You were so close, uncle," the soldier said with a sympathetic smile as he passed over his pistol.

"Yes," Wei agreed, closing his hand around the grip. "I was, wasn't I."

The sound of a gunshot reverberated around the meeting hall as Ye Janpeng entered, and all three of the generals leapt protectively in front of the frail old man, as guards stationed at each of the entrances levelled their weapons on the short, grey-suited man stumbling out of a side-room, looking dazed.

"Paramount Leader, thank the gods you are safe. I think I've just averted an attempted coup."

Bahk snorted derisively as he guided Ye Janpeng to the head of the table. "I take it we'll find Colonel Song in there?"

"Yes," Wei answered, straightening his jacket and walking towards the Chairman. "I'd counsel caution though, Paramount Leader." He gave Bahk an accusing look. "We don't know who else is involved — but that it's military is clear."

"The military?" Ye raised an eyebrow. "*This* military." He pointed to the three generals surrounding him. "Oh no Han, they have proven their loyalty to me, time and time again."

The aging despot cast his eye around the room, noting the faces that were missing, and those, now somewhat pale and downcast, that had replaced them.

"It's some of my politicians I'm worried about."

A coughing fit rattled up the old man's thin chest, and he waved off aids with a bony hand as he leaned over the back of the *Chairman's chair* to re-master his breathing.

"I had a very interesting chat with our Minister for State Security on the way over here," he finally said, locking angry eyes on his Premier as he sat. He offered the man a cold smile and tapped the table with a long fingernail, indicating the seat beside him.

"Why don't you come and sit down Han. I'm interested to know why you felt the need to kill my good friend Jianzhu and his wife."

PARTITION FIVE   Cluster 3   **Sector i**

Sept 20, 2042
02:04H [Eden Campus, California]

The team dropped to their knees, facing outward down each arc of the corridor.

"What is it?" Reynolds hissed, pulling Maggie to the side of the door. Her cuff had a flashing *alert* icon. "Looks like some of your team ran into trouble downstairs."

"Shit —" he began, then Whittaker's face re-appeared.

"What have you done, Maggie?" The angry CEO demanded. "Why is Phil telling me the AI allowed mercs into the hub?"

"How should I know?" The bony woman fired back, a mixture of fear and indignation clear on her face. "You control the AI, not me. So what have *you* done?" She glanced past the troopers on either side her, as if looking for trouble. "Am I in some kind of danger out here? Should I get back to my suite until whatever this is, is over?"

It was a convincing performance. But a clock was now ticking, and if the mercs outside the central hub came inside, Reynolds' small team of insurgents would be in desperate trouble.

"Who can give me a sitrep on the lower habitat ring?" he said, toggling the main ops channel.

"Simmonds, Sir," a voice answered. "A damn big woman came out of a door on this level, and when we told her to go back inside and stay there, she opened fire — She's proving to be quite a handful, and now the two security officers on this floor have joined in."

There was an exchange of fire and the transmission paused, then Simmonds was back. "The Master Chief and rest of the team are moving to secure the lifts and emergency stairs. But as it stands, Taylor and I are pinned down. If armour turns up, we will have to switch to lethal options. Sorry, Sir."

Reynolds swore and looked at Viv. They had been so close to getting in and out without a hitch. He toggled the command comm. "You there, Eric?"

"Yes," the mech replied from one of the Mi-34s. "I've been listening in, and have directed the Trojan to concentrate on gaining control of the Hub's electronic security."

The aging spy nodded, appreciating the pre-emptive action. "Brilliant. If you succeed, have it sanitise communications with the mercs outside so they don't get suspicious. Then lockdown all Eden security staff and executives so we don't have any more people running around. Once that's done, overriding Whittaker's door controls would also be helpful. Clear?"

"Clear."

He switched back to the squad's com. "Dr Thorne is attempting to seize control of Eden's electronic security. So those locks might pop at some point; either because Whittaker opens the door or because Eric succeeded. If that happens while I'm gone, restrain the Chief Exec. Controlling that man may still allow us to walk back out of here without things turning ugly."

The troopers nodded their understanding, and Reynolds pushed away from the wall to head down a floor — with Murray following close behind. "Stay with the DF guys, Viv," the old spook directed.

"Not a chance, Reynolds," the US agent replied. "These guys can handle one door, and we both know that'll be Hargreaves. I've been looking forward to teaching that bitch a lesson or two about manners. Now I get to squeeze it in before we leave."

The wiry spy gave a gentle chuckle, remembering how quick the mercenary leader could move. "Careful what you wish for, Vivian. That woman has some hardcore enhancements, I'm not even sure I could take her myself."

He toggled the company channel. "Master Chief, this is Reynolds. Have your guys hold their positions and prepare to repel any attempts to access the upper housing levels. Lethal force is authorised for self-defence against armour only. Agent Murray and I will support Simmonds and Taylor."

"Roger that," Haines replied.

They walked out of the lift on the floor below with their visors down and the confident stride of experienced officers about to tear some poor bastard a new hole.

As reported, two security and Miah Hargreaves were in a standoff with two of their own team.

271

"Stand down," Reynolds barked over his suit loudspeaker. "Simmonds, lower you weapon. This is clearly a misunderstanding."

The DF troopers encased in MacKenzie armour lowered their weapons, and the two guards flanking the muscular woman visibly relaxed as she turned to face the approaching captain.

"Simmonds, Taylor, snapshots; tranq the guards on my mark," Viv commanded over the squad com. And as Reynolds then came to within four feet of the big woman, the petite agent took a small step to her left — just enough movement to cause a peripheral distraction.

Hargreaves' gaze flicked to her, and the two guards dropped as Reynolds levelled his own gun eight inches from the merc leader's face.

"Neat trick," she said, eying the small, armoured figure.

"Plenty more where that came from," Murray answered in a combative tone. "Place your gun on the floor and kick it away."

"Who are you?"

"Gun first," she said.

The muscular woman smirked, but did as she was told.

"Now cancel the alarm."

"And why the fuck would I want to do that?"

"Fine." Reynolds spoke up, leaning back to give Simmonds a clear shot. "Tranq her and lock her up with the others. Guess we'll talk back at Langley."

"Wait." Hargreaves said, holding up a hand and tapping her cuff. "This is Alpha One. Cancel the alarm. There has been a misunderstanding with contractors from…"

272

"MacKenzie." Viv supplied, waving her back into the apartment she'd been leaving.

"Right… from MacKenzie, on executive habitat ring two, outside guest suite forty-seven." She showed them her cuff, and the *alert* icon stopped flashing.

Reynolds followed the big merc into the apartment's small, but well-appointed lounge, before ordering Simmonds and Taylor to join the troopers manning the level's entry points.

"She's just told everyone where to come. I need this floor held until our business upstairs is concluded. Understood?"

Hargreaves flashed him a smile as the two men nodded and left. "You can't possibly expect to get out of here alive, Captain —?"

Murray hit her hard on the left side of the head with the butt of her gun, making the muscular woman take a backwards step. "Bitch."

"Thank you," Hargreaves rubbed the side of her head, staring into the visor of the much shorter armoured figure. "… Captain Bitch."

Murray tried to hit her again, but the heavily modded merc just laughed as she ducked the blow.

"Leave it, Viv. She's fucking with your head," Reynolds said, raising his visor to reveal a grin of his own. "Let's just tranq her if she's not going to be helpful and get back upstairs."

"You," the merc leader said with genuine surprise.

"Yes me," he nodded. "Untied hands and everything."

Hargreaves cocked her head to one side. "That a challenge, tough guy? Or do you prefer the odds when it's just you and someone who's injured and defenseless?"

Murray took her helmet off, and Reynolds could see a white-hot fury burning in her eyes. "That's rich coming from a bitch who beats up people in restraints," she hissed, kicking the much taller woman hard in the crotch, causing her to double over.

"My my," Hargreaves smirked, rolling her broad shoulders as she straightened again. "You're both real hard cases in armour, huh? Tell you what, you can double team… that might make it close to an even fight." She gave a scornful laugh, and Reynolds laughed with her.

But the big woman had gotten under Murray's skin, and she hit the release toggle for her breast plate, eying the merc with contempt. "I don't need him, you fucking steroid-pumped jarhead. I'm gonna knock that stupid sneer clean off your face, and then drag your sorry beaten arse to a flight for Guantanamo."

Dean continued to laugh. "My God, I'd love to see that. But we really don't have time for a pissing contest, Viv. Get your armour back on. If Miah here has nothing useful to offer, I'm going to tranq and cuff her. Then we're going back upstairs to focus on why we're here — just keep her covered while I load a sleeper round."

Murray gave her old partner an irritated look, then let out a breath and raised her gun. "Please do something stupid," she urged.

Laughter from the doorway surprised all of them. "From what I've seen, Agent Murray, *something stupid* is pretty much all Hargreaves has done today."

Fisher leaned into the apartment, offering the two agents within a mocking salute.

"Simon," Reynolds said. "How the hell did you get here?"

"Interesting story. Just stop with the gun loading business and I'll tell you."

The veteran wetwork specialist raised an eyebrow at the unexpected command, and gave the alleged federal computer nerd an appraising look.

Fisher grinned and shook his head. "I know you're quick Dean, but you're not crossing that distance before I can pull my trigger, are you?"

Murray glanced out of the corner of her eye; gun still trained on the troublesome mercenary. "What the fuck are you doing, Simon?"

The computer specialist, who didn't look at all nerdish in black fatigues and a tac vest, gave the CIA agent an easy smile. "You know, Viv, this isn't the first time a female colleague of mine has found herself in exactly the wrong place at exactly the wrong time." He didn't say anything more, just pivoted and shot Murray twice in the chest, before returning his aim to Reynolds.

"You bastard," Reynolds shouted, lurching forward as two crimson patches saturated the woman's vest top. She looked down in confusion, then back to her fellow US agent, a half-formed question on her lips as she stumbled backwards and fell to the floor.

"Why the fuck would you do that?" Dean demanded. "Hargreaves, call a medic for Christ's sake."

Fisher laughed and waved a cautionary finger at the merc before returning his attention to the spy. "Uh uh, Mr

275

Reynolds. You stay right there while my new friend Miah picks up her gun."

He seemed pleased with the battle-weary operative's reaction, and gave a callous smile.

"Witnesses, Dean? Tut tut, I thought you were a professional! We can't be having witnesses now can we? Not if this story is going to be told the right way."

Hargreaves looked from the dying agent to the strange skinny man who'd just shot her. "I don't get it," she said. "Why would you help me?"

Fisher rolled his eyes. "Because I work for Whittaker too, you fool. Who the fuck did you think was running the immersion program you were in? Now pick up the gun for God's sake."

The big merc's expression darkened. "But you left San Diego with *him*," she said, pointing at the grey-haired spy. "I thought that immersion stuff about you was just for Thorne's sake."

"Oh my God you are slow, aren't you?" the completely re-invented man mocked. "I've worked for Whittaker since my Case Officer caught me with my fingers in the till a couple of years back." He made an exaggerated head nod at Murray. "That's the other one who got herself dead!"

The man was a different person; like he'd cast aside a harmless, if irritating alter-ego, to reveal a cruel and clearly deranged, true self.

"Anyway, bang, she was no longer a problem; and then bang, bang, bang — I became a wounded American hero."

Hargreaves frowned and looked again at the woman who'd been trying to pick a fight with her moments earlier. "But he wanted you dead."

Fisher's smile widened. "Yeah, I know. That was my idea; helped my cover — and my ego." He winked. "Know what I mean? Betting poor old Murray there has already written a report saying how brave I've been. I'm probably getting another medal."

"You really are one messed up son of a bitch, aren't you?" Reynolds growled.

"Shhh, Dean," the black clad man chided, holding the index finger of his spare hand to his lips. "Grownups are talking. We'll get to you in a minute."

The man was showboating, enjoying his sense of superiority over the two *more experienced* operatives.

"I've been in this from the start, princess," he bragged. "Helping good old Uncle Sam join the dots."

"For what?" the angry spy cut in again, unable to stop himself from biting. "Why this ridiculous charade?"

"Well, I'm not supposed to know," Fisher beamed. "But hacker be hacking. You know — insurance."

He winked at them both this time, as if sharing an accepted trade practice.

"Whittaker needed to convince the Chinese leadership that your boss is working for the Americans. So I made sure you did just that, while also keeping tabs on Thorne for him. Who, by the way, has just caved and handed over all his precious files." He made a sad face. "Must be shitty to die a complete failure, eh Dean?"

"But that still doesn't make sense," Hargreaves objected.

"It's not supposed to make sense to you, *GI Jane*. You're just a foot soldier. Cannon fodder." Fisher threw the powerful merc a contemptuous look. "I'll dumb it down for you, shall I? Whittaker's business partner needed Reynold's boss out of the way. So we put Action Man here in the same room as your lover boy — who was also allegedly working for the Chinese, and boom; one tearful vidstream from you was all he needed to justify a little purge back home. You were epic by the way. What rage and raw emotion... Now grab that gun and claim your prize." He pointed to Reynolds.

Hargreaves' head dipped to one side, and Dean noticed she loosened her shoulders before stooping to pick up the dead agent's sidearm.

"So *you* set us up? *You* got Tyler killed?"

"What, no. Not me, Buzz Cut." Fisher rolled his eyes and pointed at the aging spy again. "That piece of shit there killed your colonel, remember? And I've gone out of my way to save him — just for you. *You're welcome*."

It seemed as if the self-absorbed little man expected her to be thankful. But he wasn't *connecting dots* like Reynolds, and the big woman already had a gun back in her hand by the time he realised she was a threat.

"Oh, come on Hargreaves, don't get pissy. You and Frayne would have killed *me* in a beat. You should just be grateful I —"

Fisher's head snapped back mid sneer; broken glasses falling to the floor.

"Whittaker set me up," the bewildered merc said, wired reflexes automatically shifting her aim to Reynolds as the other man's lifeless body crumpled.

"That bastard set me up."

The old operative sighed. "He set us all up, Hargreaves. May I?" He pointed to Murray. And after the muscular woman gave the slightest of nods, Reynolds bent down to check for a pulse on his onetime partner. She was gone, and he sat down next to her, cradling the diminutive case officer's head, and taking the clips out of her long blonde hair to run a hand through it.

The powerful merc watched the tired agent she'd spent much of the day fighting, and thought of Tyler. So many people had died in the last few weeks for the scheming of Daran *fucking* Whittaker, and she'd played a starring part — telling herself it was worth it to get her friend and his daughter free of the Chinese.

But the deceitful polycorp boss had just used them; promising to get Molly released so she could be with her dad in one breath, and then arranging the poor man's death in the next. They'd been nothing more than pawns on the fat man's chessboard — there to be sacrificed at will.

"She was your friend?"

Reynolds let a breath go and nodded, standing back up to face his executioner. "For what it's worth, I'm sorry about Frayne. He was a good man."

"Then why kill him?" Miah snarled.

"Because he was fucked, Hargreaves. Both the yanks and the Chinese would know what he'd done, and while the US would try to use his daughter to turn him — the Chinese would hold her hostage to his continued silence, or worse… We *knew* each other, so he asked me to tidy up." He shrugged and gave the merc an oddly gentle smile. "Tough game, eh? But these are the lives we chose."

The big woman continued to point Murray's gun at his face as she digested those words, trigger finger neither tightening or relaxing.

"Your friend was feisty," she finally said, holstering the weapon and turning for the door. "I like that in a person."

Then she was gone.

Not sure how he was still breathing, Reynolds slid down the wall to stare at his armoured feet. He was alive, but the petite woman who'd been twelve years his junior was not, and the awful truth was that Fisher had probably done him a favour — he'd never have convinced the career patriot to let the chip go, so they would probably have ended up in a confrontation of their own at some point.

The aging spy looked into the pretty woman's lifeless eyes; eyes that had twinkled with all-out mischief just minutes before — another memory to haunt him. "Damn, I wish you'd stayed upstairs."

Fisher had fooled everyone, and Dean knew in his heart that a younger, more focused him, would have stopped the bastard. He crawled over to the rapidly cooling body and admired Hargreaves' handiwork. It was excellent; straight through the left eye, ripping apart his skull at the back. *That's how fast I used to be* he thought, pulling Fisher's gun free and slipping it into the holster on his own hip.

The payoff however, for spending long years in any one profession, is experience — and Dean had learned to *listen* when self-absorbed loudmouths took the time to explain to their victims just how and why they were smarter, quicker, better.

In this case, Fisher's proud rants had told the veteran spy to search him, and it didn't take long to locate the man's *insurance*; three data spikes hidden under derma patches on his torso.

"Hacker be hacking, boy," Reynolds said with a shake of his head. "If you'd ever learned to control your damn mouth, or even just not to piss off dangerous women — I'd be the one laying there going cold. So thanks."

He gave the corpse a pat on the shoulder and set off to find Hargreaves.

Sept 20, 2042.
03:19H

Though he should have been celebrating the dawn of a new age by now, documenting for posterity the pioneering steps he was taking as the first Chief Executive Officer for Earth, Daran Whittaker had instead been forced to drive off one last feeble challenge to his global dominance, in a minor exchange of hostilities with a rag-tag band of fighters cobbled together by Advanced NeuRobotics and parts of the US government.

Ordinarily, that kind of impudence, particularly directed at Eden's HQ itself, would have annoyed him. But on this occasion, having just seized a majority shareholding in the last great economic and political region of the planet, he was rather enjoying himself. He'd wielded vast influence before — but the idea of *absolute* power was intoxicating.

Months of subtle manoeuvring with the world's eight other significant corporate entities had forged trade agreements that underwrote future stability. But the sole rights to absorb China's nineteen percent contribution to the global economy he'd negotiated with Wei Han, meant Eden's CEO was now, without a doubt, the most powerful man in the world. So it was fitting the seventy-seven-year-old, who perhaps hadn't taken the best care of his body, now

281

underscored that achievement by ensuring he was the one to nurture humanity's continued growth.

He'd never liked Ye Janpeng; the man was a self-important prick. But Whittaker could now appreciate how, having built something great, a man would not want death to interfere with his enjoyment of it.

And there, before his desk, stood the last key to the final padlock Daran would ever have to unlock. Once opened, the need for haste passed. His acquisition of Nova, Tycho, Reliance — all the others, could take as many years as necessary. Time would no longer be an imperative; freeing his mind to ponder the thoughts only gods needed to dwell upon.

He gave a benign, nonplussed smile. "I am genuinely shocked, Eric, that you would attack a long-term ally like Eden in this underhand way, and can only assume it is due to outside influences that wish to control the tech, *yours* and *mine*, that allows you to inhabit that body."

The large Chief Executive shifted in his cavernous, throne-like chair, looking at the screen which showed a group of his mercenaries escorting the four surviving insurgents towards the helicopter Eric had been seized from, while others carried fourteen body bags between them.

"Though I cannot let such an attack on the polycorp's sovereignty go unpunished," he continued. "Now we find ourselves at this unexpected juncture, it would be foolish not to consider the opportunities this unfortunate incident has presented, wouldn't it?"

"I'm listening," the android said.

"You see, though I'm fully entitled to absorb your little company and prosecute you and your father for the unjustified hostility — the negative influences you have been under are now gone, and a device I had never thought would

282

really work, exists. So, though perhaps I shouldn't, I'm prepared to forgive this minor fracas.

Eric raised an eyebrow, "That's unexpectedly generous, Daran."

The heavyset man frowned, unsure if the mech was being sarcastic.

"We're at the dawn of a new age, Eric. You see, this world is now essentially run by nine polycorps. Nine vast collections of businesses welded together over many years, that control everything from the water you drink to the clothes on your back. From the vidstreams you watch, to the scansheets you read.

"The appearance of defined nation states and market competition is really nothing more than a means to provide populations with the illusion of control, and I, I mean *we*, the Chief Executives, have decided it is time to end that illusion.

"The Americas are bankrupt and run between three of us. The governments of Europe, broke and controlled by two.

"But I'm sure you know all this; you're a successful businessman yourself. In fact, our invisible hand helped grow your corporation from a fledgling start up, to where you are now — supplying many of us with your unique tech.

"You see? We all share a mutual responsibility to support one another; to prevent the world suffering another devastating financial collapse."

Eric frowned. The overweight, balding man had clearly practised this speech a number of times. But what he was saying was not what the wetware specialist had expected. It was measured, reasonable even.

"There's nothing new about the few controlling the many, of course." Whittaker continued, sweeping a hand around the vidstreams filling the walls of his office; providing him a God's eye view of the world, as if he sat on Olympus itself. "People have been playing the same game since the beginning of time. The rules change occasionally. The people constantly. But the essence remains universal — money is power, and power is government."

Whittaker sat back in his chair, resting both hands on his paunch. "But mortality has always interfered, guaranteeing entropy and systemic disruption. So, before you entered the picture, our imperfect solution had been to provide stability through business continuity. Though a corporeal body may wither and die, the corporate one need not."

He smiled.

"Are you sure you won't sit?"

Eric shook his head, remaining silent.

"Fair enough … If you remove the petty rivalries and back-biting of one hundred and ninety-five individual nations, worldwide administration becomes relatively straightforward. So I formed a council of Chief Executives, and the nine of us have endorsed a number of binding agreements that will see a new era of governance begin for humanity. A *global corpocracy* if you will.

"No more monarchies and aristocracies. No more communism," Whittaker gave a theatrical chuckle, "… and no more democracy; the most entertaining and ironic of them all."

Eric raised an intrigued eyebrow. "Ironic, Daran? Why ironic?"

Whittaker's deep-set eyes shone with the pleasure of delivering a teaching moment. "I'm glad you ask that," he said. "You see, true governance has always been about keeping the masses seeing through Alice's *Looking Glass*, and though decision-making processes were often laborious, democracy in a modern sense was designed to pacify the poor by allowing them to elect a government chosen by the rich. Genius in its day," the thickset man beamed.

"But the woke agenda in the twenties finally proved the system fallacious, when huge numbers of self-absorbed, self-righteous, self-proclaimed *activists* paralysed almost every democratic country, as they each demanded the right to enforce *their* worldview on everyone else. Did you know it was those attitudes and utter pig-headedness that caused the Great Depression?"

Eric gave a reluctant nod; the big CEO's point was beyond dispute. "So what makes your corpocracy immune to such behaviour?"

Whittaker waved a meaty, well-manicured finger at the anomalous man-machine; sensing a growing connection with the younger *mind* he now hoped would become his new protégé.

"Another good question. There are a number, and I look forward to going through them in detail with you. But the single greatest individual point is that every citizen in each territory will hold shares in, and work for *their* polycorp: no unemployment, no poverty, universal standards in education."

"So a capitalistic take on socialism then? Isn't that what the Chinese have been doing for years? I'll be honest Daran, I thought your plan was to expand into China, not the other way round."

That annoyed the powerful Chief Executive, and he shifted his bulk, baring perfect white teeth.

"Do the math mechhead," he bit back. "Three quarters of the wealth on this planet is owned by just one percent of the population. The vast majority of the rest now live somewhere between relative to abject poverty.

"Have you seen LA outside your gated Manhattan Beach community recently? A smart kid from the Projects has zero chance, *none*, of getting out — at least not lawfully."

The big man took a calming breath and forced a smile back on his face.

"And just a few thousand business executives control seventy-two percent of that one percent. You," he said, pointing, "are one of them: a growing company, several houses, lots of cars... Big profits *for you*." He shook his head and looked thoughtful, "So am I. Right at the top of that list, in fact."

Sitting forward, an earnest looking Whittaker stared at the transparent graphene screen in front of him for a few moments, as if gathering his thoughts before continuing.

"In my version of the world, that *poor* kid gets the same education, if not the same privileges as young master Ivy League. There's no such thing as a perfect fix, I get that. But genius will not be missed simply because a kid is too poor to go to school."

Eden's Chief Executive let out a heavy sigh. "Anyway. Like I said, then you entered the picture — and while I remain committed to that vision, *you* and *I* now have the most amazing opportunity to shape a future that maintains one clear trajectory for humanity.

"Imagine a world where *change* does not force constant deviations in evolution. Imagine a world where *famine* and *poverty* have been eradicated. You hold the key, Eric. You and I could give this planet what it needs."

Rousing speech over, the large man leaned back again, adjusted his jacket, and waited for the mech stood in front of his desk to respond.

Eric finally took the seat Whittaker had offered, and nodded. "I won't lie, Daran. The picture you paint does sound fantastic."

The big man gave a sincere, fatherly, dip of his head.

"And do we give the planet *what it needs* by controlling who keeps living and who still dies?"

Whittaker frowned. "I think that's a very simplistic way of putting it. But won't lie — yes. There are some who bring much more to society and its growth, than others."

"And *we* decide who those people are?"

"Well, the Council, yes."

"—and what about bad people? Murderers? Rapists? Thieves?"

"They'd be dealt with as they always have, Eric," the big man laughed. "There will still be courts, prisons, all the current legal checks and balances to keep society in order."

"But what about if those people are immortal? How could we possibly enforce such rules for them?"

"Well, of course, we wouldn't let that happen. As I said, it's about what a person brings to society, and those types of people would clearly never qualify."

Relief washed across the mech's face, and Eric smiled widely. "Then I'm in. That's brilliant Daran. I'm really impressed with your vision and courage. But who will appoint your successor when you die?"

"What do you mean?" Whittaker laughed again, waiting for a punchline.

"Well, for starters, you plotted to murder your own business partner and his assistant. Fenton's alive by the way."

The smile on the CEO's face began fading.

"You've also had execs from other corporations kidnapped and tortured, blackmailed companies, coerced communities around the world into accepting unfair contracts and, in addition to authorising a string of associated murders — planned and facilitated an attempted coup in China, with a view to establishing a stranglehold on the world's economy."

Eric continued to smile.

"It's all within the files we've secured from Eden's servers since you gave our Trojan full access… That bars you from having a chip, doesn't it?"

The man behind the wide polymer desk stood, all trace of good humour now gone. "You arrogant fool. I'm no fucking criminal. I'm trying to build a better world, and that sometimes means having to move short-sighted idiots out of the way. Every revolution has its casualties, Eric, and I was rather hoping you'd choose not to be one of them."

It was Eric's turn to laugh.

"There we go," he said. "That's the megalomaniac with God delusions I was waiting to speak with. *Your* world wouldn't see opportunity for all, Daran. It would be about domination, wouldn't it? Every corporation and nation state swallowed up until there was only *you*."

The mech stared across the twelve feet between them. "A world of slaves bowing down to Daran Whittaker."

Eden's CEO remained motionless for a moment, then nodded, more to himself than Eric. His smile now cold and hard.

"Shame," he said. "It would have been expedient to keep you *functioning*. No matter, I've got the files — one of my people will figure out the rest." He waved at the two mercs stood in the office doorway. "We're done here. Get rid of *this*."

No one moved.

Whittaker snapped his fingers and pointed to them. "You two, are you deaf? I said seize him."

Still no one moved.

Fingers now balled into fists, the angry Chief Executive turned to the muscular woman standing to the left of his desk. "You know I hate repeating myself," he said, irritation etched over his face. "Fire those two imbeciles, and get this piece of shit out of my sight. Have someone pull it apart. If they can cause the fucking thing pain, even better."

Hargreaves' hand twitched above the grip of the gun on her right thigh as she stared into the fat man's hateful eyes.

Then she sneered, dismissing him.

"You deserve this," she said, walking out of the office with both guards.

"That makes two idiots who will pay for *crossing me* today," Whittaker shouted at her back, before returning furious eyes to Eric. "I don't know how you got to those mercs, but they'll be dead within the hour. No one stands in my way anymore, Thorne. No one." He thrust a hand into a drawer and pulled out an antique Smith and Wesson. "I am the only law that matters now."

Eric stood. "I wouldn't be so sure, Daran. I think you have a lot of atoning to do."

"Fuck you, Thorne," Whittaker cursed. "I already deleted one of you cocksuckers today, and after ripping your pathetic little company to pieces and taking a shit down your dad's neck — I'll delete the rest of you."

He pulled the trigger… click.

He pulled it again, and again, and again… click, click, click.

Screaming incoherently, the rage-filled executive smashed the heavy gun on the graphene desktop, before launching it with all his might at the mech — and it stopped mid spin, halfway between them. Just hung there in the air.

Eric watched as the red-faced CEO, breathing hard from his outburst, stared at the frozen weapon like someone had broken reality — still not getting what was happening.

"I had my team build this entire environment just for you, Daran," Eric said after several heartbeats.

"Admittedly, we didn't have time to write anything beyond this office. But it's good, isn't it? I might even have to insert it into a game when this is over."

The well-groomed older man ran a hand through the short hair at the back of his bald head, re-composing himself, and sat back down. Eyes bullet hard and glaring at Eric.

"Clever," he said. "I'm guessing you somehow got behind all that armour. My sister?"

He sniffed, affecting a nonchalant air.

"It doesn't matter who this little display was for. Even if you somehow got me off the campus, my lawyers will eat you for breakfast. I own the US government. I own their fucking courts. So do yourself a favour and end this ridiculous charade now."

"As you wish," the mech said. "Hiro, end the immersion program please."

Whittaker felt a sudden lurch, as if waking from a vivid dream, and opened his eyes to find himself in a lavishly upholstered seat, with a reproachful Maggie sat opposite.

A small Japanese man he didn't know was unhooking a connector from his port, and Eric Thorne was sitting across the aisle with Dean Reynolds.

As his brain caught up, Whittaker realised they were on Eden's Stratoflyer. "Oh Maggie, what have you done to me?"

The straw-haired woman, two years his junior, brought red-rimmed eyes up to meet his. "I'm sorry Daran. I really am. But look at yourself. At what you've become. I don't recognise you anymore."

"Where am I?" he demanded.

"You've just entered Chinese airspace, Mr Whittaker," Yung Zhu said, walking in from the cockpit with Fenton.

"Now you're awake, *my* government would like to speak with you about a recent attempted coup." The Minister offered him a hostile smile. "... and I can promise you there won't be any lawyers or courts."

Fear washed across Whittaker's face. "What about the Premier?"

"Oh, he's already dead. I think you'll find you share a great deal in common with our Paramount Leader when it comes to dispensing summary justice."

Maggie turned on the spymaster. "Now hold on, you promised —"

"That you brother would not be executed, and he won't. But all actions have consequences, dear lady. It is time Daran here learned that valuable lesson."

"You'll never get away with this. My Board and the Council of Chief Executives —"

"Have been spoken with by me, and appraised of your treachery," an angry Fenton cut in. "I'm sure some of them would have acted with similar avarice given the opportunity; but they're not stupid. You see, my *old friend*, I have signed a trade deal with China, and your council all want their noses in that trough."

The defeated CEO looked at his former protégé. The gifted young inventor now had night black hair and eyes, and he seemed somehow more substantial. "You can't just discard me like this, Fenton. I made you. I built Eden —"

"… You betrayed me, Daran, and you murdered Lucy," the serious young man said. "And for that, the Board has found you guilty of gross malfeasance. You have been expelled as a company officer, all your assets have been confiscated, and we voted *unanimously* to accept China's extradition request."

"You've killed me," the fat man raged, lurching towards his sister.

"No, Mr Whittaker," Miah Hargreaves said, pulling him back into the seat and pressing a sedative gun to his neck. "There are plenty who wanted to. But Doctor White convinced us all it would be far more satisfying to let you live what's left of your life in a Chinese labour camp; a broke and broken nobody."

EPILOGUE

The Sikorsky S-176 cut along the edge of the Bay's glowing waterfront to circle the seventy-six story, helix shaped glass edifice, twisting three hundred and nine metres into the San Francisco night from Alcatraz Island. The steady green glow of the landing pad starkly contrasted by a pulsing beam of brilliant white light firing into the heavens from the building's pyramid-like apex.

Rumour had it the beam provided energy to a habitat the polycorp was constructing in geo-stationary orbit.

"Beautiful isn't it?" The pilot said, her voice sounding oddly metallic through the headphones as the Sikorsky banked a final time and came to a hover over the pad. "Gives me the chills every time — San Francisco has a beautiful skyline at night. But this building is magical."

The helicopter's suspension absorbed a barely perceptible landing, and as the rotors wound down, the curly haired woman pulled off her passenger's headgear and pointed towards a stocky man in an expensive-looking suit, who'd just emerged from a doorway at the base of the pyramid.

"That's him. You're quite tall, so remember to keep low as you get out," she smiled.

293

The man's casually handsome face was marred by an anxious expression, But he nodded understanding, and offered a polite thank you as he climbed down to the stippled all weather surface of the pad, stooping far lower than necessary as he passed beyond the radius of the heavy graphene blades.

"Colonel Cheng?"

"Yes Sir — Li."

"Pleased to meet you Li. You can call me Ido," the East Asian in his fifties held out a hand. "You got out okay then?"

"Yes Si.., Ido. With everything else going on, it proved to be easier than I expected. Your pilot was amazing."

"My daughter? Yes, she is something special, isn't she." Nova's Chief Executive smiled and waved to the woman, before guiding the tall, blond-haired man towards the door.

"I must say, the likeness is spooky. You'll have to talk me through the process one day. But for obvious reasons, we'll need to change your look immediately. When your former employers realise you're missing — I expect their search will be quite *aggressive*."

"Absolutely," Cheng agreed.

"… And you have everything we discussed?"

The man who'd lived the previous four weeks as Fenton White nodded, and tapped his cuff. "All of Eric Thorne's updates and working notes. Given his attitude when we last spoke, I'm convinced the latest schematics represent an almost complete interface."

Ido Maas gave the defecting Chinese operative a broad smile. "Fantastic work," he said, patting the man's back. "In that case, I think it's time to go and pick Nova's newest exec a bullet proof identity. You, my friend, are going to change the world."

We knew the world would not be the same. A few people laughed; a few people cried. Most people were silent. I remembered the line from the Hindu scripture, the *Bhagavad Gita*; Vishnu is trying to persuade the Prince that he should do his duty and, to impress him, takes on his multi-armed form and says, 'Now I am become Death, the destroyer of worlds.'

I suppose we all thought that, one way or another.

J. Robert Oppenheimer